DISTORTED

ALSO BY CHRISTY BARRITT

Standalone Books

Disillusioned
Dubiosity
Imperfect
The Good Girl
Home Before Dark
Gone by Dark
Wait Until Dark

Mystery Series

Squeaky Clean Mysteries
Holly Anna Paladin Mysteries
The Sierra Files
Suburban Sleuth Mysteries
The Worst Detective Ever Mysteries

DISTORTED

CHRISTY BARRITT
AUTHOR OF *DISILLUSIONED*

Waterfall
PRESS

Text copyright © 2017 by Christy Barritt
All rights reserved.

Scriptures taken from the Holy Bible, New International Version®, NIV®. Copyright © 1973, 1978, 1984, 2011 by Biblica, Inc.™ Used by permission of Zondervan. All rights reserved worldwide. www.zondervan.com The "NIV" and "New International Version" are trademarks registered in the United States Patent and Trademark Office by Biblica, Inc.™

Published by Waterfall Press, Grand Haven, MI

www.brilliancepublishing.com

Amazon, the Amazon logo, and Waterfall Press are trademarks of Amazon.com, Inc., or its affiliates.

ISBN-13: 9781503942868
ISBN-10: 1503942864

Cover design by Shasti O'Leary Soudant

Printed in the United States of America

Distorted: *To give a misleading or false account or impression of.*

PROLOGUE

Tennyson Walker's mission was clear: find Dante Torres, take him down by whatever means necessary, capture the insurgents, and get out.

"You have eyes on Torres yet, Ten Man?" Kade Wheaton, his commanding officer, said into his earpiece. The former Texas boy still had a touch of twang to his voice.

Tennyson scanned the dark corridor in front of him and held his assault rifle at the ready. He had a 9 mm submachine gun slung over his shoulder, just in case things turned really ugly. "Not yet."

He crept down the hallway of the elaborate estate nestled on the island mountainside. It looked like a war had broken out here. Probably because it had. Furniture was overturned, bullet holes riddled the walls, smoke lingered in the air.

He took another step, glass crunching on the tile beneath his boots. His training had prepared him for raids like this, but his instincts would keep him alive. His motivation remained over his heart: Claire's picture. He'd never let himself forget what had been taken from him.

"Is thermal imaging back up yet?"

"Almost," Wheaton said.

Tennyson ground his teeth together. He needed those heat signatures to help him pinpoint Torres's location. The system had gone down fifteen minutes ago, and techs were working to get it running again.

For now, Tennyson would have to find Torres the old-school way—on foot, using only his five senses.

The stillness of the house made Tennyson catch his breath. The whole complex felt eerie, like a trap that had been set and now waited to snap on its prey. He couldn't put his finger on exactly what made him think this. It was just a gut feeling.

Either way, he didn't plan on being a victim today.

He kept his gun close, watching each step. The smoky, metallic smell of spent ammo filled the air. Shouts sounded in the distance. But here in this wing, it was quiet. Somewhere in the vast depths of this place, Torres was hiding like a snake under a rock.

Torres was his. Not the other SEAL team members'. He was Tennyson's.

He took another step, his boots crunching more glass, as well as broken tile and splintered plaster from the walls. The men who'd hunkered down in this wing had obviously been alerted that the raid was going to happen. There'd already been a struggle here. Most of the insurgents had been captured.

But not Torres.

If Torres was here, Tennyson would find him. He wouldn't leave until he did.

He searched room after room but found no one.

His pulse raced as his options disappeared.

"The thermal is back up," Wheaton said.

"What do you see?"

"There are two possible heat signatures. You're right beside one of them."

Tennyson's breath caught. He looked over his left shoulder. His right. An open expanse of hallway stared back. No one was here. He'd already checked both of the rooms on either side of him.

"It's clear," Tennyson said.

"Look for any doors. Any hidden spaces. I'm telling you: someone's there."

Tension grew between his shoulder blades. The element of surprise could take down the toughest of soldiers. "I'll check."

"Be careful."

"Always," Tennyson said. Except he knew he wasn't always careful. If he were always careful, Claire would still be alive. At his side. They'd be married now. Maybe even have a baby or two.

"Go to the left," Wheaton said.

Staying close to the wall, Tennyson slipped into the room. He sucked in a breath. This space had somehow been spared from the damage in all the other rooms. Why?

The room was empty and strangely out of place in the otherwise Caribbean-styled home. It almost looked Victorian with a lacy spread over an ornate bed, complete with four tall wooden posts. There were flowers. Lots of flowers. An odd smell permeated the air, some sort of perfume, pungent but expensive.

Something about this room turned Tennyson's stomach and haunted his conscience. But he pushed aside those feelings.

Wheaton was sure someone was here. Thermal imaging had confirmed it. Tennyson had to figure out where.

He studied the wall. A built-in bookshelf, filled with literature that indicated someone who was well-read stayed here, took up the majority of the space. There were also pictures of the beach. Of . . . a couple on the beach. The man in the photo was older and graying, and the woman younger and vibrant. But they were clearly a couple based on the way their arms were wrapped around each other.

Strange.

Was there a safe room behind this bookshelf? It seemed cliché, but it was worth a shot.

If there was a hidden room located behind this built-in, how did he access it?

On a whim, he began pulling out various books. As he moved a particularly thick set, he saw something unexpected behind it.

A switch.

His throat tightened. This was it. This was the moment.

"I think I've found him," Tennyson whispered.

"Wait for backup before engaging."

"How far away are our guys?"

"They're rounding up Torres's men. Ten minutes."

Tennyson's heart pounded in his ear with every second that passed. Time was of the essence here. He couldn't lose Torres. Not when he was this close.

"We don't have ten minutes. For all we know, there's a tunnel below this. He could be getting away."

"You need backup."

Fire burned in his veins. This was the moment he'd dreamed about for three years. Three years.

"I need to catch Torres."

"Ten Man . . ." Wheaton's voice held a warning.

"I'm going in, Wheaton."

"I'm not losing one of my men."

"You won't," he muttered. With that, he flipped the switch. The door slowly swung open.

A man stood on the other side. His features, though shadowed, were unmistakable as he faced Tennyson.

Dante Torres.

Satisfaction filled Tennyson as he raised his gun. But the emotion was short-lived. No sooner had he spotted the man than a strange odor filled the room.

Gas.

Tennyson started to yell. But before he could, Torres pressed something in his hands.

A lighter.

Flames burst through the air. Consumed everything in their path. Consumed Torres until he was only an outline of a burning man.

The explosion blasted Tennyson across the room. He slammed into the wall.

This wasn't the way it was supposed to end. Not with Torres still calling the shots. No, Tennyson needed to see justice.

He started to push himself to his feet, ready to move toward the burning figure. But before he could, Torres collapsed onto his knees and fell facedown.

It was too late. Torres was dead. He hadn't survived the blast, and that was precisely the way he'd planned it.

Tennyson let out his breath and quickly examined himself. He appeared to be unscathed. There were no embers on his shirt or pants.

Thank you, Jesus.

"Ten Man—are you okay?" Wheaton shouted in his earpiece. "Talk to me!"

"I'm here." Tennyson's throat was dry and raspy with smoke, and his ears rang. "Torres is dead."

"Hallowell is coming now. Help is on the way."

Vengeance would have felt good—for a moment, at least. But then he'd have to deal with his conscience. He'd have to come before God and eventually admit to what he'd done and where his heart had been.

Maybe it was better this way.

Please God, let that be the case.

Just then, Hallowell appeared in the doorway. Hallowell rushed toward him and knelt at his side. Flames still licked the walls. Smoke filled the room and choked his lungs.

"Tennyson, check out that other heat signature," Wheaton said. "Now!"

"Where?"

"On the wall behind you."

"I'll see what I can do." Could there be another secret room? Was this one of Torres's right-hand men?

Hallowell helped him to his feet, and they both turned. An extravagant wooden screen stood behind them. Tennyson and Hallowell moved it to the side. The outline of a door greeted them. It was obviously created to blend in with the wall, all the way down to the handle, which looked like a piece of molding.

Tennyson's throat tightened. Did the person behind this door have another surprise just waiting to explode?

He nodded toward Hallowell before throwing the door open. They both breached the space, guns raised. Tennyson braced himself, preparing for gunfire. For resistance. For a fight for his life.

Instead of a fight, row after row of fancy dresses greeted them. A walk-in closet. Seemingly empty other than clothes.

Carefully, he flicked on the light atop his gun and stepped into the space. Though it was a closet, the room was bigger than his childhood bedroom.

Was there a deadly surprise waiting behind one of these outfits? He wouldn't put it past Torres.

Using his gun, he shoved some aside. Hallowell did the same on the other side. Slowly, they worked their way down, toward the back of the closet.

As he reached the last set of clothes and shoved them aside, he saw something that stopped him in his tracks.

A woman. A blonde. Curled into a ball. Her knees pulled to her chest.

He shined his light on her. She ducked her head behind her knees, shielding her eyes from the light.

When she drew her head up, the look in her eyes clutched Tennyson's heart. Fear glimmered there. The worst kind of fear: the kind that chained a person in silence, in speechlessness. That froze each muscle and took captive every thought.

The woman's eyes widened as she stared at him. And kept staring. And kept waiting.

Tennyson's mind paused in a moment of recognition.

Recognition? That was crazy. Why would he recognize her?

She certainly didn't appear to be a local. She was too pale. Too blonde. Too scared.

Was this one of Torres's concubines? One of the girlfriends he hired? They'd heard a few months ago that Torres had a girl here with him, but Tennyson knew nothing about her personally.

He observed her clothing. White silk pants. An expensive-looking beige tank top. Her nails were done. Her hair looked untouched. Her makeup perfect.

She wore jewelry. A lot of jewelry. Gold bangles and bracelets. Dangling earrings. Multiple rings with sparkling jewels.

Concubine? He wasn't so sure about that. This woman was well taken care of.

The truth fought to emerge from the depths of his thoughts and memories.

He lowered his weapon as he approached her. "Ma'am?"

"Please don't hurt me," she whispered.

Her eyes were wide and almost childlike, though Tennyson guessed her to be in her midtwenties. Her accent . . . it wasn't tinged with the Caribbean dialect that others around here had. No, it sounded American. Mid-Atlantic maybe.

He sucked in a breath as her features came into clearer focus.

He remembered where he'd seen her face before.

She was Mallory Baldwin. A socialite from Washington, DC.

Her family had been killed at the hands of terrorists a year ago. Her parents' bodies had been found at sea a month later. Investigators had assumed Mallory's body had been washed out into the ocean also.

But it hadn't been. Torres had kept Mallory here this whole time.

His heart stammered in his ears as he knelt in front of her. "It's going to be okay. We're here, and we're going to help."

"No one can help me."

7

He shook his head. "That's where you're wrong. No one's beyond hope. No one."

He believed those words for other people. Now if he could only believe them for himself as well.

CHAPTER 1

Two Years Later

"You're going to do great, Mallory." Grant Donovan squeezed her shoulders like a coach prepping a boxer before the big match.

Mallory Baldwin drew in a deep breath and stared at herself in the bedroom mirror. Her first stop on her thirty-city tour was a shelter for abused and trafficked women called Hope House on the Eastern Shore of Virginia. It was the perfect location to kick off her new initiative.

She stared at her reflection. Did her gaze hold the strength she'd been told she possessed? Or would people see beyond her best efforts and know that inside she was a quivering mess? Still the scared, broken woman who'd been rescued?

Two years. It had been two years since she'd been freed from the home of Dante Torres. Sometimes it felt like just yesterday. Other times it seemed like another lifetime.

She'd since been through counseling and therapy and drug rehab. She'd had solitude. She'd even tried chocolate and shopping therapy. Anything to try to mend the broken pieces of her soul.

Everyone said it was amazing how she bounced back. She wasn't sure she believed it yet. Anyone who really got to know her had to think she was fragile.

Maybe that's because she was.

And she'd always been.

And she always would be.

"Mallory?" Grant said, his hands still on her shoulders.

He stared at her reflection also, his gaze studious. Assessment was what Grant did best. He was her manager, but in the years since her rescue, she had turned to him for advice. She had come to depend on those bright blue eyes to see what needed to be seen.

But she desperately wished he would move his hands from her shoulders. He was touchy-feely, and Mallory was the opposite. Unwelcomed contact made her want to hurl. Sucked her back in time. Made her remember things she didn't want to remember.

"What are you thinking about, doll?" Grant seemed to sense how she'd prickled at his touch and removed his hands.

Did Mallory dare tell him what she was thinking about? She knew the pep talk she'd get in return. Did she even want to go there? To hear his platitudes?

No, she didn't.

She pushed a lock of hair behind her ear and stood, drawing on every ounce of her inner strength. "Let's do this."

He led her into a living room lined with chairs. Everyone quieted as she walked in. Reporters were here today, as well as local city council members, a representative from a government task force, and a local sheriff's deputy. But she hardly saw any of them.

No, her heart lurched at the sight of the women—the residents of Hope House—who were seated in the room. At the haunted look in their eyes. Because she understood it. She'd lived it.

Why had she been the one plucked out of obscurity to do this? Why had she been rescued, while so many others perished? Perhaps she was suffering survivor's guilt. She didn't know.

Grant insisted that Mallory was the perfect person for this role. Most people thought of human trafficking victims as being unlike them, he'd said. They thought of runaways. Girls overseas without family to miss them. Impoverished women, desperate to survive by whatever means necessary. Women who weren't relatable to the average American.

Apparently, Mallory was relatable. Grant, a master of PR who also had a Hollywood flair, had downplayed her family's wealth and influence and tried to make her look like the girl next door who'd been snatched away from her idyllic life in the Washington, DC, social scene and sold into slavery.

Mallory went along with his plan, trusting that he knew what he was doing. She wanted to make a difference, and she would play by Grant's rules if that's what was necessary to make this work.

As she stepped up to a makeshift stage area, everything felt like a blur around her, yet, at the same time, crystal clear. Grant introduced her, and she swallowed hard. So hard it hurt. Her hands trembled as she approached the wooden podium in front of her. The scar on her shoulder began throbbing, just as it always did when she got nervous.

She cleared her throat and forced herself to look up. Twelve women stared back at her. She had to focus on them. On helping them find healing.

"My name is Mallory Baldwin. I'm twenty-seven years old, and I'm the victim of human trafficking," she began, just as she'd rehearsed. She reached beneath the podium and pulled out a glass of water. She set it at the front of the wooden stand, a place where everyone could see it. "Water. It's essential for life. We must have it in order to survive. Yet water can also be devastating. It can drown us. Take it away, and we'll wither to nothing. It holds the power of life and death."

Water was a part of her survival story. Mallory had always been fascinated by it. Had adored trips to the beach. Then in captivity, she could see the beautiful water of the Caribbean surrounding the island. Trapping her there.

Water, essential to staying alive, had been poisoned to ensure compliance.

Good and evil had collided in one liquid. Yet it had been another form of water that had saved her—Living Water. Jesus, who'd helped her see beyond the temporary struggles of this world and into the eternal.

"If there's hope for me, then there's hope for you, too," she ended, wishing her voice didn't sound so high-pitched. "We can take our greatest struggles and turn them into our greatest victories. I'm not only talking about myself but all of you also. Our experiences, no matter how brutal, can make us stronger and tougher. Though we've been shattered, we can put ourselves back together again. We won't be the same as we were before. No, we can remake ourselves into women who are stronger. Against all the odds and statistics, we can rise above. We *will* rise above."

As she said the last word, and applause filled the space, she pulled her gaze away from the women in front of her and scanned the people standing at the back of the room. Jack and Savannah Simmons, who ran this shelter. Reporters. The sheriff's deputy.

Another man caught her eye, though. One she hadn't seen earlier. Something about the man made her heart stutter and stammer and squeeze as her subconscious scrambled to keep up.

She knew him, Mallory realized.

Knew him. Knew his face. Knew his eyes.

Her gut churned as life around her froze, and only this moment, this thought, mattered.

How did she know him? From where? It was on the cusp of her memory.

Mallory studied his features. The man was tall and lean with close-cropped dark hair that was longer on top. His frame was muscular, and his eyes looked intelligent, even from a distance.

She knew him from her time in captivity.

Alarm panged inside her, and the room began to spin.

Her thoughts twisted as she tried to pinpoint the exact instance in which they'd met. Was it in one of her drug-induced moments? Had he been a friend of Dante's?

"Mallory, are you okay?" Grant's voice snapped her from her haze.

People murmured around her. Reporters crept closer. But all Mallory could see was the man in the distance.

She stepped away from the microphone, not willing to make a spectacle of herself. "It's okay. I'm just . . ."

Sensing her unease, Grant touched her arm for just long enough to get her attention and direct her away from the podium. Mallory's gaze shot back across the room to the man.

He was gone.

Where? She scanned the entryway in the distance. He wasn't there.

Uncontrollable shakes overtook her, despite her efforts to control them.

Mallory was supposed to stay out here to mingle and do interviews. But she needed a moment to compose herself. Now.

Before all the strength she'd just shown was proven to be a lie.

• • •

Tennyson Walker couldn't get over the change in Mallory Baldwin. Last time he'd seen her, she'd been dressed up like a doll, curled in a ball, and nearly catatonic. He'd never been able to get the image out of his mind.

Two years later, Tennyson still had nightmares about finding her. Knowing that she'd been held as a slave. Remembering the depravity of the human soul that could allow something like this to happen.

"Ten Man, you made it."

He looked over and saw his former commander, Kade Wheaton, standing there. He now ran an organization called Trident International. The ex-military man had a heart of gold, and he dedicated part of Trident's mission to helping those suffering from PTSD.

"Sorry I'm late," Tennyson started. "My elderly neighbor was trying to haul bricks from his truck to his flower bed by himself. I had to help before he hurt himself."

"I'd expect nothing less. I can only imagine how this takes you back."

Tennyson exhaled slowly. "To my last mission as a SEAL? I'd say so."

"Does seeing Mallory make you regret leaving?"

"It was time for me to walk away. My mission was accomplished, and there was nothing left for me to do."

For months, all Tennyson had lived and breathed was to destroy Dante Torres. He'd told himself that when the job was done, he'd walk away from his naval career. That's what he'd done.

"You were one of the best men on the team," Wheaton said.

"And now I'll try to be one of the best men on your team at Trident," Tennyson said. "I'm looking forward to the change."

Wheaton turned as a man approached them.

"There's someone who'd like to meet you," he said. "Tennyson, this is Grant Donovan."

Tennyson shook the hand of the well-groomed man in front of him. Fortysomething, he had bright blue eyes that sparkled with charisma, and light-brown hair that curled back from his face in waves.

"Pleasure to meet you," Tennyson said. He had the feeling that Wheaton had already talked to the man and that this conversation had a distinct purpose.

Grant offered a hearty handshake. "I hear you're taking charge of the security division of Trident."

"That's correct."

Tennyson's gaze wandered across the room to Mallory as she emerged through a doorway. Savannah was talking with her, and she didn't look quite as shaken anymore.

Until her gaze shot over to him.

A flash of fear simmered in the depths of Mallory's eyes.

The look made Tennyson's gut clench.

He turned his attention back to Grant, unsure how to correct his misstep of coming here tonight. He should end this conversation as quickly as possible and get out of here. Wheaton had invited him, but he'd obviously upset Mallory. That had been the last thing he'd intended.

"I'd like to talk to you about doing a job for us," Grant said.

The only reason people would need to hire him would be because they were in trouble. The man now had Tennyson's full attention. "You're having problems?"

Grant gave a small shrug of his shoulders, noticeably trying to look more relaxed. "Problems? No, I wouldn't say that. But Mallory has had a touch of celebrity status since news of her rescue came out. There have been some unsettling messages. Some strange fans, if that's what you want to call them. Her safety is of utmost importance to us."

Tennyson let out his breath. "So no direct threats have been made?"

"No, but there's an underlying fear of things escalating."

Whenever someone became a public figure, the exposure put them more at risk than the average person. Grant had every right to be concerned.

But that didn't mean that Tennyson was in a position to take on a new role. He was going to be working behind the scenes, training ex-military to become protection experts. Tennyson had no desire to go back out into the field again, and he had a long list of reasons why.

"You have to understand that we're just starting the security arm of Trident," Tennyson said. "I'm sure Wheaton filled you in on how we operate. We want to be very careful and not jump into any contracts too soon—for everyone's sake."

"Who do you have available then? Certainly you have someone who's ready to take on the task." He stared at Tennyson, unblinking as he awaited—and expected—a response.

Tennyson carefully considered his answer. "Honestly? All of our guys are just starting the program. It hasn't gotten off the ground yet."

"*You're* trained, though."

"I'm trained only because I'm in charge of the program."

Something glinted in Grant's eyes. "We'll hire you then."

"I'm not doing any more fieldwork. I'm still recovering from a shoulder injury, to be honest."

Tennyson glanced at Wheaton, who shrugged, silently leaving the decision to Tennyson. That was one of the many things Tennyson appreciated about his former commander. There was a strong level of trust between them.

Just then, Tennyson's muscles pulled taut as he sensed someone behind him. He turned and saw Mallory.

Her gaze, once nervous, was now intense and smoldering as she stared at him.

He soaked in her features. Even though it had only been two years, she was even more beautiful than he remembered. Breathtaking even. Of course, everyone who'd ever seen her knew she was a stunner.

Her nearness caused Tennyson to suck in a quick breath. Instantly, two years' worth of guilt pummeled him.

Yes, at the time, they'd heard that Torres had a woman with him. But they had to make the call to wait. Going in too early could have compromised his mission of taking down Torres, and they weren't willing to let that happen. Hundreds of lives were at stake. As a result, Mallory had suffered—had continued to suffer—at the hands of a madman.

Tennyson would carry that guilt for the rest of his life.

"We've met before," Mallory said.

"Yes, we have," he said softly. "I'm Tennyson. Tennyson Walker."

"When?" She kept her chin high, even though her neck muscles looked strained.

Tennyson prepared himself to break the truth to her. Did Mallory remember him? Though Tennyson had saved her, she might associate him with the horror of what had happened to her.

But she had a right to know.

"The night you were rescued," he said, quickly noting that both Grant and Wheaton had backed away to give them privacy.

Mallory's eyes widened, and her lips parted with surprise. He saw the facts colliding in her head. Her gaze showed every emotion. Every memory. The raw pain there compounded his guilt.

"It was you," she whispered, stepping closer and studying his face without reserve. "You rescued me. You found me."

He offered a curt nod, not seeking admiration or thanks. Knowing he'd helped someone was enough. He'd thought defeating Torres and saving Mallory would redeem him from his utter failure when Claire died. But that wasn't the case. In fact, every day the loss still haunted him, still prevented him from moving forward.

"That's correct," he finally said.

Mallory continued to study him, and he braced himself for her next reaction.

"Thank you," she finally said. "I never got to tell you that. Thank you. Thank you so much."

At once, the scent of strawberries filled his senses.

Strawberries. When he'd first met her, she'd smelled like expensive perfume. The memory took him back in time for a moment. Flashbacks pierced him like bullets from the enemy.

"You don't have to thank me," he murmured.

He meant it. That wasn't why he'd come. In fact, he didn't deserve thanks or admiration.

Mallory stepped back, those wide eyes still on him and still full of gratitude. "Yes, I do. I should have earlier. I . . . I don't know why I didn't. I just had so much going on and—"

"Really, you don't need to say anything. I didn't do my job as a SEAL to get thank-yous."

Her perceptive gaze locked on his again. "You came here tonight. To see me?"

17

She wasn't the shrinking violet Tennyson had expected to encounter. He knew how trauma like what she'd been through could set a person back. Could break them. Could play with emotions and insecurities . . . indefinitely. But Mallory seemed to have conquered that.

"Yes, I came tonight to listen to you. I wanted to hear for myself how you were doing. My friends actually run this place."

"It's a noble cause. I enjoyed speaking with Savannah and Jack."

Tennyson shifted, unsure what to say next. There was an ocean's worth of things they could talk about, but none seemed appropriate.

"So, I hear you've started a nonprofit?" he finally said.

"That's right. I've channeled all of my efforts into Verto, from a Latin word for 'change.' It's always the first thing people ask." She cracked a soft smile, but it quickly faded. "We're trying to raise awareness on the issues of human trafficking and to help those who've been held captive to that life."

"And you're releasing a book?" Even as he asked the question, he knew he was just going through the motions of the conversation.

Other thoughts pressed more heavily on his mind. Mostly the messages Grant had mentioned. Was Mallory putting herself in danger by going on this tour? The thought caused his gut to twist.

"That's right. This weekend. I'll be kicking off a three-month, thirty-city tour, which includes book signings, public appearances, television and newspaper interviews, and even speaking before a congressional committee on human trafficking. All of the proceeds will go right back to Verto."

Tennyson tried to cast aside his anxiety. She was doing good work, and that was something to be proud of. He needed to focus on that instead of jumping into protective mode. "I hope that goes really well for you, Mallory."

A smile tugged at her lips. Something about the action made him feel alive. Made him long for more time with her. Made him want to sit down and talk with her—to really talk with her.

She tilted her head, her eyes still on him. "It was good to see you, Tennyson. Really good. I can't say thank you enough for what you did for me that night. There is no gift, no money, no anything that's big enough to show my appreciation."

"Knowing you're doing well—that's all the satisfaction I need." He meant it.

But would she feel that way if she knew that he'd played a part in delaying her rescue? In drawing out her suffering at the hands of a madman?

She gave him one last look of gratitude, then stepped away toward a reporter who was patiently waiting for a quote.

Tennyson watched her walk away. Though part of him was fascinated with the woman, another part felt unsettled. Was Mallory about to walk into the lion's den with this tour?

"So what do you say?" Grant picked up right where they'd left off, his gaze briefly trailing Mallory before his keen eyes latched on to Tennyson again. "It's obvious that she trusts you. I think you'd be a great fit on our team."

Our team. The man certainly knew how to spin things to make them enticing.

Tennyson offered a terse shrug. The idea of being around Mallory was tempting, no doubt about it. But he wasn't doing fieldwork anymore. Besides, when Mallory learned the truth, she wouldn't be able to trust him.

"I'm not really in the bodyguard business," he said.

Grant's expression tightened, and a shadow fell over his gaze. He looked around before nodding toward the corner. "Do you mind?"

Tennyson didn't know where this was going, but curious now, he excused himself from Wheaton and followed the man.

"I didn't want to mention this," Grant started. "But Dante Torres may still be alive."

CHAPTER 2

Certainly Tennyson didn't hear Grant correctly. "That's not possible."

"I'm afraid it is."

"Why would you think that?"

"Mallory was sent an e-mail from someone who claims to be Torres."

Tennyson wanted to laugh at the simple—yet unreliable—explanation. "Did you ever consider that it was a joke? A cruel prank of some sort?"

Grant stepped closer. "I did consider that, but the person who sent it knew things that only Torres would know."

Tennyson paused. "Like what?"

"What Mallory was wearing when she disappeared."

"Anyone could have gotten that information from a news article."

"That she's afraid of the dark."

"Anyone who knew her as a child would know that."

"That Torres doused himself with gasoline and lit a lighter to kill himself."

Tennyson's heart pounded in his ears with a deafening swoosh, swoosh, swoosh.

He couldn't come up with a reason why someone would know that . . . unless they were there that night. The specifics of the raid had been kept classified. Was Mallory even aware of that fact? He wasn't sure. As far as the public knew, Torres had simply died during the raid.

Tennyson's heart continued slamming into his rib cage.

"But I saw him go up in flames with my own eyes," he said.

At the peak of his reign of terror, Torres's cronies, known as Inferno, had been responsible for an embassy bombing in Russia, a shopping-area massacre in France, and the total destruction of a village in Africa.

Acts of violence such as those had died down in the years since his death. But if Torres was still alive and possibly regrouping . . .

Tennyson shook his head, snapping himself out of his trancelike state. The idea that Torres could be alive was enough to push Tennyson to the brink of . . . of what? Of uncontrolled anger? Of pulse-pounding fury?

But the fact remained that all this was probably for nothing. Torres was dead.

"I don't know what kind of game you're playing, but I saw him kill himself with my own eyes," Tennyson said through gritted teeth. "That man is dead. Burned to death at his own hands. An extensive autopsy was done and verified it was him."

Grant shrugged as if unconvinced. "A burned corpse is hard to identify, especially since they can't do genetic testing without a family member to compare his DNA to."

"We brought his remains back with us to the States for the top forensic anthropologist in the country to examine."

"I'm just saying that Torres and his network are powerful. They could have paid someone to fake the results."

Tennyson balled his hands into fists. "Everything confirmed it was Torres. His build, his height, his age. His teeth even."

"I just thought you'd want to know."

Tennyson narrowed his eyes. "Mallory didn't start her tour here by mistake, did she?"

Grant's eyes lost some of their glimmer. "No."

Grant had come with an agenda, Tennyson realized. An agenda that included running into Tennyson and having this conversation.

"How'd you connect me with her, anyway?" He'd refused to do any interviews on the subject or even let his name be leaked to the media. He didn't want publicity. He'd just wanted to do his job.

"Mallory often talks about the man from SEAL Team Six who rescued her. I knew about Trident. That Kade Wheaton was a SEAL. I did a little research and made some astoundingly good guesses."

Tennyson speculated there was more to the story than that, but he had other more pressing questions. "Why would you want me? There are plenty of bodyguards out there looking for work."

"Mallory is very particular about who she trusts, especially when it comes to men. I thought you'd be a good fit. We pay well."

"This isn't about money."

"Then make it about doing the right thing."

Grant's words hit him like a jab in the heart, but Tennyson had never been one to make an emotional decision.

"I'm not a bodyguard," he finally said.

Grant shoved a slip of paper into Tennyson's hand. "Think about it. I haven't mentioned this to Mallory yet."

Tennyson froze. "She doesn't know you're trying to hire a bodyguard or about the e-mail from Torres?"

"I monitor her e-mail, so I made sure she didn't see the one from the man claiming to be Torres. She has been getting other troubling messages, but I don't believe the senders are one and the same. I didn't want to shake her up right as this tour was kicking off. Plus, a possibility like that could undo every ounce of therapy she's had. The only reason she can sleep at night is because that man is dead. Until we know something for sure, I decided to keep it quiet."

Grant stared at him until Tennyson finally nodded in agreement. The man's explanation made sense—he supposed.

As Grant sauntered away, Wheaton rejoined Tennyson. His gaze trailed after the man. "What was that about?"

"He claims Torres is still alive. Said he got an e-mail from him and—he didn't say this outright—wonders if he'll come after Mallory." Tennyson scanned the room until his eyes landed on Mallory as she smiled at a reporter, looking cool under pressure. Unaware of the potential danger around her. Of the news that could turn her world upside down.

If it was just the e-mail, Tennyson might dismiss it. But Grant had intimated that the sender had known details about what had happened the night of the raid. The fact disturbed him.

"What do you think?" Wheaton asked.

"My mind is still turning right now." Tennyson's jaw tightened. "I saw the man die, Wheaton."

"Is there a chance Torres could have arranged the whole scenario?"

Tennyson wanted to deny it, but he couldn't. "I've learned to never say never."

Wheaton's hands went to his hips, and he followed Tennyson's gaze to Mallory. "You know, we're still a good three or four months out from being ready to get this new arm of Trident off the ground. If you wanted to take the job, the timing just might work out."

"I've already committed to helping you." Even as he said the words, desires warred inside him. If there was any possibility Torres was alive . . . Tennyson needed to see justice served.

"I appreciate your dedication. But let the decision be yours. I know how Torres affected you."

Affected him? He'd turned Tennyson's life upside down. Taken him into an abyss of vengeance and bitterness. He'd only recently started to climb out.

And he couldn't let himself go back there. Not without more proof.

No, there were plenty of other qualified people who would do a better job, who wouldn't be frozen like he was by memories of the past that tried to surface and remind him of his impossible choice.

Even if this whole scenario did capture his interest, Mallory would be better off with someone else—anyone else—besides him.

• • •

After a dinner of local clams and French fries, Mallory arrived back at the Cape Thomas rental house. The town was small—so small that there were hardly any hotels. The ones that were here claimed to be filled to the max. Savannah had said something about harvest season and migrant workers.

It didn't matter to Mallory. She liked the solitude this house on the bay brought with it. She'd stayed last night, and she'd stay tonight, before moving on down the road to Norfolk. Pit stop number one was almost behind her.

She and Grant were the only ones staying here tonight, even though the house was big enough for ten people. Originally, there was supposed to be a whole team with them, including Grant's assistant, an aide for Mallory, and various others at different points of the tour.

Right before Mallory had left, she'd decided that she'd be more comfortable with a small group. Specifically, she'd be more comfortable with just Grant, who'd become somewhat of a father figure to her. Being around too many people made her feel neurotic. Large crowds caused her calm facade to crumple as her mind scrambled to remain in control.

Currently, Grant was on the phone with someone, so Mallory decided to step outside for some fresh air. Freedom was something she'd never take for granted again, and the Chesapeake Bay glimmered at the back of the property, a temptation she couldn't ignore. She pulled on a sweater as her feet hit the deck.

The darkness was beginning to sink its teeth into the evening sky. As she glanced up, hoping to see the moon, she saw a bolt of lightning across the water instead. There was no rain or thunder or wind. Not yet, at least. Instead, she had a front-row seat to the storm in the distance.

The weather had been turbulent lately, as cold and warm air masses collided, and the season changed from winter to spring. Growing up, she'd loved thunderstorms. Now, not so much. Now, the storms seemed so ominous, a reminder of the things in her life that were out of her control.

Despite that, she stepped farther away from the house and the safety it offered. The balance between craving freedom and needing safety was delicate, at best. She'd yet to master it. Paranoia too often reared its ugly head.

A wooden walkway led from the steps of the deck to another deck overlooking the water. She inched toward it, hesitation urging her to go back, and stubborn determination pushing her forward.

Lightning cracked the sky in the distance again, and Mallory drew in a sharp breath. The violence and power in that one act of nature almost seemed like a sign for her to retreat.

But that was silly.

Nothing but woods led to the place. There was no danger out here. No reason to feel scared.

Of course, that's what she'd also thought that night at the swanky Caribbean resort where she and her parents had been vacationing. She'd felt untouchable then. She'd never be that naive again.

But knowing Dante was dead did a lot to allay her fears.

Here, on the banks of the Chesapeake Bay, the water didn't feel like an impenetrable wall preventing her from escaping. Here, it reminded her of peace and solitude.

As she leaned against the railing, the breeze picked up, indicating the storm was blowing closer. Her thoughts crashed back to her reunion with Tennyson hours earlier.

He'd been even more mind-blowing in reality than she'd imagined. In her mind, he'd been the bigger-than-life hero who'd rescued her from the consuming darkness. She'd thought of him often, yet she only had a vague memory of his exact features.

The man could have stepped off the screen of a superhero movie. Captain America maybe? He was lean and muscular. His eyes were wise and kind. He was brave and put his life on the line for others.

There really were men like him out there. Men who were truly heroes and who deserved that honor.

Or had she simply put the man on a pedestal?

She glanced across the water as the storm continued to seize the air and promise a violent awakening.

Why had Tennyson been in Cape Thomas? Coincidence? That had to be it.

Except she didn't believe in coincidences. Had Grant purposely chosen this location to start the tour? Why would he have done that? Was it because he'd hoped Tennyson would be here?

The wind gusted again, and as it did, the hair on Mallory's neck prickled.

Her spine stiffened. What were her instincts trying to alert her to? Was danger lurking close by?

She glanced around. The only light she saw came from the windows of the house behind her. Otherwise, it was darkness.

She swallowed hard, fighting the fear that wanted to consume her.

Over the past couple of weeks, she'd been sensing that she was being watched. She hadn't told anyone. They'd think she was paranoid. If they were too concerned about her, this whole tour could be canceled.

This circuit was the only thing that was keeping Mallory going. Knowing that she could take her heartache and redeem it by helping others had given her a reason to go on. She didn't want to alert anyone that paranoia could be kicking in.

And paranoia was the only thing these feelings could be attributed to. After all, who would be watching her out here in the middle of nowhere?

Sure, she'd gotten some strange e-mails from a man she called Nameless. But those messages were most likely harmless, written by an overzealous admirer. The sender had wanted to feel how soft her skin was. To gaze into her eyes all day. Thought the two of them were destined to spend forever together.

Grant monitored her inbox, sending all pertinent e-mails to a second inbox that had been set up for Mallory. She'd requested to see those anonymous messages. Part of her hadn't wanted her to read them, but she had anyway.

There had been a few fans who'd been slightly aggressive after she did an interview on the national news program *Yolanda*. One had cornered her at the airport, wanting an autograph. Another had tried to sequester her at a restaurant, ignoring her efforts to leave and essentially blocking her path. But those incidents had been isolated.

That only left . . . Torres's network, Inferno. But why would any of them want to watch her? She knew nothing. The men had spoken in Spanish when she was around, and she could hardly understand a word of it.

No, the only reason one of them would be watching was if she was a threat . . . which she wasn't.

Which meant she was paranoid.

Just then, a stick snapped in the distance.

She froze.

Something was out there. Something hiding in the darkness.

CHAPTER 3

It's nothing, Mallory. An animal. A deer maybe.

She forced herself to pivot. She faced the woods to her left, looking for a sign of where the sound had come from.

Everything had gone silent again.

She desperately wanted to get back inside to Grant, yet she felt frozen with fear. Was someone watching her?

Panic clawed at her throat.

No, Mallory. It's just an animal. Those days of living in fear are behind you. Now it's time to move on. You've crested that peak.

She drew her sweater closer.

She needed to head back. Now.

Just as she took a step, another crack sounded.

That had definitely been a stick breaking. Was someone out there?

She glanced in the direction of the noise.

A glimmer of something caught her eye. Based on the height and size . . . had those been glasses? Binoculars? Night-vision goggles?

She didn't know. But she ran.

And she knew she couldn't speak of this to anyone. Not even Grant, who was already acting concerned.

Grant would call her therapist. Her therapist would say Mallory wasn't fit to do this. Some people already thought she was rushing things, even if she knew she wasn't.

Without this tour, her life would go back to being without a purpose. She couldn't let that happen. She couldn't let her paranoia undo all the good work she'd already done. For the first time in years, she felt like she was really alive.

She had to ensure the past didn't try to draw her back and permanently wreck her future. Her therapist had warned her about it. He'd told her stories about people who'd gone through major trauma and who jumped into the limelight too quickly. One had ended up in a mental institution. Another was now addicted to drugs and alcohol, a cycle that had started as she'd tried to numb the pain.

Mallory had agreed to check in with her therapist every month. She'd also agreed to allow him to get updates from Grant on how she was acting.

Telling Grant that she thought she was being watched? That she kept thinking she'd seen a dead man?

It would only make her look weak and delusional.

She couldn't let that happen.

No, she refused to let Dante strip anything else from her.

•   •   •

Tennyson stared out the window of his new office, a space with a brilliant display of the Chesapeake Bay just beyond a few trees at the shoreline. He should be working on some notes, but all he'd been able to think about for the past twelve hours was Mallory Baldwin and Dante Torres.

His watch beeped—he'd set an alarm—and the sound pulled him from his preoccupation. He had to head back to his place and pick up some food he'd forgotten to bring in for Wheaton's surprise birthday celebration at the office.

He stood, but before he could exit, his phone rang. He glanced at the screen, and his heart stuttered.

Admiral Kline.

It had been a long time since he'd spoken with him. Since Claire's funeral, for that matter.

He sat back down as he put the phone to his ear. "Admiral, thanks for returning my call."

"Good to hear your voice, Tennyson. What can I do for you?"

Just hearing the man's deep, commanding tone took Tennyson back in time, but he couldn't let that happen. He had to stay focused. "I just heard a rumor. I wanted to find out if you knew anything about it."

"Rumor about what?"

"Dante Torres." As silence stretched on the phone line, Tennyson absently straightened the few personal items he had on his desk: a medal the navy had bestowed upon him for bravery after his last mission, the now well-used Bible he'd received at his baptism, and a photo of his family back in Indiana.

"What about him?" the admiral finally asked.

"I heard he might still be alive."

The admiral scoffed. "Alive? You and I both know better."

"So you haven't heard anything to the contrary?"

"No, why would I? We both know he died that day."

"That's what I thought also. I figured the rumor had no merit." But how had the sender of that e-mail known that Torres killed himself with gasoline and a lighter? No one would have known that except for the SEALs there that day and Mallory. The fact bothered him.

Admiral Kline let out a deep sigh. "There is one thing."

Tennyson tensed. "What's that?"

"There's rumor that Inferno is reorganizing. That there's a new leader at the helm. We don't know who this person is yet. But there's been a lot of underground chatter."

"Is that right?"

"I'm not saying that person is Torres. Of course. But there has been some activity surrounding Inferno lately."

Inferno reorganizing? The thought caused acid to pour through Tennyson. He couldn't even stomach the idea.

Tennyson chewed on the admiral's words during the short drive to his house. He didn't know anything either—if he was telling the truth. Tennyson felt certain that the admiral would tell him if he knew something. They both had a stake in the situation. If Torres was alive, Admiral Kline would be the first to hire Tennyson to hunt the man down. After all, the man had killed his daughter. Claire.

A few minutes later, Tennyson pulled up to his temporary home. It was small—a little cottage on the Chesapeake Bay, less than nine hundred square feet. But it was perfect for him. He was renting it for now, until he could move in to more permanent quarters at the new Trident facility.

Before he went inside, he walked toward the high embankment over the water. A set of wooden stairs led to a sandy beach below. He drew in a long breath of fresh air, trying to clear his thoughts.

Should he have said yes to Grant's request for a bodyguard? He couldn't deny that the idea ignited something in him. But Mallory would be better off with someone not linked to her past, who didn't hold the secret that he did. And Tennyson wasn't sure he could stomach working for Grant. Besides, Wheaton needed him here.

Put it behind you, Tennyson. Move on.

The things that he'd seen and done as a SEAL would always be a part of him, though. They'd made him who he was today. As much as he tried to forget the past, it was always there, hovering just a little too close for comfort. Taunting him. Reminding him of what he'd lost.

As he stepped away, something on the beach below caught his eye. It couldn't be . . . It was.

A body.

A blonde.

Lying on the shore.

Something about the woman's build, her hair, her clothes, drove his thoughts to only one person: Mallory. Was it Mallory?

CHAPTER 4

Tennyson dashed down the stairs. As he did, he pulled out his cell phone and called 911. He tried to control his racing thoughts.

"What's your emergency?"

"This is Tennyson Walker, five-one-three Sunset Way in Cape Thomas. There's a body on the shore outside of my property. You need to send the police and an ambulance. Now."

"I'll send someone out now—"

The operator started to ask more questions, but Tennyson put the phone back in his pocket. He reached the wet shoreline, ignoring the putrid scent saturating the sand, and rushed toward the body. Gently, he turned the woman over.

The face came into view.

It wasn't Mallory.

He released his breath. His relief was short-lived, though. It might not be Mallory, but someone had died.

He put a hand to her neck, already knowing the woman was dead but needing to confirm it.

There was nothing there. No heartbeat. No rise and fall of her chest. Nothing.

He dialed Wheaton's number as he looked for any other evidence of what had happened. He studied her skin for any visible cuts or bruises. He saw none.

How had she died? Had she drowned?

As he looked the woman over, compassion welled in him. The body hadn't begun decaying yet, so he guessed she hadn't been dead long.

As he turned her back to her side, part of her shirt slipped off her shoulder.

A circle with a flame in the center stared back at him.

He pressed his eyes closed. That was Torres's symbol. He branded his women with it, as if they were worth no more than cattle.

Anger burned through him.

"What's going on?" Wheaton answered. "No birthday song?"

Tennyson shoved the phone between his ear and shoulder, wishing he had a happier greeting for his friend. "A body washed up on the beach outside of my house."

"A body?" Wheaton's voice lost its lightheartedness.

"She's been branded by Inferno. I already called the cops. They're on their way."

"Unbelievable," Wheaton muttered. Silence stretched a moment. "This has to be connected with Mallory's appearance in town. If someone really is after her, maybe they left this body as a way of sending a message."

"I feel like they're sending me a message, not her."

"Maybe they are."

"Why would someone do that?"

"You helped disband a major terrorist network. You played a pivotal role in Torres's death. Maybe that's why. Maybe someone left that body there purposely, knowing you'd find it."

"Or maybe someone was hoping that word would get back to Mallory about this. Maybe this is one more way of threatening her."

"Whoever did this had to know that word would get back to her," Wheaton said. "With her connection to Torres, there's no way it wouldn't. Maybe you should reconsider that offer to run security for Mallory."

The sparks that had started earlier inside him grew stronger, brighter, more powerful. Torres—whether dead or alive—was still spreading his influence, still flexing his muscles. Tennyson couldn't stomach the thought of it. Inferno should have withered.

But someone was determined to keep Torres's legacy alive.

That was unacceptable.

Tennyson stared down at the body again, and his thoughts slammed back to Mallory. If someone wasn't watching out for her, she could be the next one who met this fate. Could he really live with himself if he let that happen?

Someone was playing a game, and they wanted to use Tennyson as a pawn. If there was one thing Tennyson hated it was being used.

But, against his better instincts, he knew Grant Donovan's job offer was one he couldn't refuse. Not when Mallory's life was on the line.

• • •

Just as Tennyson reached Virginia Beach, the dark clouds overhead consumed both the sky and the air. Based on the size and color of the mass, this storm would be a doozy. He just hoped he could get to the hotel before the sky broke open and unleashed its torrent of emotion.

By the time he arrived in downtown Norfolk, the wind had picked up, and a light spattering of rain had started. He parked, knowing one of the guys from Trident would pick up the vehicle later, and hurried into the hotel lobby. As the automatic doors closed behind him, thunder rumbled outside.

He paused in the entryway and spotted Grant Donovan. The man strode across the room and met him. "Tennyson, I'm glad to see you made it here okay, especially with this storm bearing down on us."

"Yes, I made it inside just before the sky broke."

"Excellent. Come on over this way. Mallory and I just arrived. You caught us just in time."

"Before we meet Mallory, there are a couple of things I'd like to discuss with you." Tennyson stopped, refusing to go any farther until Grant looked him in the eye, and they had a mutual understanding.

"Of course. What's on your mind?"

"I just want to confirm what we talked about on the phone. I'll take this job, but I want to help investigate these threats, not just be a bodyguard."

Grant nodded. "We can arrange that. In fact, I think it's a good idea."

"I'd also like to bring someone else on to help with security."

Grant squinted. "What do you mean?"

"If I'm helping with the investigation, that means I won't be able to keep an eye on Mallory at all times. I'll need someone else."

"Who do you propose?"

"There's someone I worked with. I think she would be excellent."

"She?"

Tennyson nodded, his gaze flickering over to where Mallory was standing against the wall. No one else was near. Still, he didn't like seeing her alone. He scanned the lobby but saw no one suspicious.

"Her name is Kori Burns. She's a former police officer. Top of the line. I mentioned it to her that I could have a job lead, and she said she's available to start in two days."

"Will you be okay for two days without her? You seem to think it's important that she's here."

"As long as I have a clear picture of what's on the schedule, where we're going, and I can review the routes we'll be traveling, we should be fine. The threat is minimal right now, but definitely something that I want to be taken seriously."

"You know we have a limited budget for this tour, right?"

"I'm not concerned with money. As long as I have a place to sleep and food to eat, I'll be okay. You can give my salary to Kori."

Something flickered in Grant's eyes . . . approval. He nodded. "Very well then."

Tennyson lowered his voice. "Did you tell Mallory about Torres yet?"

Grant shook his head. "I thought we could tell her together. For the record, she's opposed right now to the idea of having a bodyguard. She thinks it's unnecessary."

"We'll talk to her together tonight."

"Let's do that. Let's not keep her waiting any longer."

As Tennyson walked toward his client, he took a moment to study her. Her wavy hair was pulled back into a twist. She wore snug jeans and a tailored, red jacket that looked professional yet youthful. She exuded confidence and vibrancy, which only made him admire her more. The image was quite the change from the brokenness she'd personified when he'd found her in Torres's compound.

As he got closer, he noticed the gray circles beneath her baby blues. The tiny lines around the edges. The way her eyelids occasionally drooped.

She was tired.

But when she spotted him, she smiled and the grayness, the lines, and the droopiness disappeared. For a moment, at least.

"Mallory, you remember Tennyson, right?" Grant said with a glimmering smile.

"Of course." Mallory nodded at him, but her actions seemed almost sluggish. Reserved? Maybe. Road weary? Quite possibly.

In an instant, Tennyson wished he could wipe away some of the burden from her gaze. That he could somehow make her load a little lighter. That he'd be able to see her smile more.

But what he really wished was that he could undo her year as Torres's captive.

Another clap of thunder sounded overhead, and the hotel walls rumbled along with it. Lightning followed, then a gust of wind that pushed a smattering of debris against the building's windows and doors.

"This storm is going to be a monster. Mallory, why don't you show Tennyson up to the suite? I've got to speak with the manager about the bill, but I'll be right there."

"Sure thing."

Tennyson walked with her toward the elevator, uncertain what to say. He'd never been suave or had a way with words—nor did he even care about being those things. He only wished he could put Mallory more at ease right now.

"I'm glad you made it here okay," Mallory finally said. The clack of her shoes sounded twice for every one of his paces.

"It was a nice drive over the Bay Bridge Tunnel." He hated how mundane the conversation seemed, but maybe they were both hesitant to talk about the huge issue they had in common: the fact that Dante Torres had stolen something from both of them. Besides, it wasn't a conversation for an elevator.

The raid had pulled them together, and they had a connection that very few people would understand. Grant had been clever to bring them together now. Certainly he realized that Mallory would probably warm up to him faster than most.

"That stretch of road terrifies me," Mallory said. "The entire time I'm on it, I rehearse about what I would do if I went off the side of the bridge and into the bay. It's neurotic, I know."

He smiled at her chatter. "I think a lot of people do that."

They stopped by the elevators and waited for the doors to open. Black marble walls made the place look expensive but dark. Instrumental music played overhead. The smell of lemon-scented cleaner hung in the air.

The elevator doors finally dinged open. Tennyson took a step with her inside when two businessmen chatting about the stock market hurried in front of them, oblivious.

Mallory froze, one foot halfway into the car. Her face paled.

As the doors started to close, Tennyson tried to nudge her forward. Mallory's feet seemed to have taken root, though.

"Mallory?"

She nodded toward the two men, who suddenly noticed them. "You go ahead."

The elevator doors squeezed shut. Tennyson could guess what had caused her reaction, but he didn't want to make assumptions.

Her gaze—now listless—darted up to him, and her jaw looked clenched. "I never get in the elevator with strangers," she explained. "I can't. It's a trigger, and it causes me to panic."

"That's understandable."

She pressed her lips together, as if trying to choose her words wisely. "I'm sorry if I made a scene."

"Don't apologize. Will you be okay being inside an elevator with just me?" *Because I'll never let anything happen to you. Ever.* He kept that quiet, though. No need to further scare her with that declaration.

She rubbed her shoulder—at the location where Torres most likely branded her.

"Yes, I'm okay with it," Mallory said. "Only because I know you're one of the good guys."

Warmth filled his chest, but it quickly cooled. There was so much she didn't know about him.

Another elevator dinged to a stop. They slipped inside, and he hit the close door button before anyone could share the space.

He stood at the back of the elevator, his hands at his side, as they started up toward the fifth floor. He was all too aware of Mallory standing beside him. Though she didn't move or fidget, waves of anxiety poured from her like heat coming from asphalt on a summer day.

"I really think having a bodyguard is unnecessary." She clasped her hands in front of her, her wide eyes accentuating her high cheekbones. "Just for the record."

"It's only a safety precaution. Just for the record." He flashed a reassuring smile even though remorse pounded inside him. Soon enough, he'd tell her the truth. Part of her world would crash down when he did. He hated to think about it. But she deserved to know.

"I heard about the body." Her quiet voice broke the stillness.

He nodded, trying not to show how worried he really was. "I suppose the FBI talked to you?"

"They did. It's been . . . unsettling, to say the least." She smoothed a hair back as if it was wayward. It wasn't.

Silence passed for a moment.

"I didn't know her," Mallory finally said.

"I didn't think you did."

"She was found outside your house?"

He swallowed hard. "That's right. I'm unsure why, at this point. But I know the FBI is working diligently to find some answers."

Just then, the lights blipped.

The elevator grunted.

Lurched.

Stopped.

He glanced at Mallory in time to see the color drain from her face.

Then everything went black.

• • •

"Mallory, can you hear me?"

The elevator stopped spiraling. She closed her eyes, trying to grasp reality and pull herself out of her panic. She forced air into her lungs. Tried to remember everything her therapist had told her.

Acknowledge and accept the fact that you're panicking. Watch and wait, remembering that this moment will pass. Breathe deeply and concentrate on doing so, knowing it will distract you from overwhelming thoughts. Repeat.

Someone had spoken.

She tried to talk but nothing came out. *Speak, Mallory. Move your mouth. Force air across your vocal cords.*

"Mallory?"

That's right. Tennyson is here. He's a good guy.

His deep, calm voice pulled her back to reality.

"I'm here." Her words sounded so shrill that she could hardly understand them herself.

"It's okay. It's just you and me in here. The power must have gone out."

A power outage. That was right. The storm raged outside.

That fact made her feel only a little better. Fear still charged through her like a runaway train.

"Mallory?" Tennyson repeated, his voice soft and prodding.

"Yes?" Now her voice sounded mouselike, but she couldn't alter it.

"I'm reaching out my hand toward you. If you'd like to hold on to something—to someone—I'm here. It's okay if you don't, though. It's your choice."

His words washed over her. His hand. She could hold it. Find an anchor in him.

Was that what she wanted? Or would touching him turn her stomach in revulsion?

She wasn't sure.

At that moment, the elevator jerked. The lights blinked before going dark again.

She started to reach for him but stopped. That was one area she hadn't mastered yet. Intimacy. Touch. Human contact.

Instead, she wrapped her arms over her chest and squeezed.

"It's going to be okay," Tennyson murmured.

Her mind flashed back in time. That's what he'd said when he rescued her. He'd promised her everything would be okay. And then he'd swept her away from that year of her life and into safety.

She knew better than to have a crush on him. Honestly, she couldn't see herself having a crush on *anyone* again. Ever. It didn't matter what her therapist told her. But, against her better judgment, she had Tennyson up on a pedestal as the bigger-than-life hero who'd rescued her. As someone who could do no wrong. As a literal knight in shining armor.

"I used to hate the dark," Tennyson said.

Mallory's thoughts shifted. "Did you?"

"That's right. All the way up through middle school. I was a late bloomer, as my mom said. So when the lights went out in the school locker room once, some of my classmates decided to shove me in a locker."

She tried to picture someone doing that to the strong and capable Tennyson Walker. She couldn't. In her mind, he seemed undefeatable. "That sounds horrible."

"I was frozen with fear. I'll never forget it. Finally, one of the PE teachers found me. The boys who did it got a slap on the wrist."

"They deserved more."

"Of course they did. But they were the star athletes. Even in middle school, it made a difference."

Unfair. That was life sometimes. A lot of times. And that fact made her burn inside. "I'm sorry. How did you get over your fear?"

"I remembered that if Christ could conquer death, I could conquer anything in my life as well. We've only got one chance to make the most of each day, right? So whenever I got scared, I remembered that fear was robbing me of the joy of the moment. It sounds so simple, doesn't it? But it really did help."

"Sometimes changing our mind-set is the only thing we have control over." She cleared her throat, wishing her voice would return to normal. "That's what my therapist tells me, at least."

"There's some wisdom in that. I've found over time that the darkness is really pretty fascinating."

"Why's that?" She couldn't imagine.

"Darkness can blind you. But one flicker of light drives away the night and changes everything. The smallest flame can help us see what we couldn't see before."

Just at that moment, she realized how very close she was standing to him. Close enough to feel his warmth. To smell his woodsy cologne.

Self-consciously, she stepped back and tried to get a grip on her emotions. "I'm sorry."

He softened his voice. "I've been through SEAL training. I think I can handle a dark elevator."

She tried to shift her thoughts from her fears. Her therapist's voice echoed through her mind. *You must have focus in order to overcome. You can control your thoughts. Your emotions. Or you can let them control you.*

She cleared her throat, determined to take her therapist's advice. She needed to distract herself. "I've heard SEAL training is brutal."

"It has to be. It doesn't come close to matching what you experience out in the field."

"I suppose that's true. I'm kind of surprised you're not a SEAL anymore. You're still young. You had more years ahead of you." He was probably just over thirty years old, if she had to guess.

She sensed the air around him change, and she knew she'd hit on a sensitive subject.

"It was time," Tennyson said.

"I see."

Before she could say anything more, the elevator jerked back to life. The lights flashed on—and stayed on.

Mallory cleared her throat again and smoothed her jeans, desperate to do something to stay busy and cover the embarrassment over her panic. "Thank you, Tennyson."

"It's no problem, Mallory. It's never a problem."

•   •   •

Grant rushed into the suite fifteen minutes later, bypassing the bedroom doors and heading directly toward Tennyson and Mallory in the living area at the back. "Mallory, you're going to want to see this. You too, Tennyson."

Mallory froze. Based on his demeanor, he had bad news.

Grant held up his phone, the air crackling with energy around him. "I just got these photos in my inbox."

After a slight hesitation, Mallory took the device. She could feel Tennyson peering over her shoulder, and warmth spread through her. She scolded herself. All her life, she'd been defined by the men around her.

She was going to stand on her own two feet. That meant no tingles were allowed. No racing hearts. No dreaming of a happy ever after.

Those things were so far from her reality anyway.

As the screen came into focus, Mallory's gut clenched.

There were pictures. Of Mallory.

In one, she was sitting at a restaurant eating. In another, she was checking into a hotel—not this one, however. In the final one, she was standing in front of some large shipping containers, doing a PSA that would run on several TV stations.

A tremble quaked through her muscles, strong and furious, and the phone slipped from her hands in the aftermath. Tennyson grabbed it before it hit the floor.

Mallory wasn't imagining things. Someone *was* watching her.

"Are these from Nameless?" she finally asked, her voice cracking and giving away her anxiety.

Grant shook his head. "I can't be certain."

"I take it you had no idea someone was following you?" Tennyson asked.

Mallory stepped back so she had a better view of both men. Then she shook her head, feeling a smear of guilt. That wasn't the entire truth.

"No, I didn't see anyone who was acting suspiciously," Grant said. "But someone is obviously stalking Mallory. I think we brought you on just in time, Tennyson."

"These pictures were sent to your e-mail, Grant?" Tennyson narrowed his eyes in thought. "Why not Mallory's?"

"I'm monitoring all of her e-mails for now. I forward her any that she needs to personally reply to." Grant paced away, shaking his head still. "I'll send these to the detective in DC."

Tennyson's hands went to his hips. "You're working with a detective in DC?"

"We are," Grant said. "As well as FBI Special Agent Turner."

"This seems like just as good a time as any to debrief," Tennyson said.

Something about the way he said the words caused anxiety to ricochet up Mallory's spine. What did he mean by debrief? Perhaps they just needed to discuss the threat assessment?

That was probably it.

They sat down; Mallory in an armchair, Grant on the couch across from her, and Tennyson in the chair beside her.

The two men exchanged a glance.

What did that mean? Mallory knew: the two men had something to tell her.

She rubbed her throat, fighting unease. Fighting the urge to run. To bury her head in the sand.

Tennyson nodded at Grant, and Grant shifted, angling to face her better. "There's something you should know, Mallory," he started.

Her body stiffened. "Okay."

Grant leaned toward her, his elbows propped on his knees. "Mallory, we got an e-mail from someone who's claiming to be Torres."

The blood drained from her face. "It was a joke. Obviously. Dante's dead."

"Of course that's what we think. But we need to take every necessary precaution, just in case."

Her gaze shot to Tennyson. "You saw him die . . . right?"

He nodded stiffly. "That's correct."

"So this is all for nothing. It's someone playing a cruel joke." Images of Dante flashed into her mind. All those times she felt like she was being watched. Almost like Dante would never let her get away that easily. She was his property. His death was the only thing that had kept her safe. If there was any chance he was alive . . .

Her hands began to tremble.

"We take every threat seriously," Tennyson said, glancing at her twitching muscles and frowning. "Though this is most likely nothing, we want to explore the possibility. Plus, there have been those odd messages from Nameless. You have to understand that your safety is of utmost importance. I'd like to bring on a security team—"

She swung her head back and forth. "No, I don't want a team. That's overdoing it. All of this is probably for nothing."

"Mallory, we hope that's the case, but we need to examine this from every angle first," Grant said.

She shook her head again. "I only want you, Tennyson. I actually didn't want anyone, but if I have to have a guard, you're the only one I trust. Being around too many strangers . . . well, it's kind of like being in an elevator with people I don't know. I don't handle it well."

Tennyson shifted. "How about at least one other guard? A woman."

A woman? Mallory might be able to handle that. Better than a group of testosterone-pumped men, at least. "I'll consider it."

"There are some events I may have to bring in more guards for," Tennyson continued. "But there could be two of us traveling with you."

"If that's what we have to do."

"And Mallory, you shouldn't go anywhere alone. There always needs to be a guard with you. Do you understand?"

The reality of the situation was hitting her . . . hard. Too hard. Her mind was reeling, hardly able to keep up. "I understand."

"Wherever we go, there will be plans in place."

"Are you sure this isn't all overkill?" she asked.

Tennyson and Grant exchanged another look.

"I wish it was," Tennyson said. "But my job is to keep you safe, and I plan on doing just that."

Grant let out a long breath and stood. "Mallory, I've got to go make a phone call. It's Ashley's birthday today."

"Tell her I said happy birthday," Mallory said. Ashley was Grant's daughter, and he didn't get to see her very often because of his divorce.

"I'll do that. And maybe you and Tennyson could get to know each other since you'll be working so closely together. Are you okay with that?"

She nodded.

"I'll have dinner sent up then." He started to reach for her arm but stopped. They'd been through this routine before. Touching wasn't something she was comfortable with. She didn't know if she'd ever be comfortable with it again.

Grant settled on a nod, and then disappeared into his bedroom.

Mallory glanced at Tennyson, whose eyes had followed Grant. Perceptive. He was the kind of guy who was always watching, observing, calculating. All desirable attributes for a bodyguard.

"Grant comes across as a little flippant or self-centered sometimes, but he's really a nice guy," she finally said.

Tennyson's gaze flickered toward her, but he still didn't look convinced. "I'm sure he is. How'd you meet him?"

"Right after my rescue, my life was in turmoil." She stood and paced over to the window where drizzles of rain formed rivers down the glass. Her mind went back in time to that day. "Everybody seemed to want a piece of me, including some relatives who wanted to profit from my supposed death. The media had been knocking on my door.

Numerous managers had approached me, and I wasn't impressed with any of them."

"Smart girl."

She offered a faint smile. "Then I met Grant. He asked me to meet for coffee. I only agreed after I'd done some research on him and seen that he'd done good work in the past."

"Coffee sealed the deal?"

She glanced outside again, shrugging—though barely. "Over lattes, Grant listened to me tell my story. He asked questions. He was interested in what I had to say. Most of all, he didn't bring marketing schemes with him . . . or contracts for me to sign."

"That was . . . considerate."

"Before he left, he gave me his card and asked me to call him if I ever needed help. Since that moment, he's taken care of me and given me guidance. I've had no reason not to trust him."

"Good for you."

She finally looked at him and nodded. "Yeah, I'm not complaining."

Mallory's gaze went back to the window, and she watched the people moving down below. Even though it still rained, people scurried back and forth, most of them walking quickly in an afternoon rush.

One person in particular caught her eye. Mallory blinked, certain she was seeing things.

"What's wrong?"

She shook her head, trying to rid her mind of the thought. Her eyes were tricking her. Or it was the power of suggestion.

That's what it had to be.

Because otherwise, she'd just seen Dante Torres on the sidewalk.

CHAPTER 5

"It's nothing," Mallory finally said, raising her chin. Her eyes shifted before Tennyson could see the truth there.

"It doesn't look like nothing." Tennyson rose and moved closer, wondering exactly what had spooked her. "You look frightened, like you saw a ghost."

"My eyes were playing tricks on me." She crossed her arms and turned away from him. "I thought I saw someone, but I was mistaken."

"Who?"

She pressed her lips together. Swallowed hard. Shook her head again. "No one."

"Mallory . . ."

She pressed her lips together again, and Tennyson was sure Mallory was going to make up another excuse. Instead, she said, "I thought I saw Dante, okay? But it wasn't him. It was simply someone with dark hair who looked like him. It was just a by-product of our conversation. I'm thinking about Dante, so now I'm starting to see him. I'm sure there's a word for this type of thing."

His shoulders tightened, and he stepped closer to the window. "Is that right?"

"I mean, I know he's dead. It doesn't matter that someone sent that e-mail. It was just a joke. Believe me, if Dante was still alive, he wouldn't have waited two years to reveal himself again." She let out a fake laugh that quickly faded into a frown. "Sometimes the past just tries to pull you back. You know?"

Tennyson peered into the downtown street below. The rain had eased into a drizzle as the storm moved away. Numerous people moved across the sidewalk, but no one who looked like Torres.

"You think I'm crazy, don't you?" Mallory said softly.

"No, I don't."

The truth was, Tennyson still thought he saw Claire sometimes, too.

But besides that, there was the fact that Torres could still be alive. There was the fact that someone was stalking Mallory. And there was the fact that a dead body branded with Inferno's symbol had washed up on Tennyson's property.

He waited until Mallory went to bed before having a heart-to-heart with Grant. Tennyson motioned for the man to join him in the living area, away from Mallory's bedroom. Grant followed, seeming hesitant and slightly exhausted. The two of them needed to talk about their plan for the rest of this tour, though.

"Have you received any more e-mails from the person claiming to be Torres?" Tennyson kept his voice low as he sat across from Grant. "Did it come to your inbox or Mallory's?"

Grant looked over his shoulder, toward Mallory's door. "No, just the one. And it came to her inbox, but like I told you, I'm monitoring those e-mails."

"Who else knows about that e-mail?"

"Agent Turner. He tried to trace the IP address, but it was untraceable. He had a whole bunch of technical language he used as to why, but that's what it boiled down to."

That didn't surprise Tennyson. "Did that e-mail have any of the same markers of the e-mails Nameless sent?"

Grant released a slow breath before shaking his head. "No, the wording didn't have his usual flair or sentiment. The all caps, for example. Agent Turner didn't indicate it was from the same person."

Tennyson had replayed Torres's death over and over again in his mind, more times than he'd wanted to. "That dead body resembling Mallory that washed up on my beach was no accident. If this is a game, then the stakes are high. Too high."

Grant sighed and ran a hand through his hair. "None of this was supposed to happen. This was supposed to be a victory tour to show that Mallory had overcome her ordeal. Now it appears someone wants to make her go through agony again. That's why it's so important that you're here."

Tennyson shifted, trying to think everything through. "I'd like to see those e-mails you said Mallory received. I'd like to figure out if there's any connection between them and Torres."

"Of course." Grant strode across the room and reached into a briefcase on the couch. He handed him a stack of papers. "I've printed them all out for you."

"When did this start?" He rose, taking the stack over to the small table against the window. Rain drizzled down the glass and a dark, overcast sky goaded on dreary thoughts of danger and gloom.

Grant followed after him, some of his Hollywood facade fading under the fluorescent lights overhead. "After she appeared on *Yolanda*."

"All of these in a month?"

Grant nodded, grabbing a bottle of water from the fridge behind him. "She gets at least one a day."

"And you have no clue who's sending them?"

Grant downed a large gulp of water before answering. "Not one earthly idea."

Tennyson read the first one out loud. "Mallory, I think about you day and night. You're always on my mind. You are exquisite. We're meant to sail through this life together. I'm sorry you've been through what you have. I can rescue you before you drown. I can heal you. And I will. When the time is right."

Unease sloshed in his gut with each word. This man wasn't asking to help. He was *telling* her he *would* help. Tennyson didn't like the sound of that. And what was up with all the nautical references?

He skipped ahead several more e-mails.

"I saw you on *Yolanda*. I can't believe how strong you are. I always knew you were." Tennyson paused. *Always knew you were?* It almost sounded like this man knew Mallory before all this recent publicity. That wasn't comforting. "You need someone to protect you and keep you safe before you fall overboard. You need me. When the time is right, I'll let you know."

Grant sat back down, still nursing the bottle of water as if he was parched. "It's disturbing, right?"

Tennyson nodded. "Very. This man seems to be tracking her every move."

"That was my feeling also. I didn't tell Mallory that, of course."

"Any idea why he's using the references to the sea?"

He shook his head. "No idea."

"Torres . . . ?"

"As far as I know, he didn't have a particular affinity for the water. Mallory's never said anything."

Tennyson observed Grant for a moment. The man looked like he needed some time alone to freshen up. His shirt was wrinkled. His hair, at one time gelled up straight, now flopped downward. This situation had drained him also, Tennyson realized.

"Are you sure that Mallory is ready for all of this? The tour, the public appearances, the engagements?" Tennyson asked. "There'll be time to do this later. There are other ways to get her message out, ways that don't put her life on the line."

Sure, Tennyson had been asked to guard her physically. But he couldn't help but think about her emotional and spiritual side. Who was guarding that?

Grant stared at Tennyson a moment, something unsettled in his eyes, before he finally nodded. "I'm sure that now is the time for Mallory to do this. She would agree. This tour has helped her healing more than any therapy has."

But Tennyson thought for sure he could see doubt in the man's shadowed gaze.

. . .

Mallory lay in bed, praying for sleep to find her and for nightmares to stay far away.

Very few people knew how insomnia had claimed her nights. Getting to sleep was one of the hardest things, and she refused to take sleeping pills. She'd rather be tired than groggy. Besides, when she finally got to sleep, night terrors claimed her rest, taking her back in time to a place she didn't want to revisit.

She lay on the luxurious sheets of the hotel bed. The bathroom light was on, spilling illumination into the room. Anything to ward off the darkness.

She fluffed her pillow for the fourth time. It wasn't the pillow's fault she couldn't sleep, though. Her thoughts bounced all over the place, finally stopping on the man she'd seen outside the hotel. For a moment—and just a moment—she'd been absolutely certain she'd seen Dante on the busy street.

The man had been walking along with the throngs of businessmen and women. She wouldn't have even noticed him as she looked down at the tops of people's heads.

Except he looked up. Seemed to look right *at* her, as if he knew she was there.

Then he was gone.

And she'd known she was seeing things.

She thought she saw him often. At least once a week. It was always in a crowd. And just as soon as she thought she recognized him, he would disappear.

She hadn't told anyone. Not until she mentioned it to Tennyson tonight. Even then, she'd dismissed it. She knew how it would sound: crazy. Voicing it out loud would make people think she shouldn't be on this tour.

Sometimes *she* thought she shouldn't be on this tour, that she should check herself back into the therapy center. But this work had helped her more than therapy. Staying busy had helped her.

After what felt like hours of tossing and turning, her eyelids finally pulled downward, begging her to rest. Dreamlike memories claimed her, and in an instant, she was back in the hotel suite with her parents.

She'd just gotten back from a party hosted by her dad's friend. Her dad loved a good party, especially when there was an opportunity to network. That night, they'd gone to the home of Walter Boyce, a shipping mogul. Dad said their presence there wasn't business, just old friends getting together. Mallory had been surrounded by wealthy and influential people, yet it all felt empty for the first time.

She'd been glad to get back to the hotel room, even though the fight she'd had with her boyfriend, Jason, still pressed heavily on her. She slowly walked across the marble floor of her room, her heels echoing across the space.

She could hear the waves lapping the beach outside. Smell the lilies on her nightstand. She ran her hand across her silky bedsheets, and for a moment, she felt like a queen.

Even from her room, she heard her mom and dad arguing in the living area. Strands of the conversation drifted in to her.

We're on vacation, honey. Let's just enjoy ourselves.

The company can run itself for a few days without you.

No amount of money is worth this stress.

It was a familiar argument: Her mom had wanted her dad to stop working so much and to enjoy himself. Her dad had insisted that his making more money should make them happy.

Mallory moved closer to the door for a better look at what was going on. Her mom opened her mouth, about to continue their debate, when Dad swept her into his arms and twirled her in an impromptu dance across the floor. Her mother instantly relaxed in his embrace, even letting out a little giggle.

Her father had a way of doing that. It was what had made him a good businessman. Or so Mallory had heard. He would woo people and pull them out of any negative thoughts, putting a positive spin on the worst situations.

Mallory slipped away from the doorway as they continued to glide across the room. If only all her problems could disappear with a two-step across a marble floor. Her grandfather's death had opened her eyes to all that was wrong in her life—starting with the poor decisions she'd been making lately.

Jason had just added one more problem to her ever-increasing list tonight. They'd gotten into a fight, and Jason had stormed off. She hadn't seen him in four hours. Even though it was nearly midnight, he still wasn't back or in his room.

Why had she ever convinced her parents to allow her to bring him on this vacation? Probably because Jason had given her a guilt trip. He'd wanted to come, for some strange reason. The two had been drifting apart for a while now, and Mallory knew it was time to end their relationship once and for all. No more on again, off again.

When she got back to DC, she'd make some changes. She'd forget about that reality show she'd been talking to a producer about. She'd find new friends. She'd get a real job instead of living off her family's wealth.

Yes, that was what she'd do. This trip to the Caribbean had been eye-opening on more than one level. She'd been living with blinders on, and it was time to change things. She would do it in memory of her grandfather.

She was twenty-four. Her life was slipping past, and she had nothing to show for it except a few mentions in the gossip section of the local newspaper and the best wardrobe of anyone in her social circle. Was that the legacy she wanted to leave behind? No.

She slipped her necklace off, ready to change out of her pale blue evening gown into her pajamas, when a noise caught her ear.

She paused, trying to identify the sound. Had it come from outside her window? It was almost a rustling.

Or was it a whisper? A patter of footsteps?

Her dad had paid for a private patio area, complete with a hot tub and soaking pool. Had another hotel guest crept into the area to use it? Or maybe Jason was back and trying to sneak inside.

That's what it most likely was.

She started to take a step that way, ready to confront Jason, when something crashed.

Her heart shuddered a moment.

Her mother screamed a horrifying scream that left a hollow pit in Mallory's stomach. Something was wrong. Seriously wrong.

Her dad shouted, "No!"

Blood pounded in Mallory's ears.

Instinctively, she ran toward her door. Before she reached it, men wearing black masks and militia gear rushed into the living room. She tried to count them all. There were at least eight. Maybe more.

Mallory backed up, nearly stumbling.

One of the men raised his gun.

A scream caught on Mallory's lips. The gun fired, and her mom collapsed to the ground. A pool of blood formed around her.

"No!" The room swirled around Mallory.

Men rushed toward her. Surrounded her. Took her captive.

Her gaze shot toward her dad. He stood by Mom, despair clear in the slump of his shoulders. His eyes flashed over to her. Was that an apology there?

"Dad!"

A man raised a gun toward her father's back.

Then a black bag was jerked over Mallory's head. Men shouted in Spanish.

She was going to die, she realized. A cry of despair escaped from somewhere, guttural and deep.

She had no idea she was in for something much worse.

CHAPTER 6

Mallory awoke with a start.

It took her a moment to remember where she was. She was in the hotel. In Norfolk. On tour.

Safe. She was safe.

She was no longer imprisoned by the sickly sweet decorations of her room at the Caribbean compound where she'd been held: the Victorian lace, the four-poster bed, the flowers that had been delivered every day.

She couldn't lie in bed any longer. Her feet touched the carpeted floor, and she threw on a sweatshirt, deciding to get some water. She should be able to do so quietly and not disturb anyone.

After grabbing her phone and turning on its flashlight, she crept from the bedroom, trying not to disturb Tennyson. He lay on the couch with a blanket pulled over him and a pillow tucked under his head.

Quietly, she reached the kitchenette and grabbed a bottle of water from the fridge. As she started back toward her room, she saw a wallet beside the kitchen sink. It was Tennyson's, she realized. He'd left it open, and in the top plastic credit-card sleeve was a picture of a beautiful brunette.

Mallory shifted and shined her light on the wrinkled photo. The woman in it almost had an exotic look about her with big brown eyes that matched glossy black hair, a wide smile that hinted she'd faced the hard knocks in life and laughed at them, and olive skin that was without a blemish. Something about her looked smart, and the light in her eyes indicated an adventurous spirit.

Who was she? Tennyson's girlfriend? His wife?

She didn't know anything about his personal life. A guy like him was certain to be grabbed up by now. He didn't, however, wear a wedding ring.

Her throat felt unusually tight as she stepped away. But before she did, something else caught her eye.

The printouts of the e-mails from Nameless. Grant must have made them for Tennyson. Though she'd read most of them before, various words and phrases jumped out at her now, and her lungs froze.

I CAN HELP.

WHEN THE TIME IS RIGHT.

YOU NEED ME.

I NEED YOU.

The words made her shudder.

"You shouldn't read those."

The deep voice startled her. She gasped as she glanced over at the couch and saw Tennyson sitting up.

"You were sleeping," she whispered. Her cheeks flushed, and she put the papers down. Only they missed the counter and fluttered all over the carpet instead.

She knelt down and began gathering them. Before she could blink, Tennyson was beside her, helping. His nearness sent a shiver up her spine.

Until the memory of Dante hit her like a slap in the face and made her forget everything else.

Her mind traveled back in time to the day she found some papers Dante had left in his room. She'd begun looking through them, but when Dante had caught her, he'd put Mallory in solitary confinement for a week. Being in that small room by herself had nearly been the end of her.

"It's my job to hear everything." Tennyson continued to help her pick up the avalanche of papers on the floor. Even wearing flannel pajama pants and a white T-shirt, he still looked strong and capable. "I can get these."

"No, I made the mess. I can get them." She grabbed a few more papers. "Besides, I was quiet."

"Like I said, if you'd sneaked past, then I wouldn't be very good at my job." He grabbed the last e-mail.

As he did, their hands brushed, and a jolt of electricity rushed through her.

Not good. Not good at all.

Shivers up her spine? Jolts of electricity?

Her body might be reacting one way, but her mind told her to keep her distance. That's exactly what she planned on doing.

She swallowed hard, her throat burning. That was when she realized how neurotic she was acting—again. Tennyson must think she was a nut job.

The world might think she had everything together after the tragedy that had occurred in her life, but she couldn't fool the man who'd rescued her. Tennyson had seen her at her lowest. Now he'd see behind the veil again and realize just how damaged and bruised she really was.

She let out a long breath and sat back, leaning against the kitchen counter and trying to compose herself. "I'm sorry for waking you. I just wanted to get some water."

He eyed her, clearly trying to assess her state of mind. "You shouldn't be reading those e-mails. I know I just said it, but it's worth repeating."

Something about the way he looked at her made heat rush through her. Why was she having this reaction to him? It was ridiculous. She felt like an innocent schoolgirl with a crush, when in reality, romance was the last thing she wanted—on so many different levels.

She glanced back down at the e-mails. The papers trembled in her hands. "Why's that?"

"They spawn fear."

She put the printouts on the floor and slid her hands beneath her, trying to hide just how anxious she was feeling. "How can I get over my fears if I don't face them?"

He tilted his head and sat down on the floor, also against the counter but a good two feet away. "True."

"Should I be worried?" She hardly wanted to hear his answer.

An unreadable expression crossed his face. He reached up for the bottle of water she'd left on the counter and handed it to her. "It's hard to say at this point."

"What's your personal opinion?" She placed the bottle on the floor for later.

His jaw flexed. "Those e-mails make me uncomfortable."

"They make me uncomfortable, too." She tried to read his expression but couldn't. He was all hard lines and military tough.

"You have no idea who they're from?"

"No, should I?"

He shook his head. "Not necessarily. There are a few comments in those messages that made me wonder if this person knew you before everything that happened."

She drew in a quick breath at the idea, her mind swirling again. "I never even thought about it."

He frowned. "Is there anyone from your past who might send them? An obsessive ex-boyfriend maybe?"

She searched her thoughts, wanting an answer. But she had none. "I don't know. I honestly don't. I've lost touch with most of those people."

His eyebrows shot up. "Really? That surprises me. If you don't mind me asking, what happened when you returned home? I've thought about it since I left you at the hospital."

The memories hit her like an icy splash of water in the face. "My father's former stepdaughter eventually came and got me."

"Your father's former stepdaughter?"

The recollections churned inside her. "She's a stepdaughter from an earlier marriage. She didn't have anything to do with my father after the divorce. Didn't have anything to do with me ever. Until I returned from the dead. At first, I thought she really wanted to help."

"And then?"

"I discovered that the only reason she did was because she wanted my family's money."

"No . . ."

She nodded, her stomach turning at the thought. She drew her knees close. "She had actually filed a motion with a judge to have me officially declared dead."

"What?"

"She and her husband, Arthur, wanted to fight for their right to get more of my family's money. If I was officially dead, then that was one less obstacle for her to get through. I believe the law states that a person has to be dead in absentia for seven years before the money will go to the next in line."

"What happened?"

"I put a major kink in her plans, to say the least, when I came back alive. Not only that, she was just so money hungry that I stopped feeling sorry for her. I didn't make a big deal about what she'd already spent to supposedly 'take care' of my family's house. But she wasn't getting another dime."

"It sounds like she acted foolishly."

"It wasn't even that I wanted the money. But I decided to put it into Verto. It seemed better than funding Narnie to take lavish vacations."

"Has she always been like that?"

"According to my mother, both Narnie and her mother were really all about money. She suspected that's the only reason that marriage ever happened. Most people would say my mom had no room to talk—she was so much younger than my dad. But I really believe that my mom loved my dad. She was involved with a lot of charities. She wasn't the typical socialite who went shopping all the time and blew through money."

"That's got to be hard to stomach—these people who popped back into your life just for the money. I'm so sorry to hear that."

"It's better I find out now who only likes me for what I can do for them, right?"

He shifted, bending his knee and casually resting his arm on it. "So you've been alone since then?"

She shrugged, not wanting him to feel sorry for her. She had a lot to be thankful for—even though she was still working through her issues. "Not totally alone. I have Grant."

Tennyson studied her face a moment. "You really like him, don't you?"

"He's been a constant for me. That's more than I can say about most people. Thankfully my hope isn't in people."

She had strong doubts anyone would truly love her again. She'd always be the rich girl who was sold into human slavery. Human nature would allow very few people to see past that. She had so much baggage that she was destined to travel alone.

She was about to flee back to her room when a noise caught her ear. She pivoted to look toward the sound.

She expected to see Grant emerging from his room. They'd probably woken him up from his slumber.

But his door didn't open.

Another one did.

The door to the hotel room.

CHAPTER 7

Tennyson jumped to his feet.

Someone was trying to get into the hotel room. The only thing that had stopped them was the chain lock over the door.

He sprinted toward the entryway, drawing his gun as he did so.

The intruder must have heard him coming because the chain went slack.

Tennyson quickly undid the lock and darted into the hallway just in time to see someone disappear into the stairway.

"Stay in the room," he yelled to Mallory. "Don't open the door for anyone except me. Understand?"

He took off after the man. By the time he reached the stairway, the man was a good three floors down.

Tennyson flew down the stairs. But the man he was chasing was fast. Really fast.

The intruder's steps slowed for a moment. A masked face stared up. Brown eyes assessed the situation.

Torres? Was that Torres?

The man had the right height and build. But Torres wasn't the type to do this kind of thing himself. He'd send his underlings to do his dirty work.

Unless Mallory was so important that he wanted to handle her himself.

He only had two more flights until the bottom.

But the man suddenly disappeared.

Tennyson paused. He didn't even hear his footsteps anymore.

The man had gotten off at a floor. Most likely the second floor.

Tennyson rushed down the stairs until he reached that level. He shoved the door open, ready to continue the chase, but he stopped cold instead.

Nightlife came alive around him. Late-night patrons were drinking around a bar and tables. Some people danced. A deejay played in the corner.

He glanced around. No one looked out of place. But it was hard to see anything with the dim lighting, loud music, and crowd.

He grabbed a waiter going past. "Did you just see a man run in here?"

The waiter stared back at him like he'd lost his mind. "I didn't see anyone."

Tennyson released his arm and began weaving through the crowd, looking for anyone sweaty or out of breath. He examined each face.

No one looked or acted suspicious.

The man had gotten away, he realized.

Tennyson wasn't sure how he'd managed to escape, but the bigger question was: What had he planned on doing if he got inside?

• • •

The next morning, they headed to Raleigh, North Carolina. Mallory would be doing a book signing there, and later on, she'd meet with various city officials and give a talk for Verto.

The chilling turn of the past few days continued to haunt her thoughts. As if everything else wasn't bad enough, why had someone tried to break in last night? It just didn't make sense.

Or maybe it did make sense; she just didn't want to face the truth. The truth that danger still lurked out there. That she was still a target. That she'd tried to run from her past, but she wasn't fast enough to truly get away.

Tennyson drove, and Grant sat in the front beside him. As usual, Grant was a chatterbox, a quality she couldn't imagine Tennyson appreciated. He didn't seem like the frivolous kind of guy, even when it came to conversation. Maybe *especially* when it came to conversation.

She watched him, saw how his eyes constantly went to the rearview mirror.

Interesting.

She tried to ignore the action. Told herself Tennyson was just doing his job. Tried to stare out the window at the passing scenery.

Then she looked at the busy stretch of interstate behind her. She didn't see anything out of the ordinary. Only a few cars, traveling behind them at a safe distance. Was this just life passing by? What if there was more to it? If the intruder from last night was following them?

Was she being paranoid? She wasn't sure.

All she knew was that her muscles felt tighter than a knot, and nausea had begun to pool in her gut.

Tennyson's gaze continued to flicker in the rearview mirror, as if he was watching something. Or was he watching for someone?

At once, she felt on guard. Her heart beat faster. Her breathing became shallower.

Tennyson was worried, she realized. She needed to know why.

She leaned forward. "Is someone following us?"

Tennyson shot her a look in the mirror. "Why would you ask?"

"Because you keep checking behind you."

One shoulder pulled up in a half shrug. "Just a precaution."

She glanced behind her again. Her instincts told her that Tennyson was placating her. Everyone kept trying to placate her. If there was one thing she didn't appreciate it was being kept in the dark.

She rubbed her temples. Maybe she was being paranoid. Everyone wasn't out to get her.

Nameless might be sending her e-mails, but that didn't mean he was stalking her. But what about the photos someone had sent? Someone was stalking her. But who?

Her throat suddenly felt tight. Who was it who'd tried to get into the hotel room last night? Who had killed that poor woman and left her body in Cape Thomas?

Her mind tried to go to dark places, but she shut it down. Once she went into that black abyss, it felt impossible to get out.

Even though I walk through the darkest valley, I will fear no evil, for you are with me. Cast my fear out, Lord. Please. Help me. I need to walk on water, and I feel like I'm sinking instead.

She glanced out the window again. A passenger in the car beside them stared into the SUV, almost as if he could see through the tinted glass.

Dante.

The air left her lungs.

She jerked her gaze away. Blinked. Tried to take some deep breaths. No, that wasn't Dante. It couldn't have been. He was dead. She didn't care what that e-mail had said.

She dared to look again, only to prove to herself she was being paranoid.

The man was now staring at the road straight ahead. He talked to the man beside him, the one driving the car. Mallory couldn't see his face.

She observed his thick, dark hair, his brown skin, his muscular build.

Was that Dante? They shared the same features, but . . .

She blinked again and shook her head, desperate to control her thoughts.

No, it couldn't be. He was dead, she reminded herself again. That e-mail was fake, sent by someone intent on torturing her.

"Mallory?"

She glanced up at Tennyson. He'd noticed her reaction. He'd seen something was wrong.

She couldn't let on that she thought she'd seen Dante twice in the last twenty-four hours. She'd only sound like she was losing her mind. One time, he would brush off. But not twice.

"Yes?" She licked her lips.

"Are you okay?"

"Just fine. Thank you."

Tennyson's gaze lingered on her. She forced a smile and looked down at her hands.

The man had looked similar to Dante. That was all.

Calm down, Mallory.

She drew in a deep breath, daring to take one more look over at the car beside them. She fully expected to come to her senses. To confirm that this was all a mistake and that her eyes were deceiving her.

The man craned his neck toward her again.

He smiled and waved before racing ahead into traffic.

No, she wasn't wrong. He looked just like Dante.

• • •

Tennyson faithfully stood beside Mallory during the signing. He'd seen the change in her expression as they'd driven here. Something had happened to spook her, but he wasn't sure what, nor had he had the chance to ask her. He wouldn't for a while, at least not until the book signing was over.

Right now, he remained on the lookout for anyone suspicious. At the first sign, he would escort Mallory from the building and to the car waiting outside. He'd already checked out all the building's exits so he could identify the store's vulnerabilities.

Though the manager wanted Mallory to be set up in the middle of the store, it was too risky. Instead, Tennyson had convinced the event planner to have the signing in a corner, away from windows, where the situation was more manageable. Until Kori came, he was going to have to operate this way. If the threats continued, he'd have to convince Mallory to bring on more guards. He knew that wasn't what she wanted, but she needed more manpower.

The next hour and a half flew past. There were endless smiles exchanged between Mallory and her fans. Too many faces to keep straight. Mallory was pleasant and kind to each person who came through, which was even more amazing given the circumstances of the past few days.

Everything was running smoothly, and there were only five minutes left to go.

A man toward the end of the line caught Tennyson's eye. He was tall with stringy brown hair and oversized glasses. He wore a long black overcoat and looked like he hadn't showered in weeks.

He appeared jumpy as he approached Mallory and set his book down in front of her.

"You're an inspiration, Mallory." Sweat dripped from his upper lip as he stared at her, his eyes looking a little too lovelorn for Tennyson's tastes.

"Thank you." She signed his book and handed it back, but he made no attempt to move, despite the people waiting behind him.

"I would love to talk to you about your experiences sometime."

"It's all in the book," she assured him, her smile tightening.

Tennyson noticed the slight tremble that began in her hands. She was getting anxious.

"I think you're remarkable."

Tennyson scooted closer. The man was being a little too pushy. Maybe Tennyson's presence would discourage him.

"Surely my horrible experiences don't make me remarkable," she said. "That would be a tragedy within itself."

"I know you are. You are, Mallory. You are." He said the words low and intimately. "I dream about you all the time. About what it would be like to—"

That was enough. It was time for this signing to end. Since no one else was coming over to call it quits, Tennyson would.

"I'm sorry, sir, but we've got to bring this to a close. Ms. Baldwin has other engagements tonight."

The man scowled and, in an instant, grabbed Mallory's arm.

She gasped and tried to jerk back, but the man didn't let go.

"Please, just listen to me—"

In one swift move, Tennyson grabbed the man's hand and twisted his wrist until he yelped with pain.

"Your touch isn't welcome," Tennyson growled, appalled that the man would even consider touching Mallory.

"Fine. Fine. Fine!" The man pulled his hand back and gave Tennyson a scowl.

In a last ditch effort, the man slid something across the table. "Here's my card, Mallory. If you ever want to . . ."

"We've got to go." Tennyson pulled Mallory to her feet before she could even think about grabbing the card. Not that she would.

Was that man Nameless?

No, Tennyson didn't think so. There was something about his words that didn't match the cadence of the writing in the messages. Still, the man could be a threat.

He led Mallory away from the table, waving apologetically to everyone else in line. "Sorry, folks. Mallory has another commitment she needs to get to. Thank you all for coming."

Mallory trembled beneath his hand. She was reacting to his touch also, he realized. But he couldn't avoid it at the moment. She wasn't standing quickly enough on her own, and as her bodyguard, sometimes he would have to handle her. Knowing her background, he would only do it when absolutely necessary.

"Are you okay?" he asked her when they were halfway to the exit.

She nodded a little too quickly. "I'm fine."

Her words weren't convincing. The man had rattled her.

They were almost at the door when someone stepped into their path, and Mallory stopped cold.

CHAPTER 8

"Narnie. What are you doing here?" Mallory tried to keep the contempt from her voice. But the last person she'd expected to see was her father's former stepdaughter.

She looked as smug as ever. The woman was in her early forties, but she dressed like a college-aged girl headed for the club scene. Today she wore tight leggings, a midriff-baring shirt, and heels.

Narnie was a bottle blond, wore a lot of makeup, and still curled her hair away from her face in an eighties style.

None of those things bothered Mallory, though. It was the woman's integrity—or lack thereof—that bothered her.

Narnie lifted a pencil-thin eyebrow. "Can't I just come to support family?"

"You know we're not family. I would welcome you as a sister, if I thought you wanted anything besides my money."

The smile slipped from her face. "I heard you were in the area, and I wanted to stop by."

"Why?" Mallory wasn't going to drop this. She'd been burned by Narnie too many times since her return.

"That's it. Those were my only reasons." Her eyes traveled beyond Mallory to Tennyson. "Who is this fine hunk of man who's with you?"

"This is Tennyson. He's . . . he's part of my team."

Her gaze, calculating and cool, turned back to Mallory. "Your team, huh?"

"That's right." Mallory let out a controlled breath. "Well, thanks for stopping by. Give my regards to Arthur."

Before she could walk away, Narnie grabbed her arm. "Wait!"

Mallory paused, not really wanting to hear anything else she said. She shrugged out of her grasp and barely kept her composure as she said, "Yes?"

"I'm going to lose my house." Narnie's bottom lip trembled.

Compassion started to creep in, but Mallory squashed it. Narnie had tried to manipulate situations too many times in the past. Mallory would bet the house was fine, but that she really wanted a new wardrobe. "Why are you telling me this?"

"I need your help."

"So you didn't just stop by to support me?"

"Yes, I want to support you. We're like family."

"There's no blood relation between us."

She clung to Mallory's arm again. "I need your help."

Mallory bristled at her touch but didn't pull away. "I don't know what to say, Narnie. If you're telling me the truth, then I truly feel bad for you. But you've made poor decisions, and you're going to continue to make poor decisions until you learn your lesson."

She dropped Mallory's arm, her demeanor changing from desperate to cold. "You haven't changed at all, have you?"

Mallory kept her chin up, even though the words stung. Was she doing the right thing? She had to believe she was. "I have changed. But I'm not going to be walked on anymore. Narnie, do I need to remind you that you took me to court? When I should have been recovering and focusing on rebuilding the scraps of my life, you were focused on getting money from me."

Narnie sneered and crossed her arms over her chest. "You wouldn't understand."

"Why don't you try earning your own money?"

"That means a lot coming from a rich brat."

Mallory felt Tennyson bristle beside her, but she held up a hand, signaling him to let her handle this. "This conversation is over."

"You'll regret it," Narnie growled. "You'll regret it."

. . .

That evening, Tennyson stood at the edge of the ballroom and watched from a distance as Mallory rubbed elbows with some of the city's most prominent members. She'd changed from her casual attire and donned a simple black dress with heels. She looked like a million bucks with her hair swept back in a twist, and she had a quiet dignity about her.

Tennyson had pulled out his suit for the occasion, knowing he'd stand out too much otherwise. He straightened the knot of his sky-blue tie, feeling slightly out of place despite the suit. This wasn't his kind of crowd.

He watched Mallory for another moment. She really was carrying herself with amazing resilience.

She was almost like a different person.

He couldn't deny that he'd listened with rapt attention to the media coverage on Mallory after her rescue. Before she'd been abducted, she'd been a party girl: spoiled, arrogant, irresponsible. She'd had a sense of entitlement. Didn't appreciate working for things. Lived with the proverbial silver spoon in her mouth.

He hadn't known she'd almost starred in her own reality show. But the old Mallory did seem like the type.

The new Mallory had an understated, gentle confidence. She seemed ready to work hard. She had a deep appreciation in her expression—appreciation for life. He had to admit that the woman fascinated him and made him want to dive deeper than the constraints of the professional relationship they had in place. He knew doing so was off-limits, but his mind continually drifted toward her beautiful smile and her strong spirit.

She'd mentioned Jesus in her talk at Hope House. He was probably a big reason for her change of heart. Our most desperate times could lead to the greatest reliance on our Savior. It had been so for him.

Just then, his phone rang. He glanced at the screen and saw it was Ethan Stone. Stone was an old friend, for lack of a better word, from the CIA who now worked for the NSA. Tennyson had left a message for him earlier and hoped he would call him back. The two had a lot of water under the bridge, and Tennyson feared Stone would let the past act as a permanent, unbreachable wall between them.

He gave one more glance at Mallory and saw she looked at ease as she chatted with some members of the city council. The event was by invitation only, and the crowd was small enough to manage. He'd keep an eye on who was coming and going from his position here by the door—the only entrance and exit in the room.

He put the phone to his ear. "Stone. Thanks for calling me."

"Yeah, what's going on?" The greeting was all business.

"I heard a rumor about Torres, and I was hoping to get some details from you."

"What did you hear about Torres?" Stone's voice changed from hostile to curious.

"That he might still be alive."

Silence crackled on the other end. "I don't know what you're talking about."

"Sure you do."

"Where'd you hear that information?"

"An anonymous tip. Please. I called for more than one reason. You know how I feel about the man. But the girl Torres held in captivity could be in danger. I want to make sure Torres is not behind it."

Stone remained silent a moment, and Tennyson wondered if he would respond.

"I'm not supposed to be sharing any of this." His voice sounded low and grumbling—just as Tennyson had come to expect from Stone. The man lived in the shadows, and he'd been great at his job. He was also on more hit lists than Tennyson could count.

"I know. And I appreciate your cooperation." Tennyson's eyes remained fixed on Mallory as the mayor spoke with her. She smiled back politely and gracefully, but her eyes searched the room until she spotted Tennyson.

He offered her an affirming nod, feeling surprisingly pleased that she had sought him out.

"Two different sources say they've seen Dante Torres," Stone continued. "They also said that he looks different, that maybe he's had some type of plastic surgery to change his appearance."

Something shifted in his gut. Unease. "How can they be sure?"

"They're not. That's the rub."

Tennyson scanned the crowd, suddenly more alert and on guard. "Did they say what looked different about him?"

"He'd lost weight. His nose was thinner. His hair was even darker than before."

"Or it could have just been someone different."

"Exactly."

Tennyson bit back a frown. He didn't like the sound of any of this. "Where did these sightings occur?"

"One was in the Caribbean. The other was in the States."

"Where in the States?"

"In Virginia."

Tennyson's spine bristled. Virginia was where the first body had been found. He scanned the crowd one more time. Though Virginia wasn't far away, it would take a lot of nerve for Torres to show up here.

But Dante Torres was known for having a lot of nerve. If he was here, Tennyson would recognize him—even with plastic surgery.

"If you hear anything else, will you let me know?"

"Of course."

Tennyson hung up, but his gut still churned. Danger lurked in the distance like a savage storm. He could feel it. Sense it.

What he didn't know was when it would strike. He had to remain on guard until he had more clues.

CHAPTER 9

Nothing had felt better to Mallory than kicking her heels off when she got to her suite that night. She changed into her favorite yoga pants and T-shirt, ready to relax and unwind after her busy day.

Tennyson had switched hotel reservations on them, claiming the one Grant had previously booked was too much of a risk. This suite had a private elevator and consumed the entire top floor of the building. There was no balcony and only one way inside. Tennyson had hired another guard to stand watch by the outside door. As long as the guard didn't come inside, Mallory was okay with it.

As soon as they'd arrived, Grant had disappeared into his room to catch up on some paperwork and have a video call with his assistant. Mallory stepped from her room, hoping to watch something light on TV—a comedy maybe. She needed a distraction from everything that had happened.

As she padded across the carpet, she spotted Tennyson sitting on the couch, flipping through something on his lap.

Mallory observed him a moment.

His hair was longer now than it had been when he was a SEAL. It spiked up in uneven waves on top of his head. He wore a black T-shirt that showed off his muscular arms and chest. She'd tried not to notice. She'd failed, though.

Just like Mallory had tried not to notice how handsome Tennyson had looked earlier dressed in his suit and tie. Just like she'd tried to stop herself from constantly seeking him out at the reception earlier.

But something about having him nearby made her feel better. As long as Mallory knew where Tennyson was and that he was watching, she could breathe. He'd rescued her before, and Mallory knew he would keep her safe now.

Were those thoughts crazy? She hoped not. After all, Tennyson was her bodyguard. Mallory should feel that way about him. It had nothing to do with how good he looked in both a T-shirt and a suit.

All that, not to mention his eyes. Blue eyes that held an ocean of depth. Depth she wanted to explore.

Of course that could never happen. Dante had taken things from her that she knew she'd never get back. All the prayers in the world wouldn't change that.

She took a better look at what Tennyson had in his hands. Photos, she realized.

She walked closer and peered over his shoulder. When she recognized the face there, she sucked in a breath.

"Why are you looking at pictures of Dante's first wife?" Mallory asked.

Tennyson didn't bother to conceal the pictures. He'd obviously heard her coming—he didn't even flinch. But at least he wasn't hiding anything from her. She appreciated that about him.

"I studied everything about Torres in the years leading up to his death."

That wasn't the answer Mallory had been expecting to hear. She sat down beside him, curious to learn more about this man who'd rescued her from a living nightmare.

Throughout the past two years, she'd tried to fill in the blanks herself. She'd made up his backstory, and it included all things perfect. A perfect family. A spotless reputation. He'd probably rescued runaway neighborhood dogs as a child and volunteered at nursing homes in high school.

No doubt he'd gotten plenty of interest from females. He was that type of guy. And he probably dated women who were perfect—just like him. Ones who were named Miss Congeniality in their yearbooks. Who made cookies for people. Who were without blemish.

In other words, the opposite of Mallory.

"Why did you study Torres?" she asked.

A shadow crossed his face. "Personal reasons."

Mallory nodded, not pressing any further. She knew what it was like to want to keep things private, and she needed to respect that, even if it disappointed her. "I see."

Tennyson frowned and raked a hand through his hair, as if second-guessing his response or surrendering to courtesy. "The truth is that it's a long story. Aside from my personal reasons, I had a job to do. Torres was the most wanted man in the world. As soon as I caught him, I was done with being a SEAL. My mission was accomplished, and I figured I could finally sleep at night."

She tried to carefully measure her words. "That doesn't explain why you're looking at pictures of Alessandra now. She's deceased."

The corners of his lips tightened in a frown. "As I'm sure you probably know, her brother, Roberto Sanchez, was Torres's right-hand man."

Mallory considered what he was trying to say, but she couldn't quite piece it together. "You think Sanchez is a threat? That he's tracking me? That maybe he sent that e-mail and signed Dante's name?"

"Why would he?" His gaze latched onto hers, and his words sounded slow, purposeful. The question was asked calmly and without emotion, but the intensity in his stare showed how focused he was.

Mallory shrugged, refusing to break eye contact with him. Her dad said it showed weakness, and it did. She'd avoided Dante's eyes every time he came near her. "I have nothing that he could want."

Tennyson continued to study her. "You didn't hear anything during your time in captivity that would make you a risk to them now?"

She started to shake her head but stopped, determined to truly think the question through. She let out a long breath as snippets from the past echoed in her mind.

"I did hear things," she said. "But nothing that made sense. Usually it was in Spanish. Besides, if members of Inferno wanted me dead or back in their custody, they've had opportunity before now."

"You were whisked away and harder to find then. Now you're out in public."

Her throat tightened at the truth in his words. "Maybe."

"Were there any indications that someone was looking for you before this tour started?"

She rubbed her neck, wishing this conversation was a bad dream. "Someone did try to break into my home outside DC once. It was never connected to Dante, of course. He was dead. His terror group was disbanded."

"The police said that?"

"Of course. They figured it was neighborhood kids who assumed the house was abandoned. As soon as the alarm went off, they ran."

"More than one?"

"Two sets of footprints. Why?"

"I'm just trying to gather all the facts." He looked back down at Alessandra's picture. "She looks like you, you know."

A weight pressed against her chest. "I know. I think that's why Dante chose me."

She had Tennyson's attention now. "Is that right?"

She nodded, not bothering to fight the nausea in her gut. She wasn't sure if that would ever go away when she mentioned Dante's name or talked about her time with him. "In his own way, Dante really loved her. When she died from breast cancer, he was devastated. He used to call me Alessandra sometimes. He bought me designer clothes that looked like hers. Had me cut my hair to match hers."

His face paled. Whose wouldn't when processing that information? But at least Mallory had spoken the truth. There was no need to hold back. In fact, she almost felt a driving need for Tennyson to know the truth. Maybe it would help circumvent this attraction she felt toward the man. If he knew the truth about what had happened to her in captivity, they'd have no chance.

"He was sick," Tennyson muttered.

He studied her face a moment, and she sensed he wanted to ask questions. "What is it? You can ask me."

His jaw flexed, and he rubbed it before asking evenly, "How did he treat you?"

"Treat me?" She hadn't expected that.

He swallowed hard. "I know it's a strange question."

"No, I guess it's not so strange. No one's ever asked me that way before, though. They've asked what he did to me. I guess the answer is that he was generally kind—in a bizarre way, of course. I was very homesick, to say the least, when I first arrived. Dante actually found a snapshot of my mom and dad. He had it framed for me."

"I saw that picture the night of the raid."

She nodded slowly. "Yeah, it was there. It actually did make me feel better. This sounds weird, but I suppose it could have been worse."

His look clearly showed he didn't believe her.

Mallory raised a hand, begging for him to wait as she explained herself. "Don't take that the wrong way. What happened to me was horrible. Devastating. I wouldn't wish the situation on my worst enemy. But you learn to count your blessings."

He didn't say anything, as if waiting for her to continue.

So she did. "So many girls who are trapped into human trafficking are passed on from man to man, from city to city. They're living in the slums and don't have medical care, even though disease is rampant in those environments. They're beaten and discarded and drugged. In the overall scheme of things, I was treated . . ." What was the word she was looking for? Finally, she shrugged. "I was treated okay. I had shelter and food. He . . . he didn't beat me."

"That takes a lot of strength to say."

She wasn't so sure about that. "Someone once told me you can't be a victor and a victim at the same time. I choose to be a victor. I choose not to ask 'Why me?' and make the best of things."

"Sounds wise, Mallory."

"The last two months were two of the hardest. Dante was becoming unhinged and acting erratic. I . . . I almost ended my life once." She swallowed the lump in her throat. She had to change the subject. She'd never intended to go this deep with Tennyson. "Anyway, none of this really tells me why you're looking at pictures of Alessandra."

A new emotion clouded Tennyson's face. Was it . . . regret? What did he have to be sorry about?

He cleared his throat. "I'm just trying to familiarize myself with everyone who was in Torres's network."

"She's dead, though."

Tennyson nodded. "I know. But the people we surround ourselves with tell a lot about us."

"All I know is that Alessandra was the love of his life. Something snapped inside him when she died. At least, that's what I heard."

"Do you know how they met?"

Mallory let out a long breath. "I heard that Dante saw her when she was walking on the beach. He approached her, and it was love at first sight. They were married for five years."

"Did he tell you that?"

"No, one of the maids at the compound—her name was Gabriella—did. We would talk on occasion." As the words left her lips, her throat tightened, nearly choking her.

Tennyson waited, not saying anything.

"The maid . . . I think she died because of me."

Tennyson's eyes narrowed. "What do you mean?"

"She tried to help me escape once. Dante found out, and I never saw her again."

"You think he killed her?"

"He must have."

"I'm sorry, Mallory. That was noble of her to help."

She was desperate to change the subject. "Now, on a happier note, I suppose Grant gave you my schedule for the next few months?"

He nodded.

"So you know I'm doing another television interview tomorrow? I'm being reunited with Jason, my former boyfriend." Her throat tightened at the words.

Something crossed Tennyson's gaze. Disapproval? Why would he disapprove, though? "I did hear that. You haven't spoken with him since you've been back?"

She shrugged. "There are a lot of things unsaid between us. I haven't reached out to him, and he hasn't reached out to me."

"So how did this televised reunion come about?" The words were said with a bitter edge that surprised Mallory.

"Grant, of course. He thinks it will help give me closure."

He studied her again before asking, "Why on TV?"

"Everything I do is to help raise awareness, even if that requires sacrificing my privacy."

"Even if it means sacrificing your own peace of mind?"

Her throat suddenly felt dry and achy. "If that's the sacrifice I have to make to open people's eyes, then so be it."

He nodded. "As long as you're okay with it, and your eyes are wide open, then I guess no one can argue with you."

His words resonated in her mind. She was okay with all of this . . . right? Because she'd had a touch of anxiety about the televised reunion with Jason since Grant mentioned it. But she didn't want to be afraid anymore. And meeting Jason face-to-face seemed like the perfect way to accomplish that.

Victor not victim, she reminded herself again.

• • •

After Mallory was asleep, Tennyson pulled out her book, *Unfettered*. The title seemed unconventional, but he liked it. It brought to mind the image of a bird being released from its cage. Like that bird, Mallory was now free to become herself, not in the wild way of her youth, but in the strong, principled way she was trying to live now.

He stared at the picture on the front cover. It was a nice photo, taken with the beach behind her. The wind blew her hair back, but she stood there with her hands on her hips and her chin raised. Her smile wasn't large and wide, but it was subtle and confident. Her pose screamed "overcomer," which only seemed accurate.

He opened it to the first page.

Dedicated to my Lord Jesus Christ. I couldn't have gotten through this without You.

He smiled. He knew what that was like. Jesus had turned his life around as well and pulled him out of the pit of despair. Reminded him that he was a victor, as Mallory had said.

His smile quickly faded as he began reading. The beginning contained mostly things he already knew about Mallory, her upbringing, and the start of her vacation in the Caribbean. He hadn't realized that her grandfather had died only three months before that fateful trip. She talked in the book about how his death affected her, and she could sense something changing inside her.

She'd vowed when she returned from the Caribbean that she was going to get serious about her life. Though she'd been working for her dad and using her business degree, she really hadn't applied herself fully. She hadn't had to. She had a trust fund and total job security.

He slowed as he began reading about her time in captivity. There were things in there that he knew. There were other things that he'd expected. There were other details he didn't want to know. Though she never shared too much about what Dante had done to her, every time he thought about it, his blood burned with anger.

He paused as he reached another section that talked about how she passed the time when she was locked away in her room. She dreamed of home. Mourned her parents. Wondered what her friends were doing.

She'd made a handcrafted mancala game, using some old cups, and she would play against herself. She'd mark the days that passed on the inside of a dresser drawer. She'd dream about what she would do with her life if she ever got it back.

Sometimes she would even listen through the vents for a clue of what was going on outside of her room. She'd make up what the conversations were about when she couldn't identify it. She likened it to playing telephone as a child—the old game where people would sit in a circle, and someone would whisper something to the person beside them. The next person would whisper what they thought they heard, until the phrase made it all the way around the circle.

That revelation made Tennyson pause. Maybe she'd intended on being lighthearted with that information, but other people could see that as threatening. What if she'd heard something that could incriminate someone?

After she'd been rescued, the government had debriefed her on her time in captivity. Certainly she'd mentioned this to them. He knew the interviews had been extensive. They would have warned her not to share any sensitive information.

Still, something about seeing those words in print made him feel unsettled.

If there were any of Torres's men left out there, fighting for him, they wouldn't like hearing this. In fact, he was surprised the publisher had put this in the book. The revelation could put Mallory at risk.

Who was looking out for her? It seemed like everyone was looking out for their bottom line instead. Was this whole experience greed in action?

Unease jostled inside him at the thought.

He picked up his phone and left a message for an old friend, Leigh Sullivan. A forensic anthropologist. She didn't answer, so he left a message asking her to call him back.

There was only one definitive way to know if that man had really been Torres. That was to reexamine the body, which had been shipped back to the States. Even in two years, technology had advanced.

Tennyson just had to figure out how to convince the right people that his idea had merit.

CHAPTER 10

The next day, Mallory had a million doubts about whether or not she should be reunited with Jason, but here she was, at the station, waiting for him to arrive.

The reporter—a hotshot named Dana Cavanagh—volleyed between checking and double-checking her makeup in a handheld mirror and reviewing her notes. Though they were in a studio, the space was set up to look like a living room, complete with gaudy wallpaper, dark tables, and dimly lit lamps. Lights in the background flooded the two chairs where Mallory and Jason would sit. Camera crews scurried around, and producers called out directions to their underlings.

Grant had assured her that this would all help to bring awareness to her cause. Everything that happened in Mallory's life was to bring awareness. She hoped he was right. The only thing she'd learned about publicity as a teenager was that the squeaky wheel got the grease. It wasn't exactly the mantra she wanted for her nonprofit, however. Not by a long shot.

Mallory pushed a lock of hair behind her ear as she sat in an armchair, lights glaring down on her. She rubbed her lips together and pulled her gaze up until she met Tennyson's. He sent her a reassuring smile.

"You ready for this?" When Grant stepped into the room, the air around them seemed to change from relaxed but nervous to super-charged and uneasy.

Mallory immediately went tense and nodded, sitting up straighter.

The crews got into place, cameras lined up for the reunion, and Dana sat in a chair and crossed her legs. Finally, a man stepped into the room.

Jason Wentworth hadn't transformed that much from the party boy he'd been when they first met. Tragedy had a way of making some people grow up, but others regress. She didn't know what side of the spectrum Jason fell on yet, but her gut feeling wasn't favorable.

He was still the same Jason on the outside: five feet ten inches with a stocky build. His brown hair had a hard part on the side, a trendy style that she would have loved three years ago. Now, she thought his jeans were a little too tight and his T-shirt too silky.

She stood as he walked into the room. The two paused in front of each other.

This was the first time they'd seen each other since that fateful night more than three years ago. Mallory had thought he would be one of the first people to rush to meet her after what had happened. But maybe guilt had held him back. Maybe he was self-absorbed. Mallory didn't know, and she tried to reserve judgment.

Reluctantly, she stepped toward him.

"Mallory . . . ," Jason muttered.

"Jason."

They embraced quickly.

"It's good to see you," Jason whispered.

Mallory nodded but didn't return the phrase. "Please, let's sit."

The cameras rolled, catching every minute.

Mallory stared at Jason, trying to keep the contempt out of her voice. Maybe it was a good thing there were cameras rolling because, as much as she'd tried to tell herself that she'd forgiven Jason, bitterness rose inside her now as she stared as his all-too-pretty face.

Jason tugged at his pant legs, rocking from one side of the seat to the other. His facial muscles were tight and drawn, and his voice sounded slightly high-pitched. "You look great."

Of course Jason would start with a comment on how she looked. He'd always cared too much about appearances. Then again, at one time she had also.

"Thank you. How have you been?" She figured she'd start with something basic. It seemed better than jumping in with "How could you have left after what had happened? Did you look for me? Did you even care?"

"I've been . . . hanging in."

The reporter gave some kind of little spiel that was meant to put them at ease and set the stage for the rest of their conversation. Mallory hardly heard a word she said, though. All she could think about was this conversation. She wasn't nervous. No, she just wanted answers.

"Where would you like to start, Mallory?" Dana asked.

"Tell me about that night, Jason." Mallory had told herself she would ease into the conversation, but she hadn't wanted to waste any more time. Her questions pressed at her with an unrelenting urgency.

Jason's neck muscles visibly strained. "That was a rough night."

"Yes, I know."

"Sorry," he mumbled, appearing slightly self-conscious—a trait he'd rarely shown before.

"What happened to you?" Every detail of that night was etched into Mallory's brain. It felt like it had happened just yesterday. But she'd never heard Jason's side of things.

Mallory could feel the cameras moving in closer, but she didn't care. She wanted to know.

He broke eye contact and looked at his hands. "I did some things I wasn't proud of, Mallory."

She waited for him to continue.

When he didn't say anything, she started with "You disappeared."

Finally, he raised his head. "I did. We got into that argument earlier in the day, at the party."

"We did. I thought you had a wandering eye."

He shifted and wiped sweaty palms on his jeans. "I did have a wandering eye. I was supposed to go back to your family's suite that night, but instead . . . I met a girl."

Mallory expected to feel anger, but she didn't. His words came as no surprise.

"I was mad at you and determined to do my own thing. I knew I was acting like a jerk, but back then, I didn't care. I stayed out late, partying."

"What was her name?"

His cheeks flushed. "Her name? It was . . . it was Jasmine."

Jasmine. Jasmine had probably saved his life. Mallory was sure he'd thought about that before.

"When did you come back?"

He swallowed hard. "I got back to the suite around four a.m. I walked in and saw the whole place had been destroyed. I had no idea what had happened. I called the police, and they showed up around ten minutes later."

"What were those ten minutes like?" Dana Cavanagh asked, her gaze intense as it slid back and forth between Mallory and Jason.

"Horrifying." He swept a hand through his hair. "When I saw the mess, I kept going through worst-case scenarios. It turned out they were all correct."

Dana leaned closer. "After Mallory's parents were found, did you assume, like everyone else, that Mallory was dead, too?"

"I did. It just made sense. I couldn't believe it when I heard she was alive."

"How did you move on after that night, Jason?" Dana asked.

"I just did my best. I stayed in the Caribbean another week. My family met me down there. We kept hoping that Mallory would be returned . . . alive. It all seemed like a bad dream. But it wasn't."

"What kind of questions did the police ask?" Dana pressed.

His jaw flexed. "Everything under the sun. I had to verify my alibi and make my case several times that I wasn't involved in this."

"Why would they think you were?" Dana's eyes lit up.

He shrugged, this time actually tugging on his collar. "Don't they always look at the people closest to you first? My family owns one of the largest technology companies in the world—of course we're going to be scrutinized. It wasn't a fun time."

Why did he look so nervous? He was always the one who enjoyed being in the limelight, and Mallory had assumed this would be no different.

He leaned forward, sweat beaded across his forehead. "I waited for a ransom demand. I was going to pay it to get Mal back. But it never came."

"You became somewhat of a celebrity after her disappearance," Dana said. "You were featured in magazines. You went on TV. You even wrote a book on it."

"It was all to get Mallory back. After we thought she was dead, it was to preserve her memory."

His words didn't ring true to Mallory. Unless Jason had changed, he'd never been that selfless. Most likely, he wanted to cash in on his fifteen minutes of fame.

She hated to think so little of her ex-boyfriend. But he'd always had a hunger for popularity and money. People and their well-being were near the bottom of his list.

Jason turned toward her. "I guess the main reason I wanted to meet was to tell you how sorry I was. For everything."

"Why'd you wait so long?" The words burned her throat as she said them.

"I didn't know if you'd want to see me. I knew you were going through rehab. Then I wasn't sure how to find you." He shrugged. "All excuses, I know. But I'm glad we could finally talk. I've thought about this moment for a long time."

The conversation meandered along after that, mostly a blur to Mallory.

Finally, the reunion ended. Just in time because she wanted to go lie down and take a nap. It would take her a while to process all of this.

After Jason thanked everyone and said good-bye, Mallory walked him toward the door. He paused there and leaned close to her, his voice low.

"I really am sorry, Mallory, and I hope you'll forgive me." His eyes seemed pleading, but there was something else there also, something hard to identify.

Did he deserve to be forgiven? Did it matter if he deserved it or not? Mallory had needed him, and he hadn't been there for her. Over and over again.

She raised her chin. "I'm working on it."

"There's one thing that's bugged me since that night, Mallory."

Her heart rate quickened. "What is it?"

He leaned even closer. "That night at the party, before everything happened . . . I saw your dad talking to Dante Torres."

CHAPTER 11

Mallory blinked, certain she hadn't heard correctly. "My dad? No. That's impossible. Why would he?"

He shrugged. "I don't know. I couldn't figure it out either."

She glanced behind her to see if anyone else was listening. Everyone else seemed distracted—except Tennyson. Even from across the room, she could feel him watching them.

"Did you tell the police?" she whispered, turning back to Jason.

He shook his head, his eyes crinkling as if the idea was absurd. "No, of course not. I didn't want to betray your father like that."

She nibbled on her bottom lip a moment, trying to gather her thoughts. Her father talking with Dante Torres? Why would he do that? She couldn't come up with one single reason.

"I . . . I don't know what to say."

"I wanted you to know. I'll keep it quiet. I know how this could ruin your family's reputation . . . the business."

Her mind whirled as he walked away. It wasn't her family's reputation or business that she worried about. It was her father's integrity.

Her father would never align himself with someone like Dante. The crime had been random. It had been because the family was wealthy. Because Dante had seen Mallory while she was dining at a restaurant with her family. He'd realized she looked like his first wife, and that delusional side of him had kicked into overdrive.

Not because her dad was crooked. Or had betrayed him. Or anything else.

"Look, here's my card in case you need anything," Jason continued, his voice low. "Anything at all."

As Jason sauntered away, Tennyson appeared at her side. "That's over."

She nodded, trying to bring herself back into the moment. "Yes, it is."

"How do you feel?"

How did she feel? Like she wanted to crawl under a rock. But she couldn't let on to that. Nor could she do anything to implicate her father. Not without cold hard facts. Maybe not even then.

"I'm just glad it's done. I can cross that off my list."

He studied her until she squirmed. He knew there was something she wasn't sharing. It unnerved her that he could read her that easily.

"All right, you two." Grant's voice sliced through the room, an unnecessary amount of rosiness in his tone. "How about we get an early dinner?"

Mallory forced herself to smile and nod.

But all she could think about was her conversation with Jason.

• • •

Tennyson stared at Mallory as they sat across the table from each other at an upscale Italian restaurant not far from the TV station. The scents of cheese and garlic wafted around them. Lively music played overhead. The lights were dim enough to add atmosphere but bright enough to see by.

Grant rambled on and on about the reunion, muttering things about how it would make for great TV. Mallory's eyes looked glazed, as if she didn't hear a word of it.

A break from the babble came when the waitress delivered the food: chicken scampi for Mallory, lasagna for Tennyson, soup and salad for Grant.

The savory scents made Tennyson's stomach growl.

"How do you think the reunion went, Tennyson?" Mallory asked, picking at her food.

He lowered his fork and cleared his throat, surprised that she wanted his opinion.

"It's hard to say," he started. "Some people would say it will make for great TV. How do you feel about it?"

She frowned. "I thought I'd forgiven Jason. Some old feelings—some hard feelings—came to the surface, though."

"It was a pivotal moment for you."

Something unsaid stretched between them, a moment of understanding.

"Well, I think it was a great move." Grant's voice snapped them out of their unspoken conversation. "The public is going to eat it up."

"Some things aren't meant for the public to witness," Tennyson said.

Grant narrowed his eyes. "What are you saying?"

Tennyson put his napkin down. "I'm just saying that there are more important things in life than PR opportunities."

Before the conversation could spiral out of control, his cell rang. Agent Turner. Tennyson excused himself and slipped toward the bathrooms, anxious to hear if he had any updates.

"What's going on?" Tennyson kept an eye on Mallory to make sure she was both safe and nowhere close enough to listen. The last time he'd spoken with the agent, he'd requested to be the point of contact in his investigation, and Mallory had agreed that it made more sense than having Grant as the contact.

"I thought you should know there's another body."

His spine stiffened. He wished he'd heard incorrectly, but he knew he hadn't. "Another body? Where?"

"Norfolk."

It didn't take an expert to put it together. The first body had been in Cape Thomas. The second in Norfolk. Those were the first two stops on Mallory's tour.

His jaw clenched as he let that news settle in his mind. "Was she branded?"

"She was. A circle with a flame, again. Inferno."

His stomach sank. The threat against Mallory was becoming more and more overt. None of this was an accident or coincidence. The message was clear: Mallory was in danger.

"How'd she die?" Tennyson asked.

"Strangled, just like the first woman. We're still trying to identify both of them, but they appear to be foreign. They haven't matched anyone in the missing persons database."

"What can I do?"

"Besides keeping an eye on Mallory? Not much. Speaking of which, I'm going to need to talk to her again."

Tennyson glanced across the restaurant at her. She and Grant were chatting, but Mallory looked less than enthused. When she learned this news, it would be one more blow to her psyche. "I know."

"How about if I come down tonight?"

"I suppose that's just as good a time as any. I'll let her know you're coming, if that's okay."

"Of course."

As Tennyson hung up, he felt a knot in his gut. The storm brewing in the distance was only growing stronger by the moment, and he needed to solidify his plan to keep Mallory from becoming drenched in the downpour.

· · ·

After dinner, it was time to meet Kori Burns, the new guard Tennyson was bringing on. He'd told Mallory a little about the woman. She was a former police officer who'd been married to another Navy SEAL. Tennyson seemed to think highly of her, and Mallory was anxious to see if she shared his opinion.

As they walked into the hotel lobby, Mallory spotted a woman in the distance and knew it was Kori when the woman's face lit up when she saw Tennyson. The two met with a brief hug.

Were they just friends? Mallory wondered. And if they were more than friends, why did that thought cause a surge of jealousy in her? That was ridiculous. She didn't want a relationship. Someone like Tennyson should be taken and happy. He was a hero, and he deserved to be happy. To have what Mallory never would.

Mallory observed the woman. She was petite—much smaller than Mallory imagined a bodyguard to be. But her eyes were lit with fire. She had glossy brown hair that curled near her shoulders.

Something about her appeared tough. Maybe it was the way she carried herself. The confident set of her shoulders. The definition of her muscles. The no-nonsense outfit she wore—black utility pants and a long-sleeved gray shirt.

The two stepped back from the warm hug. Again, a touch of envy panged in Mallory's heart. Would she ever be able to share that kind of affection with someone? It was so abandoned and free . . . so unlike Mallory, who tensed whenever someone even started to touch her.

"Mallory, this is Kori," Tennyson said. "Kori, Mallory and Grant." They all shook hands.

"I'll debrief you later," Tennyson said. "For now, let's get up to the suite."

"I'm going to run to the store down here for a moment." Grant nodded. "I'll meet you up there."

Part of Mallory was relieved that Grant was giving them a moment. It would allow her to breathe easier and not worry about the building tension she'd felt all day. Tennyson had made it clear at dinner that he didn't approve of Grant's methods.

"I'm honored to be a part of your team," Kori started as they walked up to the suite. "I admire what you're doing."

"Thank you."

"Kori has extensive experience as a bodyguard. She even guarded Lady P," Tennyson said. "So don't let her size deceive you."

"Lady P?" The singer used to be one of Mallory's favorites, back before her life had been turned upside down.

"I mostly had to protect her from herself," Kori said with a smile.

They stepped into the suite, and Tennyson indicated that he planned to leave Mallory with Kori while he checked out the space. As Mallory cleared the hallway, she froze.

Tennyson paused near her. "What's wrong?"

Mallory scanned the room, trying to pinpoint the cause of her alarm. Like many of the rooms and suites she'd stayed in, there was a living room in front of her, complete with a leather couch and two armchairs. A kitchen area was to one side and a bathroom to the other. Three bedrooms branched off from the main area.

"Mallory?" Tennyson repeated.

She stared at the room again, looking for something that was out of place. There was nothing. The pillows on the couch were fluffed to perfection. The chairs perfectly tucked under the table. Each of the bedroom doors was closed.

"I'm not sure what's wrong," she finally said.

Tennyson stepped closer. "What do you mean?"

She shook her head, wishing she had more answers. "I don't know, Tennyson. My gut is telling me that something's different."

He surveyed the space also. "I'm sure housekeeping has been here."

"It's not that."

"Let me finish checking everything out. Kori, stay with her."

Mallory watched as he drew his gun and snapped into guard mode. Carefully, he opened the door to her room and disappeared inside. He emerged a moment later, but said nothing. Instead, he searched Grant's room, his own room, and then the living room.

"There's no one here." Tennyson joined her, slipping the gun back into his shoulder holster. "Did you figure out what was bothering you?"

Mallory shook her head, wishing she could shake the tension plaguing her. "I have no idea."

"It's safe to look around, if you need to. Kori, would you mind standing guard outside? I'll debrief you on our plan of action a little later."

Kori nodded and stepped outside.

Mallory tried to ignore the tremble in her hand as she reached for the wall to steady herself. Each step felt tentative. She didn't want to miss anything.

She went through her room, detail by detail. There wasn't as much as a wrinkle on the bedspread or a footprint in the neat lines where the carpet had been vacuumed.

She stood in the living room. The trash had been collected. There was nothing between the couch cushions. The fridge contained only the basics.

Everything appeared to be in place.

"I guess it was nothing," she admitted.

But Mallory had felt so sure something was different.

"It's been a long day," Tennyson conceded.

"That's probably it." She looked up at him, her heart suddenly stuttering out of control. "I should probably turn in for the night. We leave in the morning for the next leg of the trip, after all."

His intense gaze captured hers. "Probably a good idea."

She slipped into her room and shut the door, her cheeks warm. Tennyson had an undeniable effect on her. She had to put an end to that. The last thing she needed right now was to be looking for a normal, settled down happy ever after. Her life didn't lend itself to being that simple.

Maybe never would. Not after what had happened to her. What guy in his right mind would want to be with someone who'd been damaged as much as she had? No one, she realized. She had so much baggage that no one would be able to get past it all.

Besides, she'd always been defined by the men in her life. First her dad. Then Jason. Then Dante. She needed to stand on her own two feet. To prove—to herself and to everyone else—that she was more than arm candy. She had a lot to offer society, and no one was going to take that from her.

She hurried across the room, hoping a warm shower would clear her thoughts.

Before she could slip off her clothes, something on the bathroom counter caught her eye. It was between her foundation and lipstick. Something that seemed out of place to her, but that no one else would have noticed in the jumble of cosmetics.

She held her breath as she picked up the bottle there.

Perfume.

The same kind Dante had made her wear.

She vomited into the toilet beside her.

CHAPTER 12

Tennyson heard Mallory gasp and rushed into the room, fully expecting to encounter danger.

Instead he saw her crouched beside the toilet.

He put his hand on her back and waited while he scanned the room for a sign or clue of what had caused her reaction.

He saw nothing.

He wet a washcloth and handed it to her. She placed it over her mouth as she straightened.

When he saw her face, he noticed how pale she'd become. Something had shaken her.

"Mallory?" he asked quietly.

She nodded toward the counter. "Perfume," she croaked.

He picked up the bottle. Perfume had upset her?

He raised it to his nose and took a sniff. Realization bolted through him. This was the same scent he'd noticed when he'd rescued her. Not her normal scent of fruit and flowers. No, this was the pungent odor of expensive perfume.

She hadn't left this here.

Someone else had. Someone who'd wanted to send her a message.

Tennyson steeled himself against the anger bubbling inside him.

"No idea where this came from?"

She wiped away the moisture underneath her eyes and brought herself up to full height. "I have no idea."

He frowned. "The rest of the place is clear. Let's get you out of here while we wait for the police."

Mallory didn't argue as he led her back into the living room.

He tried not to let his concern show through too much. But how had someone gained access? How had someone known about the perfume? She hadn't named it in her book or in any interviews he'd seen or read.

He waited until she was on the couch. She sat stiffly, almost robotically.

He knelt beside her, worried about her well-being. "Can I get you some water?"

She shook her head, her eyes still dull and her demeanor shell-shocked. "No thanks."

"I'm going to get Kori to stay with you while I check out the suite again, okay?"

She nodded, and a couple of minutes later, Kori sat down beside her and began speaking in soft tones.

Tennyson couldn't ignore how Mallory crossed her arms over her chest, almost like hugging herself. She was fighting to remain in control, he realized. It would be really easy for her thoughts to spiral into a pit of despair right now.

He hesitated before taking a step away. He didn't want to leave her. But time was essential right now. He had to call the police. Wheaton. Grant.

He called people in that order. The police promised to come out. Wheaton promised to look into the situation. It was his call with Grant that surprised him. The man was downstairs meeting with more PR people.

"What?" Grant let out a grunt after Tennyson told him what had happened. "Don't tell anyone. Let me handle this."

Tennyson's jaw hardened at his insensitive words. "It's too late. I already did. The police are on their way."

Grant muttered something underneath his breath. "You should have contacted me first."

"You hired me to look out for her safety." The argument seemed so futile at a time like this. This wasn't a time for a power play.

"Do you know what a PR nightmare this is going to be?"

Anger flared inside Tennyson. How dare Grant think about the PR nightmare of this? Was that more of a concern to him than Mallory's safety? He took a deep breath and calmed himself.

"Look, can we talk about this later?" he muttered. "Right now, we need to figure out who left this perfume. That's the most important thing."

Grant remained silent a moment. When he finally spoke, his voice had softened. "Of course. I'll be right up."

Tennyson wandered back over to Mallory, praying the anger inside him would smolder, and she wouldn't be privy to his conversation with Grant. He sat beside her on the couch, soaking in her pale features. Kori sat on the other side of her, holding a glass of water.

Someone had wanted this. They'd wanted the shock value. Whoever was behind this could have tried to harm her or tried to snatch her. They hadn't. Instead, they'd wanted to scare her.

But why?

Mallory's perceptive gaze shifted up to him. "You and Grant were arguing."

He shrugged. "It doesn't matter."

"Sure it does. You don't like him. Why?"

He set his jaw as he tried to find the answer. "I question his motives."

"You think he's in this for money?"

Tennyson shrugged. "I don't know exactly. It's not important right now."

She pursed her lips but didn't say anything.

In record time, Grant barged into the room and rushed toward Mallory, as if he was beside himself with concern. His earlier politicking was nowhere to be seen.

"Doll, are you okay?" He knelt in front of her.

Tennyson looked away, unable to stomach Grant's phoniness. Maybe there was a part of the man that cared about Mallory, but too much about him screamed Hollywood, and Tennyson still wasn't convinced he had Mallory's best interests in mind.

"I don't know who would do this," Mallory said.

"Who knew about the perfume?" Tennyson asked.

She didn't hesitate before responding, "Dante. His men. I'm sure he got one of them to purchase it for him."

"Did you mention the perfume to anyone?" Tennyson continued.

She shook her head. "No one."

• • •

Mallory wished she could disappear. She wished the conversation around her was a bad dream. But it wasn't, and she had no choice but to wade through it.

"We need to cut this tour short," Tennyson told Grant.

"Don't be ridiculous," Grant shot back. "Someone's trying to scare Mallory, but that doesn't mean it should turn her life upside down."

"Look at the stakes," Tennyson continued. "This isn't all one big PR opportunity. Her life isn't your opportunity to capitalize on your career."

Grant bristled visibly. "What are you implying?"

"I'm implying that I think you're looking out for your bottom line more than you are for Mallory."

Mallory sighed. Was what Tennyson implying true? Had she put her trust in the wrong person?

"Kori, guard the door outside until the police get here," Tennyson said. "I need to go downstairs and talk to some of the hotel staff."

Mallory closed her eyes, her head suddenly pounding. Dwelling on Tennyson and Grant's argument was tempting, especially considering the alternative. Yet all she could think about was that perfume.

That perfume . . . Alessandra had worn it. That was why Dante liked it so much.

But who would have left it here? And why? Just to torture her? *Think, Mallory. Think. Who else knew about the perfume?*

Tennyson had left, and she waited for the police to arrive. As she did, her mind searched through the faces of the people she'd encountered in captivity. Her thoughts raced and scampered and skidded all over the place.

She stopped at one person.

Sanchez. Sanchez was Alessandra's half brother. Apparently, that was how he and Dante had met—through Alessandra. That was the impression Mallory had after talking to the housekeeper, Gabriella, at least.

Sanchez had never been captured, and Mallory knew he could still be trying to run operations from some isolated place. He could still have contacts with Dante's former network.

But why would he take time out of doing his reprehensible deed of selling illegal arms in order to sneak into Mallory's hotel room and leave that perfume? It just didn't make sense. She wasn't a threat.

Memories of that scent hit her again. Was it a remembrance? Or had the fragrance somehow been absorbed into her hair or skin? She wasn't sure.

She feared she'd throw up again at any minute. Images of Dante haunted her. His voice. His touch. His scent.

She leaned over a trash can and purged again.

"There, there, doll." Grant rested his hand on her back.

Mallory jerked away at his touch.

He raised his hands. "Sorry. Sorry. I didn't mean—"

"Don't apologize," Mallory muttered, knowing her reaction was an overreaction. She had to get a grip.

Mallory turned toward Grant, wiping her mouth with a napkin. "Do you know how that perfume got in here?"

He shook his head, concern etched in his gaze. "No idea. I don't know who would do this. It's cruel. The good news is that the police are on the way. We'll get to the bottom of this."

As she shook her head, her temples pounded, aching with each motion. "Maybe all of this isn't a good idea. Maybe I've brought too much attention to myself through this tour and made myself more of a target. I should have disappeared into obscurity."

"Who would be after you, Mallory? They have no reason to want you back. Dante is dead."

"Then who left the perfume? What kind of message was someone trying to send?"

Just then, there was a knock at the door. Kori let the police inside. Mallory gave her statement to the detective while a forensic tech collected the evidence.

Her mind kept going back to the perfume. She had so many questions about how it had gotten there. The only people with keys to the suite were her, Tennyson, and Grant. And, of course, the housekeeping and hotel staff. Certainly there were cameras placed around the hotel. Would they have recorded the person?

An uneasy feeling continued to slosh in her stomach.

She was tired of sitting back and waiting for this person to make his next move. She needed to figure out who was behind these acts before everything fell apart again.

● ● ●

Tennyson approached the front desk of the hotel, knowing the police would be down here soon to ask the same questions he wanted to ask. He considered it his job to protect Mallory by whatever means possible, and that didn't just include keeping her physically safe from harm. If he could head off any trauma to her, he needed to do that.

The woman at the front desk was a pretty brunette whose eyes lit up as she soaked him in. He plastered on his best smile and leaned on the desk toward her.

"Can I help you?" Her voice sounded flirty, and her eyes sparkled with interest.

He drew in a deep breath and offered his most friendly smile. "I'm hoping you can. Do you keep security footage for the hotel?"

"Well, of course. What kind of establishment do you think we are?" She laughed and batted her eyelashes, then rested her chin on her hand and stared up at him.

He leaned toward her, glancing at her name badge. "How can I get to see some of the video feed, Angie? It's important."

Her smile faded. "Well, you can't. What's wrong?"

"Someone got into the suite upstairs, and I need to find out who."

She studied him. "You're with that girl who was abducted, aren't you?"

He nodded, not willing to lie. "I'm security for her."

The sparkle in her eyes returned. "Security? Like a bodyguard?"

"Something like that."

"That's . . . very admirable."

He lowered his voice. "I really need to see that footage as soon as possible."

She glanced at her computer screen. "I guess since you're officially security, then you would have the right to see the footage. I'll bypass my manager, but only because of the timeliness of the situation. Follow me."

Awesome. He followed her back into a room behind the front desk. A fiftysomething man sat there in front of about eight screens.

"Hank, can you pull up the video footage for the eighth floor?" She smiled sweetly at the man, who immediately perked up at the sight of her. "Near the suites up there. Eight-oh-four."

"Can't do that," he muttered.

Tennyson stepped closer. "Please. You heard about the woman who was rescued from that terrorist? It's her suite. We've got to figure out if someone is targeting her, and we need to resolve this quickly."

The rumpled, red-eyed guard muttered under his breath and began punching something on the computer. A minute later, the footage came up.

There was approximately an eight-hour window when Mallory, Grant, and Tennyson were gone, and the perfume could have been placed in the room. The guard fast-forwarded the video, slowing whenever someone came down the hallway. Only two people went into the room during that time period.

The housecleaning staff.

Had one of those women left it?

Tennyson turned toward Angie. "Can I speak with these ladies? Are they still here?"

Angie's eyes narrowed in thought. "Rosie should still be here. Let me call her."

Tennyson stared at the screen. The minutes seemed to stretch, each second ticking like a time bomb. Who had left that perfume?

Finally, a woman entered the room. The twentysomething maid wrung her hands together as she stepped inside. Her dark hair was pulled back into a loose bun. Tendrils escaped and sprung from her hairline. Her uniform was too large for her slim frame.

The guard closed the door behind her, and the sound made her jump. Her eyes drifted to the floor. The wall. Anywhere but to someone else's gaze.

"Rosie, this man would like to speak with you," Angie said, her voice warm and friendly. "I need you to answer his questions."

"Yes, ma'am. What can I do?" Her hands continued to twist together as she turned toward Tennyson. Her brown eyes finally met his—but only for a moment. She quickly looked back down at the floor.

"Did you leave anything unusual in suite eight-oh-four, Rosie?" Tennyson asked.

"Leave anything?" Her gaze shifted nervously, and her breathing became heavier.

He nodded. "It's important that you tell me everything."

"I don't know, señor—" Worry rose in her voice.

"I think you do." Tennyson leveled his gaze with hers before she tried to weasel out of telling the truth. "I need to know, Rosie. Someone's life depends on it."

The woman's eyes widened, and she fanned her face. "Life depends on it? It not supposed to be like that. It was gift. From boyfriend. That what he say."

Tennyson's thoughts churned. "Tell me more. Where did you meet this boyfriend?"

Rosie wiped her hands on the skirt of her uniform before fanning her face with her hand again. "He caught me on the elevator. Said he wanted to surprise his girlfriend. He gave me perfume and ask me to leave it."

"That's not against your policy?" Tennyson glanced at Angie.

"It is," Rosie said with a frown. "But I thought there be no harm. He say they apart for many months. I thought he military." Rosie's voice rose with panic.

"Did he say that he was military?" Tennyson asked.

She shook her head. "He say he out on mission. I think he military."

"What did this man look like?" Tennyson didn't like what he was learning. But he had to get to the truth.

She shook her head, her eyes shifting wildly. "He tall. Dark hair. Very handsome."

That could fit the description of Dante. Of course, it could be the description of many other men also.

"What was his voice like?"

"He have accent. Spoke Spanish."

That was something to go on. "Where are you from?"

"Mexico City."

Tennyson nodded, trying to put all the facts together. "Did his accent sound Mexican?"

She nodded, a little too eagerly. The woman obviously wanted to help and stay out of trouble. "I think so. Maybe Sonora."

"Is there anything else this man told you?"

Rosie shook her head a little too quickly. "I no think so. I so sorry. Please—I need job—"

"You're fine, Rosie," Angie said. "Thank you for your help."

Tennyson slipped her his card. "If you think of anything, call me."

He turned back to the security guard. "Do you have any video footage from the elevators? Can we see the one Rosie was on?"

"Of course." The guard asked Rosie a few questions to determine which one she had taken, then pulled up the correct elevator at the right time. Rosie appeared in the elevator. On the fourth floor, a man wearing a crisp suit stepped inside. He kept his back to the camera, as if he knew he was being recorded.

Just as Rosie had said, the man was tall with dark hair. Tennyson guessed, just by looking at the video, that the man was in his thirties.

Was it Dante? He just couldn't tell.

"Can you scroll back? I want to see the footage before he got on the elevator. I need to see his face." He glanced at his watch. The police should be here at any minute. At that point, they'd take over, and he might not be privy to this information.

The guard did as he asked. He spotted the man walking down the hall. He wore the same crisp suit. But he'd pulled on a baseball cap. His face was still shadowed.

Tennyson's jaw hardened. Whoever this man was, he'd thought of everything. He knew where the cameras were, and he knew how to avoid them. He'd somehow known which room Mallory was staying in, which housekeeper serviced the suite, and when Mallory was gone.

More and more unease churned inside him. This wasn't good. He needed to get Mallory out of this hotel. He needed to increase security measures.

But right now, he needed to get back up to Mallory.

CHAPTER 13

Mallory stood as soon as Tennyson walked back into their suite. She was still talking to the detective and had filled him in on everything that was going on, detail by painful detail. Kori had been beside her the whole time, and though she appreciated the woman's presence, she wasn't Tennyson.

Upon seeing him, some of Mallory's unease faded, and somehow, she knew everything would be better.

Their gazes connected. He'd discovered something, she realized. Tennyson joined their circle and introduced himself to the detective.

"A man asked one of the housekeepers to leave the perfume in the room as a surprise for Mallory," he told the detective. "I confirmed the details with the hotel staff downstairs."

Mallory's hand went to her stomach. She had nothing left inside her, yet nausea still roiled. "Who? Who was it?"

Tennyson shook his head, the lines on his face taut with concern. "We couldn't make out his features. He was careful to keep his face away from the cameras."

"Could you tell anything about him?" the detective asked.

Tennyson paused before responding. "He was tall, thirtyish, with dark hair."

Grant shook his head tersely, obviously frustrated by the lack of information. "That could be anyone."

Tennyson raised his chin. "I know. It's not much to go on."

"Did the housekeeper say anything else?" the detective asked.

He pressed his lips together before answering. Mallory's blood spiked. What was Tennyson so hesitant to say?

"He had a Mexican accent. From the Northwest region probably."

"A Mexican accent?" Realization hit her like a punch in the gut. "He's one of Dante's men. Sanchez, maybe. Sanchez was tall with dark hair." And he was bound to know about the perfume.

"Don't jump to any conclusions yet. There's still a lot we don't know." Tennyson's compassionate gaze nearly felt physical as he offered her reassurance.

"Don't worry. We'll look into this, especially given all that's happened," the detective said.

"If you learn anything, I'd appreciate being kept in the loop," Tennyson said.

"I'll share whatever I can."

"We're going to need to get on the road," Tennyson continued. "It's not safe to stay here. You have our contact information."

As the detective walked away, Tennyson turned to Grant. "Who knows her tour schedule?"

Something flashed in Grant's eyes. Annoyance maybe? "Her appearances are posted on her website."

"Who knows what hotels she's staying in?"

"No one. Just me and a few other people with Verto." Grant stared at him challengingly.

"What are you getting at, Tennyson?" Mallory asked. The subcontext of the conversation unsettled her.

"Someone found out you were staying here," Tennyson said. "There could be a leak from within."

Grant pulled his lips back in defiance before letting out a bitter sigh. "No one on my team would do that."

"Then explain how this person knew where Mallory was staying." Tennyson's hands went to his hips.

Mallory felt her gut clench. She watched Grant, waiting for his reply. Finally, he shook his head, and his shoulders slumped.

"I can't. I can't explain it. I wish I could."

"I'm going to need a list of everyone who knew where she was staying. We need to end this before someone tries to take it any further."

She expected an argument, but instead Grant nodded. "Seems like a good idea. I'll make that list for you. Mallory's safety is of the utmost importance."

"Exactly."

But Mallory wasn't sure her safety was even a reality at this point. Someone wanted to terrify her, at the least. At most, they wanted to harm her. She feared they might succeed.

•   •   •

"Mallory, I need to speak with you," Tennyson said.

She looked up from the couch where she sat. They'd moved to a new hotel for the night. They'd only arrived ten minutes ago, long enough to deposit their belongings. It was late—nearly midnight already. Yet she was wide-awake and craving coffee. Grant had obliged her and gone downstairs to find some since the machine in their room wasn't working.

"Sure thing. What's going on?" The serious tone of his voice put her on edge.

He sat stiffly beside her. "I need to let you know that Agent Turner is on his way up. I wanted to tell you sooner, but things kind of got crazy."

Alarm shot through her. "Agent Turner? Again?"

"That's right." Tennyson drew in a long, slow breath.

His eyes latched onto hers, and she could see the hesitation there. He didn't want to tell her. But why?

"There have been some developments," he said.

Before he could go any further, there was a knock at the door. Tennyson stood and looked down at her a moment. "I'm going to be here if you need anything, Mallory. Just know that."

Her apprehension only grew at his words. She also stood as the agent walked into the room. She nodded toward the middle-aged man with thinning blond hair and a thick neck. The man had always been kind and professional toward her.

"Good to see you again, Mallory." Agent Turner set his briefcase on the coffee table.

Mallory directed him to sit down, anxious to find out what was going on. He lowered himself onto the chair across from her. Tennyson sat beside her—closer than she'd expected.

Was it because he anticipated she'd need moral support?

Dear Lord, help me get through this. Whatever this is.

"I won't waste any time," Agent Turner started. "Last night, this body washed ashore at the port in Norfolk."

Agent Turner slid a picture across the table.

"In Norfolk . . ." The facts collided in her head. The first dead body had been found in Cape Thomas. Now Norfolk. Those were both places she'd been . . .

Agent Turner nodded. "At the Gazette Suites."

Her heart rate ricocheted at his announcement. "The hotel where I stayed?"

He nodded grimly.

Her throat squeezed as she took the next picture Turner handed her. It was another lifeless woman.

"Have you ever seen these women?" Turner asked.

She shook her head, no sign of recognition flashing in her. "No, I haven't."

She set the pictures side by side and narrowed her eyes. "These women . . . they both look . . . like me."

Tennyson grimaced beside her. He'd realized it, too.

"Yes, that's true," Agent Turner said.

"I don't understand." She squeezed the bridge of her nose, trying to make sense of everything.

Turner leaned toward her. "Mallory, both of these women were branded."

Her eyes widened. "With the Inferno symbol?"

He nodded solemnly.

She leaned back, trying to right her world before it started to spin more.

"Is someone trying to send me a message?" she asked.

"We don't know. Is there anything that stands out in your mind? Anything that happened that might explain this?"

"Dante's dead. He couldn't have done this."

The agent nodded slowly. "But he still has men out there."

"That symbol is pretty well-known." Her own scar from where someone had branded her began to throb. "Someone could have found out about it. This could be . . . I don't know. I don't know what this is."

"We're looking into this, Mallory. We're going to figure out what's going on."

When Agent Turner left, Mallory turned to Tennyson. "I need you to do me a favor, Tennyson."

Curiosity flashed in his gaze. "What's that?"

"I need you to track down Jasmine, the girl Jason was with the night my parents were killed."

His eyes narrowed. "Why?"

"Because I need to know if she saw anything that night. Mostly, I need to know if my dad really was working with Dante Torres."

"Why would you ask that?"

Pressure simmered inside her. "Because when Jason pulled me aside after the interview, he claimed he saw my father with Torres."

A strange emotion washed over Tennyson's expression—but only for a moment, and then a neutral expression returned. "I'll see what I can find out."

CHAPTER 14

The next morning, they traveled south to Atlanta. Tennyson had informed Mallory that he'd changed their accommodations to a new hotel and put the reservation under his name.

She had a book signing scheduled for tomorrow and a television interview the next day. She'd need to replenish herself today in order to give her best. She sat on the couch, attempting to write a few thank-you letters, and tried not to fret.

Kori stood at the door; Grant had disappeared into his bedroom; and Tennyson had excused himself for a moment.

"Penny for your thoughts."

She looked up and saw Tennyson standing over her. He truly was handsome. Breathtaking, for that matter.

The old Mallory would have flirted until she got her way—and her way would have been getting his phone number, having him ask her out, having a good time until one or the other lost interest.

But it was more than physical appearance that intrigued her—he acted with integrity. He showed respect to her. He seemed to value self-control.

He moved around the couch, coming to sit beside her. Her heart rate sped as their arms brushed.

She didn't remember ever feeling so nervous around a guy.

She recalled his inquiry about her thoughts. "I'm just thinking about how quickly life can change."

"I agree. In the blink of an eye."

"Scents have the amazing ability to take people back in time," she said softly.

He frowned. "They do. I'm sure the perfume yesterday has been hard on you."

"Every time I think about that smell, I try to replace it with memories of the apple orchard my grandparents owned. Replace troubled thoughts with happy thoughts, right?"

"It sounds like your grandparents meant a lot to you."

"They did. They brought me down to earth, and I always felt like I could be myself with them and not the person my parents had wanted me to be. They were salt of the earth people who worked hard for every dime, and treasured the simple things in life."

"They sound like great people."

"When I was with them, I wanted to be the same as they were. I did a lot of things I wasn't proud of as a teenager, Tennyson."

"Most of us did."

She shook her head. "Since I was rescued, I've learned to make it on my own. Honestly, I've had no one to depend on but myself. Sometimes the thought of it is daunting, and other times it's empowering."

"That's the beautiful part about life—the ability for second chances." His eyes crinkled as he turned his full attention on her. "So, what brought this about?"

She put her pen down and leaned back. "When I talked with Jason, I realized what a jerk I was. To be honest, I don't think it's ever who I truly was. Maybe everyone who's a spoiled brat says that. But I remember when I was with my grandparents, I always felt like I could be who I was instead of who I was raised to be." She shook her head. "I'm not sure that makes sense."

"Your dad was high-powered. I imagine he had a lot of expectations for you."

"He was so different than my grandparents. When he was a teenager, he began working at an appliance shop. He learned how to repair washing machines and dryers. He scrounged together enough money from that to pay his way through college. Before he was thirty, he'd opened his own store. Before he was forty, he decided to go into business for himself manufacturing washers and dryers. Now the Baldwin name is in most households."

"Where did you fit into that timeline?"

"It sounds cliché, but my father married my mother when he was sixty and she was twenty-five."

"Wow."

She nodded. "Yeah. I was born two years later. My dad's only biological child, even though he'd been married twice before. Everyone really knew that he was only truly married to his job. That was the most important thing to him."

"That had to be hard on you."

She shrugged. "He spent every waking moment trying to better his business. His ultimate success—or failure—was based on his capital worth."

"That's a hard way to live. He does indeed sound very different than your grandparents."

"They were my father's roots. Granddad owned a farm. He worked hard, making use of the land. They had a simple life. My grandma died when I was eleven, but my grandfather lived into his nineties."

"Your granddad and dad were opposites, it sounds like."

"In every way—except the working hard part, I suppose. The way my mom told it, my father had offered to build my granddad a mansion anywhere he wanted. Grandpa never wanted anything to do with it."

"He sounds wise. You know what the Bible says about the love of money."

"It's easier for a camel to get through the eye of a needle than for a rich man to enter heaven. It's the truth. With money, you feel self-sufficient, like you have no need for God. But I bet my parents . . ." Her voice caught.

"I'm sorry."

She drew in a deep breath. "I've talked enough about my family. I really don't know anything about you."

His jaw flexed, but just for a moment. Mallory wondered what had happened in his past to cause that reaction. There was something painful there. Would he ever share what it was? Or was she reading too much into their relationship?

"There's not much to share."

"A man who became one of the military's most elite? I bet there is."

He shrugged. "I grew up in Indiana."

"Indiana? I pegged you for a Midwest type of guy."

"You pegged right. I'm the middle of six children. My dad was a cop. He's retired now and living on a golf course. He deserves it."

"Your mom?"

"She was a part-time nurse for a while. On and off during my child-hood, for that matter. When she wasn't working or being with us kids, she loved walking."

"Walking?"

A smile played on his lips, and Mallory could see his fondness for his family. "She did all of the races. In fact, some people called her the speed-walking champ."

Mallory let out a chuckle. "That sounds like a nice childhood. Do you still talk to your family a lot?"

"All I can. I only make it home three or four times a year. I wish it was more."

"That's pretty good." She pulled a leg beneath her, delighted that he was sharing. She found this other side of him fascinating. "How'd you become a SEAL?"

122

"It's what I always wanted. I played some football in high school and was offered a scholarship to play in college. I decided to go into the military instead. Went through SEAL training. I actually made it." He raised his eyebrows and his eyes twinkled, like the fact still surprised him.

"Not only did you make it—you made it into the elite of the elites. SEAL Team Six."

He nodded slowly, humbly. "That's right."

She bit down, contemplating whether or not to ask her next question. "But you got out."

The lightheartedness slipped from his demeanor. "It was complicated."

"I see."

"I lost someone I loved." Hard lines appeared across his face. "Her death wasn't the reason I got out of the military, but it definitely factored into my later decision to leave. Her name was Claire."

"Pretty name." She remembered the picture she'd seen on top of his wallet the first night he'd been on duty. Was that olive-complexioned, dark-haired beauty Claire?

"She was the love of my life." His lips pressed together a moment.

Mallory waited, hoping he would share more and giving him the space to do so, if he wanted.

"She died—"

Before he could finish his sentence, the door burst open and Grant stepped inside. He glanced at his watch. "All right, I've got lunch. Who's hungry?"

Mallory fought disappointment. What was Tennyson about to say? Would he ever risk opening up again?

CHAPTER 15

When Tennyson's phone rang, he slipped away from the lunch Grant had brought up to the suite.

"Stone, what's going on?" Tennyson asked.

"Where are you?"

"Atlanta."

"Listen, we need to talk."

"Go ahead. I'm all ears."

"No, we need to talk in person."

Tennyson bristled. That didn't sound good. "I can't leave Mallory."

"I'll come to you then. I'll catch a plane from DC. I can be there in a few hours."

Tennyson glanced at his watch. That would put him here this evening. "Okay, if it's that important."

"I'll be in touch when I land. I'll come to you."

Mallory looked up at him with curiosity when he returned. "You look very serious."

He forced a smile. "Just taking care of some business . . . Where's Grant?"

"I think he ran to the bank."

Tennyson put his phone away. "Listen, I'd like to go through some self-defense moves with you."

Her eyebrows shot up. "Self-defense?"

He nodded. "You have Kori and me watching out for you, but it never hurts to know some moves of your own. What do you think?"

She swallowed hard. "It seems reasonable."

He hesitated a moment, and she wondered what he was thinking. "I'm going to have to touch you . . ."

So he'd noticed just how badly she reacted when someone made physical contact with her. Of course he had. He was observant. He was *paid* to be observant, for that matter.

She cleared her throat. "I'll . . . I'll be okay."

He studied her another moment before nodding. "Why don't you go get changed into something more comfortable then."

They met five minutes later in the living room. Tennyson had already cleared away the furniture, leaving an open area. Mallory's nerves buzzed with anticipation.

Was she ready for this?

No, she was past ready for this. Self-defense classes should have been one of the first things she'd done. How silly of her to think that since she'd been rescued she was out of danger.

"I just want to run through a few moves with you," Tennyson started. "First of all, if you have a choice, run. If someone grabs you, go for the knees. If you're able to reach their face, go for their eyes. Let's look at a few scenarios. You're sure you're okay with this?"

She appreciated his concern and his attention to detail. She forced a nod, ready to get this over with. "Let's do it."

He studied her one more minute before nodding. "Okay, let's say someone comes at you from behind."

He motioned for her to turn around. With a touch of anticipation, Mallory pivoted away from him. Her blood pounded in her ears as she waited for what would happen next.

Breathe, Mallory. Breathe. None of this is real. Just practice.

"You're walking, and someone grabs you." Tennyson seemed to hesitate before putting his hand on her shoulder.

Her stomach squeezed as memories pummeled her. She pushed them away, determined not to shrink from his touch.

"I want you to pull your knee up, and then slam your foot back into my knee," Tennyson instructed.

Feeling slightly light-headed, she did as he asked.

"Perfect. That will throw someone off guard and give you the chance to run." He paused. "But what if that doesn't work?"

"I have no idea." Maybe under normal circumstances, Mallory would. But all she could think about right now was Tennyson's hand on her shoulder. She had to concentrate on staying lucid.

These were important lessons. She needed to learn them. Her life could depend on it.

"I'm going to put my hand over your mouth for a minute," Tennyson said.

He stood close behind her, close enough she could feel his body heat. His breath was warm.

Part of her wanted to run. The other part wanted to drink in the moment.

"Are you okay with this?" Tennyson asked quietly.

Was she? She had no idea. She nodded anyway, not wanting to seem as weak as she felt. "Yes."

He pulled her closer, wrapping one arm around her midsection and pinning her arms. "Any time you feel uncomfortable, tell me, and this is over."

It's over! It's over!

She forced herself to remain quiet. Forced herself not to think about the night she was snatched. Forced herself to remember that this was Tennyson, that she could trust him.

"If someone pins your arms like this, and then places their hand over your mouth like this, you're going to feel defenseless." Tennyson's hand went over her mouth. "You won't be able to scream."

At the moment, she didn't want to scream. No, her thoughts volleyed from terror to realization about how firm Tennyson's abs were as he pressed into her. About how good his leathery cologne smelled, about how—despite her fears—she'd even gotten this far with this training.

Maybe most people couldn't see it, but this was a big step for her.

"Your first move should be to elbow me. But what if that doesn't work?"

Her heart pounded in her ears.

"I want you to use all the strength you have in your core, and I want you to try and propel me over your shoulder."

Okay, she could do this. She counted to three, grabbed his arm, and tried to leverage him off of her. It didn't work.

"Think of me as one of Torres's men, Mallory. You can do this."

One of Torres's men? Her blood wanted to freeze at the thought. She closed her eyes. Their pictures flashed through her mind. But they only stopped at one image.

Dante Torres himself.

Revulsion welled in her. For the past. For what he was doing to her now from the grave. For how the memory of him affected her future.

She let out a grunt and jerked Tennyson's arm. The move wasn't graceful, but she managed to flip him over her shoulder and onto his back.

Then she stood there, a trembling mess as she stared down at him. She'd halfway expected to see Dante lying there.

"Good job, Mallory." He sat up, that concerned expression in his eyes again. "I know that wasn't pleasant. But you did it. You should be proud."

A surge of adrenaline rushed through her. She had done it. She'd overcome not one but two fears today. The fear of Dante. And the fear of being touched.

Part of her wanted to fall into Tennyson's arms and celebrate this victory.

Instead, Tennyson grinned and raised his hand. "Fist bump."

Her heart sank, but she raised her arm anyway. "Fist bump."

• • •

After Tennyson showered, he picked up his phone and saw he'd missed a call from his friend Leigh Sullivan, the forensic anthropologist. He only knew Leigh through his relationship with Admiral Kline, but he was glad he did.

He called her back.

"Tennyson, long time since we've spoken," she started.

"Too long. I'm sorry for that."

"No apologies necessary. What's going on?"

"How would we go about reexamining Dante Torres's remains?" he asked.

She remained silent for a moment. "What?"

"I know this sounds strange, but some new revelations have come to light. There's more than one person who believes Torres may have survived."

"I examined his remains myself, Tennyson."

"And they were hard to identify, correct?"

"Well, that's correct. But all the marks—"

"Are you a hundred percent sure, Leigh?"

Silence stretched again on the line. "No, I'm not. But it's not as simple as making a request. This is a big deal, Tennyson."

"I know it is. That's why I'm asking for your help. What do I need to do?"

"You're going to have to go through someone more powerful than me."

"Admiral Kline might have some pull."

"He would be a great starting point. But you've got to realize that he's not going to want to open this can of worms. He's just now recovering from his daughter's death—if that's what you'd call it. A parent never fully heals when they lose a child."

"I know, Leigh. I do. And I wouldn't be asking if this wasn't important."

She was quiet another moment. "Let me talk to him. I'll be in touch."

"Thanks, Leigh."

He stepped from his room and saw Mallory pacing in the living room. His stomach clenched. She'd been a trooper during their training. He knew she was uncomfortable with both his touch and the scenarios he'd presented. But she hadn't shrunk away from it either.

Now he just had to resist the urge to take her into his arms and tell her everything would be okay. Not only would it be professionally inappropriate, but she also wouldn't welcome the action. But sometimes she just got that lost, far-off look in her eyes and that screamed to him of her need to have someone in her life. A support system. An honest one, full of people who really were looking out for her best interests.

As soon as she spotted him, she hurried toward him. He could tell by the set of her shoulders that something was wrong.

"Tennyson, I'd like to go for a walk." She nodded toward the window, where the sun shone brightly, and a blue sky waited.

"A walk? That's not a good idea. What's going on?"

She pushed her hair behind her ear, and the familiar scent of strawberries wafted toward him again. She'd just gotten out of the shower, and the amazingly clean scent that surrounded her made his throat go dry. He shoved his hands into his pockets and tried to push those thoughts aside.

"You're going to think I'm crazy." Mallory stared up at him with big, luminescent eyes that were a strange mix of woman and child.

"I don't think you're crazy, Mallory." He cleared his throat, hoping his voice didn't sound as hoarse as he thought it might.

Her cheeks reddened, and she looked away. "Earlier, when you were teaching me those moves . . . that was a victory for me. I'm glad you taught me what you did. But right now, I feel like I can't breathe. Like I'm in prison again. I can't really explain it. I just need some fresh air. I know it's risky, but . . . please?"

"Any time you're in public, there's more risk."

She stared at him. "So is that a no?"

"I would need to scout out the area first. I haven't done that."

"Because it's spontaneous, no one else should realize I'll be out there either, right?"

His jaw flexed. "I can only make recommendations to you. I don't think it's a good idea."

"What if I want to do it anyway?"

"Then I'll make it work."

She stood. "I don't want to be difficult. I just want some fresh air."

"I know, Mallory. But my job is to keep you safe."

"If you're with me, I should be okay. Right?"

Flashbacks of Claire hit him. If only he were invincible. But he wasn't. And if something happened to Mallory on his watch, he'd never forgive himself.

"I guess Kori can walk with us also and keep a lookout."

"Thank you." Gratitude filled her voice. "I appreciate this. Let me grab something warmer, though." She slipped inside her room.

A few minutes later, they stepped out onto the sidewalk of downtown Atlanta. Tennyson walked beside Mallory, while Kori trailed behind.

The day was brisk but sunny. As they strolled down the street together, Tennyson wished they were doing so to enjoy each other's company. Instead, he was on duty. He needed to remember that.

Mallory tucked her hands in the pockets of her black coat, looking slightly preoccupied but overall content.

"Anywhere in particular you want to go?" Tennyson asked.

"No, I just want to stretch my legs."

"Let's keep going then."

He scanned the area as they walked, looking for any sign of danger. His eyes stopped on a man across the street, walking a dog. Not any dog—a poodle.

Tennyson glanced at Mallory, watching her reaction. Her gaze was transfixed on the animal, and her skin looked a little paler than before. The sight could definitely be a trigger for her, a cause for unpleasant memories.

Tennyson's gaze swung back across the street. The sixtysomething man with gray hair appeared ordinary enough, and a lot of people had poodles for a pet, he realized. But he had to take every precaution and be careful not to let down his guard.

"Mallory?"

She glanced at him, snapping out of her daze. She continued to walk, a little more somber now. "Dante liked poodles."

"I know."

She kept facing straight ahead, and her voice sounded duller than it did before. "He had six of them. I wonder what ever happened to those dogs."

"They weren't there when we raided the compound."

Her lips twisted with disbelief, and her steps slowed, but only for a second. "Really? That surprises me."

Tennyson pulled his gaze away from the man across the street, determining he wasn't a threat. "Why's that?"

"Dante took those dogs everywhere with him." Her lips pulled downward, as if the memories were ones she didn't want to recall.

"Maybe he caught wind that we were coming and sent them somewhere safe."

Finally, she nodded and raised her head to the breeze. Her eyes didn't look sad, or happy. They simply looked contemplative. "Maybe."

Tennyson continued to study everything around them. Cars coming and going. People taking strolls. Business people hurrying along.

No Torres. No Sanchez. No sign of any apparent trouble.

He was thankful for Kori's silent but watchful presence behind them.

"Any updates on Jasmine?" Mallory asked.

"No, I've been unable to trace her. I haven't given up yet, but she's been harder to locate than I anticipated."

"I wonder why that is."

He shrugged. "Some people are more challenging than others. It doesn't help that we know so little about her."

As his gaze drifted across the street again, someone familiar caught his eye. He squinted, unsure if he was seeing correctly.

Was that Grant?

Tennyson slowed his steps, trying not to let Mallory know what was bothering him.

He watched another moment. It *was* Grant. Mallory's manager was approaching a restaurant. And he wasn't alone. He was talking—leaning in, as if the conversation was secretive—with a tall, dark-haired man.

Before Tennyson could reach them, both slipped inside the uppity burger joint.

There was nothing strange in itself about going into the place. But Grant had told Mallory he was going to the bank. Why would he hide the fact that he was meeting someone?

Unless he had something to hide.

He almost told Kori to take over so he could follow the men. But he decided against it. Mallory's safety was the first priority.

"Tennyson?" Mallory asked.

He realized Mallory had been talking. With one last glance at the restaurant, Tennyson took her arm and urged her down the street. He'd talk to Grant later—once Mallory was safely tucked inside.

"Sorry about that. What were you saying?"

But even as she spoke, his mind remained on Grant.

· · ·

That evening, Tennyson stepped out into the hallway and quietly closed the door behind himself so he wouldn't wake anyone up.

Ethan Stone stood against the wall, looking as mysterious as ever. Everything about him screamed spy. He had dark features—black hair that always looked ruffled, a five-o'clock shadow—and wore a black leather coat. Yet his eyes were an icy blue.

"You made it," Tennyson said.

Stone straightened. "Of course."

"What was so urgent that you had to speak in person?"

His expression was grim as he stepped closer. "It's about Torres."

"What about him?"

Stone bit down before answering. "The scope of this is much bigger than we anticipated."

Tennyson tried to imagine where he was going with this. "He's alive?"

He gave a slight shake of his head. "It's worse than him being alive or not. It's what members of Inferno are doing. Rumor has it that they just sent a major supply of weapons to the rebels in Berna."

Tennyson's shoulders sagged with relief, at least temporarily. What Stone had shared wasn't new. "We knew Inferno was going to do that. They've *been* doing that since before I got out of the navy."

Stone gave a terse shake of his head. "You don't understand. If this rebel group overthrows the government there, they'll have access to the country's nukes."

Tennyson felt himself go still. "Berna has nuclear capabilities? Are you sure?"

Stone's shoulder pulled up in a half shrug. "That's what I heard through the grapevine. A very reliable grapevine."

Tennyson raked a hand through his hair, trying to process the news. "So what does this have to do with us? I'm not sure how telling me this in person is helping anything."

Stone looked left and right before pulling something from his jacket pocket. "These are the pictures of the man that some believe to be Torres."

Tennyson took the photos and began shuffling through them. He squinted, studying glimpses of the man in each one. There was certainly a resemblance to Dante Torres, but he wouldn't call this definitive proof.

"This still doesn't give me any answers," Tennyson said.

Stone raised his chin. "Until we catch this guy, we won't know any answers."

Tennyson continued to study each photograph. There was a picture of the man drinking coffee at a street-side café. Another one of him wearing sunglasses, walking on the beach. A third of him on a cell phone while in a car.

"Did you run the plates?" Tennyson pointed to the license plate in the photo.

"It was a hired driver. The man paid cash."

"Did you find out where he was picked up?"

"A hotel in Louisville. The man checked in under an assumed identity."

"Isn't Louisville where ROZ is?"

Stone's eyebrows shot up, and he nodded. "You know it."

Tennyson let out a sigh, not liking where any of this was going. ROZ was one of the leading manufacturers of guns and other weapons.

This could be Torres. Or this could be a man who was planted to throw everyone off the trail of what was really going on. What better way to pull the wool over someone's eyes than to distract them with a look-alike? In the meantime, a faceless leader—possibly Sanchez—could be planning these arms deals under the cover of darkness.

He looked up and observed Stone for a moment. Stone was doing the same to him, those cold eyes holding a hint of disdain still. He wasn't sure that would ever change.

"You heard about the women who've been found?" Tennyson asked. "Women who've been branded by Torres?"

Stone nodded tightly. "I heard. People keep saying that he became unhinged. Something snapped inside him after Alessandra died. Maybe he's obsessed with your girl Mallory. Maybe he's trying to send a message that no one else will do."

Tennyson's blood went cold at his theory. Nameless. Could Torres secretly be Nameless? No, he couldn't believe that a terrorist leader would spend his time on stalking someone. It didn't fit the bigger picture. Those letters were being sent by an overzealous and possibly unstable fan.

"Certainly if Torres is alive, he has better things to do than to follow Mallory around the country," Tennyson finally said.

"Who else would be responsible for those dead girls?"

"Someone else in Torres's network. Maybe someone who despised Mallory because Torres favored her. Maybe someone who feels threatened by Mallory. Someone who fears Mallory knows something, or who doesn't like leaving things unfinished."

"No one's walked away from Torres and kept their life."

Tennyson stared Stone down. "You did."

Stone shifted, as if he'd been caught saying more than he intended. Stone was on his side, right? Or had he embedded himself so deeply in the spy world that the man couldn't tell which end was up anymore?

"They think I died," Stone said. "But every time I show my face, I put myself at risk. It's a risk even being here. But I needed to look you in the eye."

Tennyson decided to drop it. Instead, he held up one of the photos. "You really think this could be him?"

Stone rubbed his jaw, settling against the wall again. "Honestly, I have no idea. This is what I do know. It's become a matter of national security. That means that whether she likes it or not, Mallory is involved. If Dante or his men are following and threatening her, then Mallory could be the one to lead us right to their nest of vipers."

Tennyson swung his head back and forth with force. "Absolutely not. You cannot draw her into this."

Stone raised a hand and tilted his head, as if Tennyson's reaction had surprised him. "Calm down. I don't want to draw her into this. I think you and I both know that she's already a part of this somehow. I just want to trace her. I think she could lead me to Torres."

The longer this conversation went on, the more uncomfortable Tennyson felt. "How do you plan on doing that?"

"Can you bring me on as extra security?"

That sounded like a terrible idea. Just terrible. "I don't know if she would go for that."

"Certainly you've got some pull."

Stone's words made Tennyson tense and put him on the defensive. "Why would you say that?"

Stone shrugged, as if enjoying the fact that he'd rankled Tennyson. "Just a guess."

Tennyson stepped toward him, keeping tight control on his emotions before they spun out of control. "Have you been watching us?"

Stone didn't answer.

Tennyson shook his head and backed up. His emotions were threatening to boil over. He ran a hand through his hair as he realized the truth of the situation. "You didn't just fly in, did you, Stone? You were in town already."

Unease flashed through Stone's eyes, and Tennyson knew he'd nailed it.

"You know that nothing is simple when it comes to terrorism, Ten Man. Nothing. Especially not love."

The words hung between them. Claire. They'd both been in love with her. They'd both mourned her death. But in her final days, she'd chosen Tennyson.

Stone had never forgiven him.

"I'm not comfortable deceiving Mallory about who you really are," Tennyson said.

"You're already deceiving her, aren't you? You haven't told her the truth about that raid at Torres's compound. Am I right?"

Stone's words felt like a slap in the face. Tennyson's thoughts reeled, and guilt hit him hard. "That's not important."

Stone raised his chin. His gaze was patronizing. "Whatever you say. Listen, I'll be around."

Before Tennyson could argue, Stone walked away and disappeared down the stairwell.

CHAPTER 16

The next day, Tennyson stood beside Mallory at another book signing. The store was large—large enough that a high school ensemble had set up in the corner to do a miniconcert. The music hadn't started yet, but commotion abounded as parents and teachers rushed around to make sure everything was in place. The store had planned to run the events simultaneously to draw more attention and bring in more people. That's what the manager had told him, apparently not realizing what a security nightmare this was for Tennyson.

Kori stood at the main entrance, keeping watch there. They'd gone over a plan. If any trouble arose, Mallory would be whisked away to the car outside. There weren't any safe areas within the store.

Tennyson hoped Mallory didn't have to utilize that plan, though.

He shifted beside Mallory as the line continued to grow. With publicity and attention also came an increased risk factor. He was glad he could be here to help, even though he'd been hesitant at first. But Stone's words continued to echo in his mind.

He scanned the crowd again, looking for any sign of someone suspicious. A lot of women were in line. Some had kids in tow. A fair share of men stood there also. Did any of them work for Dante? Or could Dante himself be alive and be here?

The thought caused his gut to squeeze.

His phone buzzed in his pocket. After taking one last glance around the room, he pulled it from his pocket, curious to know if Stone had discovered anything new.

It wasn't Stone. It was a message from Wheaton that read: Look what showed up online.

He quickly clicked it. It was a video of him and Mallory being reunited at Hope House.

He glanced at the details. It had been posted by a user with the name of Eagle Eye. Grant was visible in the background. Grant obviously hadn't made this, but had he sanctioned it? He wouldn't put it past the man. Half a million people had already watched it.

Brilliant marketing move, but blatantly disrespectful and lacking boundaries.

He was going to have a long talk with Grant next time he saw him. Not only about this video and if he was behind it, but also about who he was sneaking around with in Atlanta.

At that moment, he sensed Mallory tense beside him. Something subtle in the air changed. What was it?

He surveyed the room but nothing seemed out of place.

Before the next patron made her way toward Mallory, he leaned down. "What's wrong?"

She leaned close enough that her warm breath hit his ear. "I thought I saw him."

His spine tightened. "Saw who?"

"Sanchez."

He bristled at the mention of the man's name. "Where?"

"By the bookshelf over there." She pointed across the store.

Tennyson called Kori over to take his place. Then he cut through the crowd, searching for a familiar face. He knew what Roberto Sanchez looked like. He knew how all of Dante's right-hand men looked. Their faces had been burned into his mind.

Tennyson rushed to the other side of the store. He quickly surveyed each face he encountered.

He didn't see Sanchez anywhere.

Was Mallory mistaken? Or had Sanchez gotten away?

Tennyson swung toward the right side of the store. Maybe the man had hidden or tried to slip out.

In the background, the ensemble played a haunting melody, riddled with minor notes, which only added to the pressure on Tennyson's shoulders.

The shelves of books were high—too high to see over easily. Sanchez could be behind any one of those.

Picking up his pace, he moved between each of them, looking for a sign of anyone suspicious. He still didn't see Sanchez.

Finally, he reached the back of the store. He bypassed a lounge area where patrons sat reading magazines and books. No Sanchez, though. He followed the back wall.

Movement ahead caught his eye.

A man looked up at him just as Tennyson spotted him.

Sanchez.

Or was it?

Tennyson took off at a sprint. As he did, the man barged out the back door.

An emergency alarm began wailing overhead. Tennyson blocked the sound out. His muscles burned as he propelled himself toward the back door.

He pushed it open, and brisk, cold air surrounded him. He surveyed the alley behind the store; then his eyes froze on a car in the distance.

The Sanchez look-alike paused by the car door, and turned long enough to make eye contact with Tennyson. The man offered a sardonic smile before climbing inside. The next instant, a bullet whizzed through the air.

Tennyson ducked back inside the bookstore just as the bullet hit the brick wall beside him.

Before he could draw his gun, the car sped away.

•   •   •

With every wail of the alarm, Mallory's muscles coiled tighter and tighter. What was going on? Was Tennyson okay? Had that really been Sanchez?

Kori and Grant stood beside her, but their presence didn't calm her like Tennyson's did.

"What's going on?" Mallory whispered.

Kori surveyed the store. "I'm not sure."

Grant scanned the store also. When he looked away from his perusal, his gaze fell on her, and Mallory saw the worry there. Grant hardly ever looked worried. Anxiety surged through her like hot lava exploding in waves from a volcano.

Kori took her arm. "Let's get you somewhere a little more private. I'm sorry, everyone. We've got to run, but thank you all for coming out."

Mallory grabbed her purse from the floor, not even thinking of arguing, and allowed Kori to lead her across the low-pile carpet of the bookstore. Grant followed behind them. As they rushed through the store, Kori craned her neck, looking for any signs of danger.

They stopped in front of the checkout counter. The clerks behind it looked just as confused about the alarms as Mallory felt.

"Stay here until we know something," Kori said. "I'm still waiting to hear from Tennyson. This could be nothing."

"Or it could be something."

Kori remained silent.

Once tucked near the counter, Mallory scanned the store. The line of people at her book-signing table was disbanding. The music in the background had ground to a stop, much like a broken record being jerked from the player. Several people stopped in their tracks, searching for answers as to the commotion around them.

Where was Tennyson? What if Mallory had led him into a trap? What if that really had been Sanchez, and he had wanted her to spot him, just to lure Tennyson away?

She remembered the faces in the photos of those lifeless bodies. Deadly. Whatever game someone was playing, the stakes were life and death. Stakes she didn't like, in a game she didn't want to play. But someone had pulled her into it without her permission.

At once, she remembered last night. She remembered hearing Tennyson sneak out of the hotel suite. Out of curiosity, she'd slipped out of her room and peered from the peephole. Tennyson had been meeting with a man dressed in black. She couldn't hear the conversation, but it had looked intense.

She couldn't stop wondering what it was about. What had upset Tennyson so much? Why was he meeting with the man in the middle of the night? And why hadn't he mentioned it to her? When the time was right, she would ask.

Right now, she hoped she would have the opportunity to ask.

Her shoulders tensed as a familiar face appeared in the distance . . . maybe. It was hard to tell from where Mallory was standing. But something about the cadence of the person's walk told her it was Tennyson.

Her heart pounded in her ears.

Finally, Tennyson appeared around one of the aisles.

Relief filled her, followed by surprise. The stony look on his face and the stiff set of his shoulders clearly stated that he wasn't happy. What had happened?

"Are you okay?" Mallory rushed out from her place by the counter as he reached them.

She'd never forgive herself if something happened to someone else because of her. Just like she feared had happened to Gabriella. Even though Tennyson clearly looked unharmed, the worry nagged at her subconscious.

He offered a terse nod, his stance making it clear that he'd snapped into military mode. "I'm fine. But the man got away."

"Where he'd go?"

"He jumped into a car waiting out back before I could reach him."

"Did he say anything? About why he came here?"

"No, we didn't speak. I have no idea why he was here, but he's clearly trying to send a message of some sort." He peered out the glass front doors and frowned. "We need to get you out of here."

As Tennyson motioned for them to follow, she noticed that Grant was staring at his phone. A wrinkle had formed between his eyebrows, and the lines on his face deepened.

"What is it?" Tennyson asked.

Grant glanced up from his phone. "Mallory, you just got another e-mail from Nameless."

Mallory felt the blood drain from her face. That hadn't been what she'd expected to hear. "Nameless? What did he say this time?"

Grant frowned and hesitated a moment. Finally, he read from the screen, "Don't look so scared. I'm watching out for you. No one else can help."

Fear trickled down her spine. "Was he here just now?"

Mallory scanned the store, looking for a familiar face. Certainly she'd recognize the man. Even if she'd never seen him before. If he were here, there'd be something to give away his presence—a look, an odd action, something.

"He could have been."

She shook her head. "I just don't know what to think anymore."

CHAPTER 17

When they arrived back at the hotel, Mallory's mind was still reeling from what had just happened. Sanchez? Could he really be after her? Was he trying to harm Tennyson in order to more easily snatch her again?

They were all quiet as they walked back into the suite. But as soon as the door closed, Tennyson, who'd been exuding tension, turned toward Grant.

"Do you know anything about what's going on here?" he asked.

Grant's eyes widened with offense. "No, of course not. Why would you ask that?"

"Did you post that video of my reunion with Mallory at Hope House?"

He blanched. "No. Of course not."

"But you knew about it."

"It's my job to monitor these things, so yes, I did know. But I didn't authorize the production of it. My goal is not to exploit Mallory, just for the record." Irritation tinged his words.

Tennyson wasn't going to let him off the hook that easily. "How about the man you met with yesterday? Why all the secrets?"

A flash of surprise shot through Grant's eyes. "I don't know what you're talking about."

"Stop lying, Grant," Tennyson said. "I saw you meeting with someone when you were supposed to be at the bank. Someone is leaking information and playing a very dangerous game. I need to know if you're involved or not."

"You're out of line. Of course I'm not involved. I think of Mallory like a daughter."

Mallory put her purse down on the couch, never taking her attention off the confrontation. She wanted to hear what Grant had to say. If he'd gone against his word, then Mallory wanted to know, because that meant Grant wasn't trustworthy. She *deserved* to know.

"Grant?" Mallory said. She'd never seen him look so angry. His eyes flashed. His entire body looked ready to spring. His fists were clenched.

"Why don't we get to the real heart of the issue: Sanchez is apparently stalking you," Grant said.

She wanted to argue, but he was right.

Mallory turned to Tennyson. "Are you sure it was Sanchez?"

Tennyson shook his head. "No, I'm not. But why would he want to do this to you?"

"Maybe he resented me because Dante always favored me."

"Why come at you now?" Tennyson asked.

"I have no idea. Unless . . . Dante really is alive, and he wants me back."

Tennyson's jaw flexed, and he looked away.

Mallory's hands went to her hips. "I need both of you to stop treating me like I'm fragile. If there's something out there that I should know about, I want to know."

"You know what we know," Tennyson said. "There's too much at stake here. Too many unknowns. And I think you need to cut this tour short."

"That's not your call." Grant's nostrils flared.

"It needs to be someone's call. The threats against Mallory are escalating."

"You're overstepping your bounds." Grant edged closer, just daring Tennyson to defy him.

"I'm doing my job."

"Your job is to do what I tell you to do."

"Both of you—stop! I'm right here. Don't talk about me like I'm not."

Grant studied her briefly before turning to Tennyson. "Now see, you've upset her. The purpose of having you here is to make her feel better."

Tennyson clenched his teeth. "The last thing I want to do is upset her. But her feeling better won't make her safer." He turned to her. "Mallory, you understand that, don't you? There's more on the line here than just raising awareness. Your life is at stake, and I feel like I'm the only one who sees it."

Grant threw his hands in the air and stepped back. "You know what? I've had enough of this. You're fired. I'll find a replacement for you."

Mallory's heart pounded in her ears. Fire Tennyson? He'd been the one bright spot in all of this. "Grant . . ."

"You put me in charge of this tour. I can't work with him anymore."

Tennyson pressed his lips together. "You're being irrational."

"If there's one thing I expect from my employees it's that they respect my authority—something you obviously have a problem with. You're done."

Mallory couldn't stand the thought of continuing this without Tennyson. "I'm overriding your decision. Tennyson stays."

Both men turned toward her, almost like they'd forgotten she was there.

"What are you talking about?" Grant sputtered.

She raised her chin. "I don't want anyone else on my security team."

"Mallory, this is a mistake—"

"Don't talk to me about mistakes. I'm a grown, capable woman, and I can make my own choices. If Tennyson isn't on my team, then I'm canceling my tour. He's the only one I feel safe with. You two are going to have to work it out somehow, because I'm the one who's calling the shots. And frankly, Grant, if you continue to talk to me like this, you're going to be the one who goes."

Grant remained silent a moment before taking a step back. His voice was notably calmer when he spoke again. "I'm the reason this tour has gotten so much attention."

"Grant . . ." Her voice held warning. If he hadn't been such a good friend to her, she would fire him right now.

Finally, he nodded. "I'll respect your decision. We'll talk more tomorrow. Right now, I'm going to burn off some steam in the gym downstairs."

With that, he stomped into his bedroom and shut the door.

• • •

With Grant gone, Tennyson turned toward Mallory. His heart hammered in his chest. He hadn't intended on having that conversation with Grant in front of Mallory. He didn't want to upset her. She had enough on her mind as it was.

But he didn't want to see anyone take advantage of her either.

His pulse quickened as he looked at Mallory, and he realized just how much she'd come to mean to him. He didn't just want to guard her as a professional. He wanted this job because he cared about her.

Caring about her could compromise his effectiveness at the job, though. He couldn't go there again. Couldn't let someone else get hurt on his watch.

That's why he had to squash these feelings before they grew any stronger. That was one reason, at least.

"I'm sorry about that," he started.

Mallory raised her head, her eyes daring anyone to defy her. "Don't be sorry. It needed to be said."

He stepped closer, something internal drawing him toward her. "Why did you want to keep me around?"

"You're a part of this team, Tennyson. I was at the mercy of a man who had total control of my life for a year. I don't want that again. I need the freedom to make my own choices."

"I think that's healthy. You should be the one calling the shots."

She released a deep breath and took a step back. He wondered about her reaction but said nothing as she paced away from him.

"I do wonder if I need to increase my security. You and Kori are doing a good job, but I'd really like for you to focus on figuring out who's behind these threats. You can't do that if you're watching me."

"That's not a bad idea."

Should he ask about Stone joining the team? Tennyson mentally shook his head. No, he just couldn't do it. He wanted to trust Stone, but the man wasn't playing straight with him.

Mallory leveled her gaze at him. "There's one other thing: I want to help."

"I'm not sure that's a good idea."

"I don't want to sit idly by."

"You just need to concentrate on staying safe."

"Tennyson . . . I'm a big girl. No one has more at stake here than me."

He swallowed hard. "I can understand where you're coming from."

"You're certain you saw Sanchez today?" Mallory pulled her arms across her chest.

He nodded, the earlier encounter flashing back to him. "It definitely looked like him."

She sat down and let her head rest against the back of the couch. "How about the women who died. Have you heard any updates on them?"

"I talked to Agent Turner this morning. They think the women are from Germany, but they're still following some leads. There are no answers yet."

"I'm in a pressure cooker. Everything keeps squeezing in tighter and tighter. I don't want to make any mistakes that put other people in danger. On the other hand, I don't want to live in fear."

The honesty in her words gripped his heart. "How about you just take it day by day?"

"That's what I'm trying to do, but the answers feel far away. In fact, it seems like the only way I'll find out any answers is if more threats are made against me." She looked away toward the window and the nighttime sky outside.

"Fear isn't always bad. It's our body's natural defense mechanism. It keeps us alive."

"But living in fear every moment is no way to live."

"No, it's not." Nor was living with bitterness or vindictiveness. The decision not to go there was a daily one.

"Do you really think Grant isn't trustworthy?"

"What do you think?" He didn't want to be the one to burst her bubble. She needed to draw those conclusions herself.

"I think he's brilliant when it comes to PR. He's an expert at taking tragedy and making it marketable."

"That's . . . quite an attribute."

"He was behind Lynette Davis, the only woman who survived that mass shooting down in Texas five years ago. She's practically a household name." She frowned. "However, I don't care about being famous. I could disappear and be perfectly content at this point. But I do want to raise awareness. That's what all of this is about."

He believed her. He saw the sincerity in her eyes. "That's noble."

"I have to do something to turn this tragedy around. I don't want to think that all of the . . . the trials, the heartache, the pain . . . that it all happened for nothing. If I can help someone else in their healing, then maybe I can find healing myself."

Their eyes met. Something unseen and magnetic seemed to pull him toward her. But he couldn't fall under its power.

"I think that's wise," he said quietly.

She cleared her throat and reached into her purse. She'd felt it too, he realized. There was a connection between them—a connection stronger than their pasts, than this situation, than the momentary.

"I have an interview tomorrow," she continued. "What do you think? Will it be safe?"

As he started to answer, Mallory's gaze traveled to the ground. A piece of paper had fluttered out of her bag and onto the floor. She reached down to grab it. When she opened the folds, she sucked in a breath.

In an instant, Tennyson was by her side. He read over her shoulder.

Hide before I do something I regret.

CHAPTER 18

Hiding Mallory away was exactly what Tennyson wanted to do.

But Mallory wouldn't go for it. *I won't let him silence me again.* That's what she'd told him after finding the note. *Hiding isn't the answer.*

But the threat was real, and it was becoming more real by the moment. How was he supposed to get through to her?

Until he could, he had to up his game plan. He and Kori had met earlier and discussed ways to increase security and limit risks.

The note in particular had left Tennyson unsettled. The only time someone could have left it was when he was chasing Sanchez, and Kori and Grant had pulled Mallory away.

That meant there was more than one person involved in this. Bringing a third guard on wasn't a bad idea. So was canceling this whole tour, but Mallory wasn't ready to do that yet. She had too much at stake. She wouldn't let people threaten her into retreating.

Just like now. Despite everything that had happened during the day, and after finding the note, she'd still insisted on going out to eat. In public. Not in the safety of their hotel room. He sat with her, while Kori had been stationed at the restaurant's entrance.

Tennyson glanced at Mallory as they sat across from each other at dinner. At her pensive expression. At her quiet dignity. Just what was going through her head? He wanted to grab her hand as it rested on the table.

But he couldn't let himself do that.

"Grant texted me," Tennyson started. "He thinks one of the reporters who'd been at Hope House took that video. He's trying to get in contact with him now about taking it down."

"That's good to know." She played absently with her fork, her eyes still troubled. "What do you think the note means?"

"It sounds like someone feels these acts against you are out of his control."

"So he's psychotic?"

Tennyson let out a soft breath, contemplating how much to say. "Possibly. He's oddly concerned yet admitting he could harm you. I'm not sure what to think about that, honestly. I called Agent Turner and let him know about it."

She stared at him another moment, her gaze penetrating and deep. He waited for her to say whatever was on her mind.

"I keep thinking about Dante still being alive," Mallory finally said.

Tennyson blanched, startled. "You do?"

She shrugged. "Humor me a moment. What if he really did somehow survive?"

Tennyson didn't say anything for a moment.

"In a way, it makes sense," Mallory continued.

Tennyson squinted. "What does?"

"That he could be alive."

"What are you saying, Mallory?"

She nibbled on her bottom lip before saying, "I've been afraid of how people would perceive me if I ever voiced my thoughts aloud. I didn't want to be taken off tour because it would mean going back to being alone with my thoughts. But . . ."

"What are you thinking?"

She pulled her eyes up to meet his. "It's always struck me as strange that Dante set himself on fire. Why would he do that?"

Mallory had never wanted to release the thought into the open. But now she had no choice but to face it head-on.

"You don't believe Dante would set himself on fire?" Tennyson's gaze looked intense as it met hers.

She shook her head, surprise etching through her as she realized that Tennyson didn't think the very idea was crazy. "I've always thought it was strange the way things played out that night."

"Why?" His smoldering gaze remained on her.

The intensity of it nearly took her breath away.

Even if she'd had doubts in the back of her mind about that night, she had simply tried to be grateful that the man who'd enslaved her was dead.

But now, if she could share them with anyone, it was Tennyson.

"Dante had an ego. I suppose, in one way, setting himself on fire would maintain his control of the situation. But that wasn't the Dante I knew. He was too confident. He didn't think he could be defeated. So to plan something like that . . ." She shook her head, not wanting to believe there was any truth to her words.

"Did you ever tell anyone that theory?"

It wasn't the question she'd expected him to ask. "No, I figured they'd think I was crazy. Besides, no one ever asked. In the long run, it didn't matter. Dante was dead, right? So all of my intuition didn't mean anything in the face of the truth."

Tennyson's shoulders seemed to relax some. He pulled his gaze away from her, before finally looking back at her.

"You're not crazy, Mallory."

Mallory drew in a long, deep breath. She needed to make sense of her jumble of thoughts and get a grip. She couldn't think in worst-case scenarios. Because the worst-case scenario of Dante being alive . . . it was the stuff of nightmares. The stuff that would send her back to therapy.

"What if Dante is really out there calling all the shots?" Mallory asked.

Tennyson shifted. "You really think that's a possibility? That he's reappeared after two years?"

She rubbed the edge of her napkin. "I'm not sure. I just . . . I just keep thinking I see him."

"Do you?" Tennyson leaned closer. "I thought it was an isolated event.

She shrugged. "I know it's ridiculous. I know it's just my mind playing tricks. But I keep thinking I see his face in crowds."

"What would that do to you if he was still alive?"

"I don't know." She licked her lips. "Honestly, the very thought of it sends me reeling. It makes me want to do the very thing that note warned about: it makes me want to hide. Forever. And never come out."

His voice softened. "I can only imagine."

"It's almost like I can face this, knowing he's dead and can't harm me anymore. But the thought of ever coming face-to-face with the man again . . ." She visibly shuddered. "I don't know if I can handle it. Everything inside me wants to die at the thought."

· · ·

Tennyson wrestled with his thoughts as they returned to the room after dinner. What if Mallory really had seen Dante? Tennyson wondered. If he was alive and following her? Was this part of the evidence they were looking for? His mind raced with possibilities and that old, familiar sense of vengeance tried to rear its head again. If Dante really was alive . . . Fire burned in Tennyson's blood.

He stepped into the suite while Mallory waited with Kori in the hallway. Right before he flipped the lights on, he saw a man's silhouette sitting in one of the living room chairs. He snatched his gun from the holster.

When he turned on the lights, a familiar figure came into view. "Stone . . . ," he muttered.

Mallory stepped inside behind him, despite Kori's protests. "Do you know him?"

He sighed and lowered his gun. "Unfortunately. What are you doing here?"

Ethan had his most charming smile plastered on his face as he sat in an accent chair, looking like he belonged in a space that clearly wasn't his.

"Who is he?" Mallory asked, curiosity saturating her voice.

"I'm an old friend of Tennyson's. Ethan Stone."

Mallory glanced at Tennyson. "Is that right?"

After a moment of thought, Tennyson nodded. "It is."

"He's always been quite the charmer with the ladies, you know." Stone winked at Mallory. "He could have any woman he wanted. And that he did. Single, taken, it didn't matter."

Anger simmered inside Tennyson, but he knew he couldn't let Stone get the best of him. That was exactly what the man wanted. "Why are you here, Stone?"

"We need to talk."

"About what? How'd you get in here?"

"That's not important."

Before Stone could say anything else, his phone rang. He put it to his ear and muttered something in Spanish.

Mallory gripped her stomach. Her skin paled.

She was remembering something, Tennyson realized. He took her arm, trying to pull her back down to reality. "Mallory?"

When she looked up, her gaze flew to Stone. Her shock disappeared and anger replaced it.

She pointed to Stone. "I know that voice. You're one of Dante's men."

CHAPTER 19

Stone lost his cool composure, but only for a second. His gaze was noticeably darker; his glib tone was gone. "I don't know what you're talking about."

Fear and anger collided into a surging whirlpool inside Mallory. What was going on here? Had all of this been planned? Was Tennyson in on it?

She backed up, putting as much distance as she could between herself and this man . . . this supposed friend of Tennyson's. "I didn't realize it until I heard you speaking Spanish. I'd know that voice anywhere."

Stone let out a chuckle. "I'm sorry, sweetie. You're wrong."

Betrayal smacked her like a punch in the gut. Had she done it again? Had she been too trusting of the wrong people? Tennyson had seemed like a good guy this whole time, but what if he wasn't?

"No, I'm not wrong." Her gaze turned to Tennyson, and she took a step back. "You're a part of this. You're somehow in Dante's pocket also."

"Mallory, I need to explain—" Tennyson started. He reached for her hand, but she jerked farther back. She rushed toward the door, desperate to get away.

"Mallory—wait!" Tennyson pleaded.

She grabbed the door handle, but her hands shook so badly she couldn't open it.

Tennyson stopped behind her, his voice pleading. "Please let me explain. This isn't what it looks like, nor did I realize Stone would be showing up here."

She paused.

"Mallory, you can trust me. Please."

She thought about it. Questioned her sanity. Questioned her safety. Finally, she stopped and turned toward him. "You've got five seconds."

"I know this is difficult to hear, but this is my fault. I'll start." Stone raised his voice from where he was sitting. He glanced at Tennyson. "Yes, Tennyson had no idea I was going to show up here tonight."

Her eyes bounced from one man to the other. "How do you know each other?"

"We know each other from Iraq," Tennyson said. "He works for the NSA now."

Her fiery gaze fell on Stone. "The NSA?"

"Formerly CIA." He nodded. "I was embedded in Inferno, trying to get information."

His confession echoed in her mind. He'd been there. With Dante. Acting loyal to the man.

She wasn't sure how she felt about that. "So you were a good guy who was on the inside?" she clarified.

"Right. Deep cover, as we call it."

She narrowed her eyes. "Did you know I was there?"

Regret washed over his face. "I didn't. I only knew he had a girl. I didn't know it was you. I wasn't a part of his inner circle."

"I guess that one girl wasn't enough to provoke a rescue?" Bitterness soaked her voice.

Stone's eyes softened. "We're talking about the life of one person versus the lives of thousands—hundreds of thousands. I worked hard to get into that organization, and I couldn't blow it. Not when the stakes were so high."

"A lot of good it did."

"You'd be surprised at what we were able to stop with my information," Stone said. "A bombing. A village being raided. A terrorist attack right here on American soil."

Her heart skipped a beat. "Dante was planning all of that?"

"He had his hand in it," Stone said. "He had his hand in a lot of bad things. I was able to provide information that helped us in the raid that night."

Her shoulders softened slightly as she let that sink in. "I see."

"I asked Tennyson to meet with me last night," Stone continued.

"Why?"

"I've been following Dante's network since his . . . since his death," Stone said. "We believe his network is still strong and still planning acts of terrorism across the globe."

Her pulse quickened. But all the pieces still weren't fitting together. "What's that have to do with Tennyson exactly?"

Stone exchanged a glance with Tennyson. "It's not so much Tennyson as it is . . . you."

She pointed her finger to her chest. "Me? What do I have to do with any of this? Last I heard, terrorist attacks weren't on my agenda for this tour."

Stone lowered his voice. "I know about the dead bodies that look like you. We're concerned that there's a connection with Inferno."

A pit in her stomach grew larger and deeper with every new tidbit of information. She still wasn't sure why that meant a former spy needed to show up here. Now. "You think those dead bodies are going to lead you to a terror cell? You think this terror cell is following me?"

"Not exactly. But we've wondered if someone associated with the terror cell is following you. We're just trying to cover every base."

"So why come here tonight under these circumstances?"

Ethan and Tennyson exchanged a look. Finally, Tennyson spoke. "Ethan and I don't always see eye to eye, to say the least. I thought he should keep his distance."

Her gaze volleyed to Ethan. "You didn't."

He shook his head. "No, I didn't. There are larger matters at stake here, Mallory."

Her jaw set in thought. More secrets. More deceit. More danger. How much could she take?

"I'm sorry, Mallory," Tennyson said. "I wasn't at liberty to discuss the subject. Besides, my job is to protect you."

"Keeping me in the dark isn't protecting me."

He pressed his lips together. Her words had hit him hard. Harder than she expected. Was there more he was hiding from her? She prayed that wasn't the case.

"I understand," he said.

Her trust in him had been fractured. To think that earlier she'd been dreaming about kissing him. Wondering what life would be like after this tour, with Tennyson at her side. "I'd like some time alone."

Tennyson said, "Of course."

"Mallory, if you would consider talking with me sometime . . . ," Stone said.

"Maybe. Probably. But right now, I just need to clear my head."

CHAPTER 20

Mallory disappeared into her room. She needed to be alone. There was too much happening, and it was all making her head spin.

She sat down on her bed, pulled out her phone, and began scrolling through her text messages. Grant didn't screen these since so few people actually had this number. She stopped at one from Jason.

I'm in town tomorrow. Meet for lunch?

Jason was in town? In Atlanta at the same time she was? Could this really be a coincidence? And why was he texting her? After so many months of silence, they meet for an interview, and then he contacts her again as if they're old friends?

She stared at the message, unsure how to respond.

Before she could type a reply, someone knocked at her door. Mallory's heart sank when she saw it was Grant and remembered their earlier argument.

He came inside and sat across the bed from her. "What's going on out there? Who's the new guy? I decided it was in my best interest not to ask Tennyson."

She pressed her lips together. "Long story. Let's just say he's an old friend of Tennyson's."

Grant's frown made it clear he wanted to ask more questions. Instead, he said, "You don't look happy. Want to talk?"

Did she want to talk? She wasn't sure. There was just so much to process and think about right now.

Finally, she decided to sum up what had happened for him. He deserved to know about the new developments.

"So this Ethan guy wants to work with you?" A wrinkle formed between Grant's eyes.

She shrugged. "I'm not sure."

"Do you think you can trust Tennyson?"

She thought about it for a long minute. It seemed like she regretted giving her trust to anyone, including Grant. Grant may have made some poor choices, but he'd always been there for her. She *wanted* to trust him, to think that he offered some kind of safety net.

"I do think I can trust Tennyson," she finally said. "I just wish he'd told me that the NSA was also investigating this in an effort to locate members of Inferno."

"I know you decided to keep him on despite what I advised—"

"It was ultimately my decision," she said, her words sharper than she intended. "It's not up for discussion."

Grant nodded, visibly backing off. "I understand. And I apologize for my role in your current stress. I can be a bit of a control freak at times. It's what makes me good at my job, but it also makes me an occasional pain to work with."

"I suppose."

"Look, Mallory. I really am sorry. I'm just trying to look out for you, even though it may not seem like it at times."

"I know. Apology accepted."

"I do think you should hire someone else to be on your security team," Grant said. "With these threats escalating, it only makes sense."

She thought about the dead bodies. The perfume. The note. The e-mails. She had to be wise here.

She slowly nodded. "I agree. But who?"

Grant's gaze locked on hers. "I have someone in mind. I found another guard who comes highly recommended. His name is Logan, and I took the initiative to find out if he's available. He is. How would you feel about bringing him on?"

"Shouldn't we hire someone from Tennyson's company? That makes more sense."

"Tennyson himself said there's no one else on staff who's qualified yet. Their program is just beginning."

"Before you hire anyone, I insist you run them past Tennyson first since he is in charge of security."

He smiled. "Great. I'll talk to Tennyson and get right on it."

"Have there been any updates on those letters from Nameless? Or on the identities of the deceased girls?" *Murdered girls,* she silently corrected herself.

Grant shook his head. "I spoke with both the detective in DC as well as Agent Turner today. Both assured me they're still looking into things, but there are no definite leads yet."

"Thanks, Grant."

He stood to leave.

"Oh, and Grant?" She stopped him before he left. "Jason texted me and wants to meet for lunch tomorrow. That should be okay, right? My interview isn't until afterward."

"If that's what you want to do."

Was it what she wanted to do? She wasn't sure. But she wouldn't let fear stop her from living life. She couldn't give it that much control. "Thanks."

●　　●　　●

Tennyson had walked Stone out and was lingering in the hallway where Kori stood duty.

"Everything okay?" she asked, her shoulders back and gaze scanning the hallway.

"I need you to stay at the door," Tennyson said. "I'm going for a walk to clear my head."

He needed to cool off. A little walk should do the trick.

Something flashed in Kori's eyes. Curiosity. Perceptiveness. "She's getting to you, isn't she?"

Tennyson paused, and his hands went to his hips at her implications. "What do you mean?"

"You like Mallory."

"Mallory's a good person." He knew exactly what Kori meant, though.

"You watch her all the time. And I'm not talking about just for the job."

He pressed his lips together. "Do we really have to have this discussion right now?"

"You'd talk to me if the roles were reversed. You know the number one rule of body guarding is to not let your feelings get involved."

"I know that, Kori." He lowered his voice, trying not to let his irritation show through. He was irritated with himself, not Kori, but she was the one who'd brought this up.

"Up here you might." She tapped his temple before pointing to his heart. "But down here, I'm not sure you do."

"If anyone knows it, it's me. You do remember what happened with Claire, don't you?"

Her eyes softened. "I can't forget. That's why I thought it was important to remind you to keep your feelings in check."

He raised his chin, refusing to admit anything. He and Mallory had a professional relationship. Maybe slightly more than that. Maybe they were becoming friends. But that was it. Just because he thought the woman was beautiful and fascinating and strong didn't mean he wanted to explore a future together.

Even as the thoughts flashed through his mind, Tennyson wasn't sure he had himself convinced. If circumstances were different, he wouldn't mind getting to know Mallory as more than a friend. But it was complicated. On Mallory's end. On his end.

The truth was he didn't deserve to be happy after what happened with Claire. No, he deserved to live every day with guilt at his failure. And when Mallory learned the truth about the decisions he'd made in the past, she'd resent him. Anyone would. That had been clear by her reaction to Stone when she'd learned he knew that Torres was keeping a woman at his compound.

So all this was a nonissue. He and Mallory would never happen.

He stepped outside and into the crisp night. The city streets were surprisingly quiet, and the air was just brisk enough to invigorate him. He started at a quick pace down the sidewalk.

Kori was right. He cared about Mallory. He knew he did. But they could never be together. He was damaged and undeserving of love. And Mallory was his client. There were professional boundaries in place, and feelings would only get in the way of him doing his job.

Just as he reached the corner, he felt something whiz by him.

A bullet, he realized.

Someone was shooting at him.

CHAPTER 21

Tennyson ducked behind the corner. He counted to three before daring to peer around the edge. Despite the streetlights, it was too dark to locate the shooter. Too many shadowed spaces lined the street.

Tennyson guessed that the gunshot had come from the upper floor of one of the surrounding buildings. He looked for the glint of metal or the reflection of glasses. Anything that might tip him off.

He saw nothing.

Had someone just been waiting for him to emerge from the hotel?

He didn't have time to think about that now.

Another bullet hit the wall beside him. The musty smell of dust and the metallic scent of a fresh bullet filled the air. His mind tried to transport him back to the war zones he'd fought in. He didn't want to go there now.

Right now, he was in his own war zone.

Whoever was shooting at him was using a silencer. Which would only make locating the shooter that much harder.

Tennyson glanced at the bullet hole, noting the direction it had come from. It had come from above. His suspicions were right—someone was hiding in one of these buildings.

He dropped to the ground behind a car.

Pulling out his phone, he dialed the local police.

"My name is Tennyson Walker," he rushed. "I'm a private security guard, and I need to report an active shooter situation."

"What's your location?"

He glanced around until he saw the street sign, and he rattled off the cross streets.

"We'll send someone right out."

Another bullet pierced the air and hit the side-view mirror of the car he was against.

Where were those bullets coming from? The hotel across the street? This wasn't good.

He had to get out of sight.

He glanced around again. There was an entrance to a deli about ten feet away. The restaurant was closed, but the alcove where the front door was located might be the perfect shelter.

If he could only get there without getting shot.

He had no choice but to try.

Before he could move, a group of college kids rounded the corner, totally oblivious to what was going on.

His heart rate ratcheted. "Get down!"

All five of the young adults looked at him like he was crazy.

"There's a shooter!"

They still didn't react.

Another bullet ripped through the air, hitting the window of the shoe shop behind them. The glass shattered.

The group screamed as one; some people ducked, and others darted away.

Tennyson had to figure out who was doing this. But by the time he could pinpoint the person's location, they'd be long gone. He knew that. The shooter knew that.

Sanchez. Was this Sanchez?

Or was it Dante?

He hoped the police arrived before he got shot.

• • •

After being questioned by police, Tennyson started back up to the suite, desperate to stay close to Mallory after the shooting. He was lucky to have gotten through that with only a sore shoulder from where he'd dropped to the ground. It could have been much worse.

He called Kori on his way up, explained what had happened, and instructed her to keep an eye on Mallory.

Then Tennyson called Stone.

"I just got shot at. You know anything about that?"

"What? Why would I know anything about that?"

"Because I'm fully aware that there's something you're not telling me." Tennyson didn't really think that Stone would be shooting at him. He was smarter than that.

"I may not like you, but I'm not going to try and kill you either."

He hung up and rushed toward the room. Kori stood outside the door.

"Did you see anyone in the hallway?" he asked.

Kori shook her head. "No one. It's all been quiet. So what happened?"

Tennyson filled her in.

"You didn't catch the person who pulled the trigger?" she asked.

Tennyson shook his head. "Whoever it was, he was good."

His muscles tightened as he felt someone approaching. He turned to see Stone.

"I got back here as soon as I could. Nothing new?" he asked.

Tennyson shook his head.

"Why would someone shoot at you?" Stone asked.

Tennyson had thought about that himself. "Maybe this person wants to get rid of me so he can get to Mallory."

"Sounds very Dante-esque," Stone said.

Tennyson couldn't deny it. He walked to the other end of the hallway, determined to check the stairway. Stone fell into step beside him.

"I'm surprised that Mallory wants to make herself a public figure considering Torres could still be out there," Stone said.

"She feels very strongly about her mission."

"Does she know you had the chance to rescue her but didn't?"

His gut clenched. "No. It doesn't seem important."

"Based on her reaction earlier, I'm not sure she'd have you on staff if she knew that."

"I told you, it's not important. Not right now."

Stone let out a grunt. "I've seen girls who've come out of human trafficking. Most never recover."

Tennyson paused by the stairway and bristled. "What are you saying?"

"Just that that kind of trauma can mess up the most stable of people."

Tennyson refused to believe that. "Mallory is different."

Stone narrowed his eyes, studying Tennyson a moment.

"You like her, don't you?" Satisfaction tinged his voice.

"And if I do?"

"Then good for you. Challenges make life interesting."

Tennyson fought to keep his emotions under control. He couldn't let Stone bait him, and he had to be the bigger person. "Look, I'm sorry about what happened with Claire. Is that what you want me to say?"

All the smugness left Stone's expression. "I know I can't hold it against you. Claire chose you. Neither of us ended up winning that one, did we?"

At the thought of Claire, Tennyson's heart began pounding. He realized that lately Claire's picture had begun being replaced in his mind with Mallory's image. He wasn't sure when it had happened. He hadn't even realized it had happened until this moment.

"Claire was a good woman," Tennyson said. "She didn't deserve to die at Torres's hand."

"No, she didn't. For her sake, let's make sure he doesn't kill someone else who's innocent. Put the past behind us?"

Tennyson nodded. "Put the past behind us."

•   •   •

Tennyson stood when Mallory walked into the living room the next morning. Her demeanor was different—more businesslike—as she went into the kitchen and grabbed some coffee and yogurt.

He hadn't seen her since she, Stone, and he had talked. He'd hoped that with some space things might resume as normal, but that obviously wasn't the case. She appeared standoffish.

"Good morning," he said.

"Morning." She paused, but her expression looked strained as she turned toward him. "I assume that Grant has talked to you."

Tennyson braced himself at her cold tone and set his own coffee down. "Only briefly this morning. Why?"

"Then he ran our plan past you?"

"What are you talking about, Mallory?"

She frowned. "We're going to hire someone else for the security team, just like you and I spoke about doing. You'll be in charge of the team, however. Grant promised he would run his new hire past you."

He fought a sigh. This was just another power play on Grant's end. However, Tennyson wanted to be careful and not also become a power player. That would put him on the same level as Grant, and he wouldn't do that to Mallory.

"He didn't run anyone past me."

She didn't say anything for a moment, but he saw the deep angst in her eyes. "Grant knows how to hire quality people. I'm sure he'll do a good job. I didn't see any harm in allowing him to bring on someone he trusts."

Tennyson had to bite his tongue. *Trust her, Tennyson. Trust her.* "As long as you're comfortable with all of it, Mallory."

She seemed to let out a breath, followed by a quick smile. "Okay. Great. He'll be coming in later this morning."

"That quickly?"

She nodded. "Grant worked on it last night."

"Do you know anything about him?" Tennyson at least wished that he could vet the guy first.

Curiosity flickered in her gaze. "Why? Are you going to do a background check?"

He shrugged, realizing she had him pegged. "Maybe."

She continued to examine him, not bothering to hide it. "You really don't want anything to slip past you, do you?"

His jaw flexed as his past mistakes began to play like an old movie reel in his mind. Never again. "Failure isn't an option."

"Good. I don't want you to fail either. I'd really prefer that I wasn't in this situation at all, but since I am, I'm glad you're on my side."

Silence stretched for a moment. "I'm sorry about yesterday."

"I know."

"I don't ever want to hurt you." His words weren't professional. This conversation wasn't professional. But he knew the lines were blurring for him.

She sat down beside him, her cheeks reddening. "Thank you."

"Look, I want to be the one to tell you this. I slipped outside last night for a walk, and someone shot at me."

Her gaze darted toward him, and her lips parted. "What?"

He nodded. "Thankfully, I just have a few bruises."

"Who?"

"I don't know. The police are looking into it. I can only assume they won't find anything. I haven't heard from them yet this morning."

Before he realized what was happening, Mallory reached over and squeezed his hand. As soon as she touched him, the air between them changed. Electricity crackled between them.

Electricity? Was he crazy? Mallory probably wasn't interested in ever attempting to trust another man. Sure, she'd overcome a lot, and she was an inspiration. But that didn't mean she was going to be in a hurry to fall in love.

Nor was he.

Her touch was just an act of kindness and compassion. But the fact remained: she'd reached out. Tennyson knew how hard that was for her, how she didn't easily offer any physical contact.

His conversation with Stone came back to him. When Mallory found out the truth, she was going to hate him. Hate him.

He stood. "I need to go check my e-mails. You okay?"

She nodded a little too quickly and withdrew her hand. "Of course. I need to review my notes for the interview today."

And before either of them could do anything they'd regret, they both escaped.

CHAPTER 22

The new guard showed up at their hotel suite midmorning.

"This is Logan Hagen." Grant extended his arm toward the towering man behind him.

Mallory stared up at the new guard. He looked Nordic in his features. His eyes were crystal blue. His teeth perfect and white, and his smile blinding. He was tall with a strong, angular face, hair so blond it was almost white, and arms full of defined, bulky muscles.

Tennyson had muscles also, but his were more subtle. Mallory had the distinct impression that Hagen wanted everyone to know how strong he was.

Mallory fought a wave of anxiety at his quick appearance here. This was her decision, she reminded herself. She'd given Grant the go-ahead.

Still, there was a peace-loving side of her that knew there would be tension over this choice. Tennyson, though he was trying to conceal his emotions, wasn't happy about this. Hagen was oblivious. Grant was gloating.

"Glad to have you on board," Mallory said.

"Nice to meet you." His voice sounded as stoic as his demeanor.

"This is Tennyson. You'll be working with him—" Grant started.

"You'll be working *for* him," Mallory corrected, knowing she needed to establish that up front. "Tennyson is in charge of our security plan. He'll ultimately call the shots."

Something flickered in Hagen's gaze, but he still reached out his hand toward Tennyson.

"Nice to meet you," Hagen said. "We should sit down and talk."

Tennyson nodded. "As soon as you're settled in, we can meet for a few minutes."

Grant clapped his hands once. "Now that this happy meet-and-greet is over with, Mallory, I need to prep you for your interview this afternoon."

Mallory thought about the gunshots last night. "Are you sure the interview is a good idea? It's one thing if I'm in danger. It's another thing entirely if I put any of you in danger."

Grant frowned. "You know about what happened with Tennyson last night?"

She nodded. "Of course I do. Tennyson told me this morning."

Why did he make it sound like she wouldn't know? She fully expected Tennyson to keep her in the loop about what was going on.

"The news station is secure," Grant said quickly. "They've got their own guards at the door, metal detectors, et cetera. You won't be out in public. But of course, ultimately, this is up to you. Mallory, what do you think?"

Did she want to do this? To continue on like nothing had happened?

Mallory finally nodded, knowing the issue was more complex than that. "I don't want these guys to control me any longer. If I instantly go into hiding, they'll win. That's probably what they want."

Tennyson's jaw flexed. He didn't agree with her choice, she realized. But it was her decision, and she had to make it.

"I'm going to go prep for the interview. I'll let you two talk about the security detail, and I'll be back out in an hour so I can meet with Jason before the interview."

• • •

Tennyson had only been around Logan for five minutes, and he already didn't like him. He had to try to give the man the benefit of the doubt, but he wished that Grant had let him at least help pick out who else would be working with them. He wanted to read his resume and not have to play this all by ear.

But that hadn't happened, so now he needed to make the best of things. For Mallory's sake. He wasn't usually a control freak. He just hated to see Grant trying to manipulate every situation. He hated to see Mallory in the crosshairs.

But he could be a team player. He *would* be a team player. Again, for Mallory's sake.

"I assure you, I'm experienced. I was navy for four years, and then went on to work for the Baltimore PD," Logan said, as if he could read Tennyson's doubt.

They were in the living room, reviewing the notes for the rest of the tour.

"Why'd you leave?" Tennyson asked.

"I got a job offer I couldn't refuse for Steele Security."

Tennyson had heard of the firm before. They were supposed to be one of the best. But Tennyson was very careful about the trust he gave out.

Logan crossed his arms and leaned back against the couch. "So, what's your game plan?"

"I have her tour schedule. We check out the layout of each building and hotel where we'll be staying. We assess risks. We develop emergency plans in case things go south. I've made some notes."

"Why not just cancel this tour?"

"It's not a bad idea, but Mallory calls the shots here. We're available to help her in whatever decisions she makes. That's the game plan."

His eyebrows flickered upward. "That's not what Grant made it sound like. He sounded like he was running this show."

Tennyson stood and grabbed a water bottle. "I'm not here for a power struggle. You shouldn't be either. We answer to Mallory."

Logan nodded slowly. "A guy who's not afraid to give up control. That's got to be admired."

Tennyson felt himself bristle. "You must be new at this, because that's one of the first rules: control belongs to the client in this line of work."

Logan's smile faded, and he shifted. "So what's on the agenda for today?"

Tennyson reviewed everything with him. Until his phone rang. He recognized Stone's number. "Excuse me a minute."

He stepped into the hallway to take the call. But just as he stepped out, Stone appeared.

"I found out a few things you might want to know."

"I'd love to hear them."

"The first is about Walter Boyce."

"Who's Walter Boyce?" The name sounded vaguely familiar.

"He was a friend of the Baldwin family. He has a place in the Caribbean. It was his party the Baldwins went to the night they were killed."

It was starting to come back to Tennyson now. "Okay."

"He owns one of the largest shipping businesses in the world. The man's filthy rich."

"What's this have to do with anything?"

"Some people believe that Boyce is helping to ship arms for Torres."

"What? No . . ." Could Mallory's father have been involved with this after all? What if her family hadn't just been randomly targeted?

"There's more," Stone said. "Apparently, Baldwin was married before he married Mallory's mom. Married twice, actually."

"That sounds right."

"His second wife had a daughter—"

"Narnie."

Stone's eyebrows flickered up. "You've met her?"

"Unfortunately."

"Well, it's going to get even more unfortunate. Rumor has it that Narnie is mad. She thought she was going to be able to stake claim to some of her former stepfather's fortune since she was the only surviving heir."

"Okay . . ."

"Mallory turning up alive really put a kink in her plans. Now, she claims to have some dirt on Mr. Baldwin—proof that he was working with Walter Boyce in order to transport these weapons."

"How did you hear that?"

"I've been keeping my eye on good old Narnie for a while. As soon as the Baldwins disappeared, she went after their money. That's always suspicious, if you ask me. People who are that desperate for money are also desperate in other ways. Apparently, she's in a heap of debt."

Tennyson didn't like where this was going. He'd met Narnie and wouldn't put anything past the woman.

"She says she has evidence to bring the family down. She threatened Walter Boyce."

Tennyson remembered Narnie's threat to Mallory at the book signing. *You'll regret it.* Was she acting on that threat now?

"Anyway, this is what it boils down to: Narnie is missing."

"Missing?"

Stone nodded. "She had a hotel room here in Atlanta. All of her things—including her purse—were found there. There was also a sign of struggle."

"Atlanta? Why was she here?"

Stone shrugged. "That's the question of the hour. We can only guess that she was following Mallory."

Tennyson sighed and glanced at his watch. "I've got to get ready to take Mallory to lunch."

He didn't want to take her anywhere right now. Not when the stakes had just risen so much. As soon as lunch and her interview were over, he wanted to whisk Mallory away, somewhere out of sight and safe.

Humor crinkled Stone's gaze. "Sounds cozy."

"She's meeting someone else," Tennyson told him. "We're strictly professional."

"Sure you are."

CHAPTER 23

Mallory wasn't sure why Jason had wanted to meet her. What more could he have to say after the interview with Dana?

She straightened her dress and looked around the upscale restaurant. At her request, Tennyson had taken a seat at the table beside her. He'd be close enough if trouble flared up, but far enough away to allow her privacy. Kori stood at one door and Logan at the other.

Tennyson was quiet as they waited. Did he not approve? Why wouldn't he? And why did she care?

Mallory took a sip of her water and flinched. Drinking out of an open cup always made her cautious. She preferred bottles without the seal broken. It was probably because Dante had drugged her glasses of water when she was in captivity.

She glanced across the dining area and spotted a familiar figure step inside. Jason.

She rubbed her hands against the skirt of her dress before standing.

He offered a nervous smile as he approached. It was strange. Jason had never been nervous before. Had he changed?

"Thanks for agreeing to meet me—without any cameras." He kissed her cheek before his gaze skittered behind her to Tennyson. His eyes darkened. Jason hadn't been expecting her to have anyone with her, she realized. He was going to have to deal with that fact, especially in light of everything that had happened.

Mallory glanced at Tennyson and saw that he was giving them the illusion of privacy by holding a newspaper. She'd bet he wasn't reading a word of it and was subtly listening to everything going on instead.

"Please, have a seat," she told Jason, nodding to the chair across from her.

Before he had the chance to help with her chair, Mallory quickly sat. He was the type who could be charming when he wanted to impress someone. Or he could be a total jerk. Mallory was tired of people who put up fronts so that things could work to their advantage. Authentic . . . that was who she wanted to be.

He glanced around before seating himself. A server appeared, and Jason ordered a glass of red wine.

"You sure you don't want anything stronger than that?" Jason gestured toward her water.

Mallory nodded. Truth was, she never wanted to take anything again that would inhibit her senses. "I'm sure."

"You look good." He offered an approving glance.

"Thank you."

Jason hadn't aged well. She hadn't noticed it as much during the interview because she'd been so distracted by the monumental task of speaking with him. But now that she was getting a good look at him, away from any media scrutiny, she noticed how his hair thinned on top. How his midsection had gotten softer. How his shoulders were thicker, but not necessarily with muscle. He was two years older than she, which would put him at twenty-nine. Did he have a real job yet? Or was he still living off of trust funds?

"I'm glad there are no cameras this time," he said.

Was he really glad? He had always liked attention.

He drew in a deep breath, as if about to launch into something heavy and deep. Before any words left his mouth, the server appeared again with Jason's wine. They both ordered—and Mallory got something for Tennyson also.

He looked over from his Queen's Guard–like stance for long enough to offer a weary smile. But he said nothing.

Jason's eyes subtly narrowed, however. What was that about?

As soon as the emotion appeared, it was gone. "We used to have good times together, didn't we?"

Mallory cringed, not wanting to reminisce like old friends. They had too much history, too much water under the bridge.

"Did we?" she finally said.

A grin cracked his face. "You remember that time we took that yacht on a joyride on the bay? I thought my dad would never let me leave the house again."

"We were lucky we didn't go to jail for that." It had been irresponsible, at best. Criminal, at worst. The only reason they'd gotten off was because they had good lawyers.

"Or that time we raced down that mountain road with your dad's Viper? I thought we were going to crash."

Her cheeks burned. None of these memories were ones she wanted to hold onto. No, she'd rather forget them.

"Someone else did get run off the road because of that," she reminded him.

"They didn't get hurt, though. And they got a new car out of it. Thanks to your dad."

She straightened, smoothing her napkin in her lap. "Why'd you want to meet, Jason?"

She got right to the point. She had little interest in rekindling their friendship. He'd proven his character when he'd left with Jasmine that fateful night. He'd proven it again when he'd avoided her while she was in rehab.

He leaned closer. "I just want the chance to make things right."

"What do you mean, 'make things right'?"

"I've hardly been able to live with myself these years."

It was funny . . . Mallory had looked up news articles on Jason a few months ago as a matter of curiosity. He'd certainly seemed to have recovered well. He'd continued to party, to make stupid choices—and headlines.

Nothing about those articles had indicated he was remorseful. That said, she also realized that different people handled trauma in various ways. Some covered their pain with substance abuse, with living hard and fast, by doing whatever they could to forget.

Compassion, Mallory. Compassion and grace . . . with a good dose of wisdom.

"There was a lot of trauma that night." She swirled her water and eyeballed some of the bread that had been left at the center of the table. "For everyone involved."

"I blamed myself, you know."

She fought a sigh. Had he asked to see her only so he could make himself feel better? Maybe there was nothing wrong with that, but it summed up most of their relationship. He'd been selfish. A taker. Not a giver.

Maybe some things never changed.

"You shouldn't blame yourself, Jason. You obviously had nothing to do with the actions of Dante Torres and his men."

"But if I'd been there—"

"What ifs mean nothing. We can't change the past. We can just learn from it."

He lowered his gaze. "I wish we could. I would do things differently."

"We could all say that."

"I suppose you're correct."

She studied him another minute, looking for a sign of sincerity. Mostly what she saw was superficial and polished—far from authentic. "Is that the only reason you wanted to meet with me?"

"The whole experience has opened my eyes to some things." He reached out and grabbed her hand. "I still care about you, Mallory."

She flung her hand back, nearly knocking over her water. She could hardly catch her breath when she looked back up at him.

"I wasn't expecting that," she muttered.

"I shouldn't have—"

"No, don't apologize."

Awkward silence fell between them. The server finally came and set their food on the table, breaking up the tension with her perkiness.

She watched as the woman gave Tennyson an extra wide smile. Tennyson seemed unaffected by it, which brought Mallory an unexpected satisfaction. She really needed to get that thought out of her system. There was nowhere healthy it could go.

"Mallory?"

She turned back toward Jason. How long had he been talking to her? She wasn't sure. Her thoughts had been on Tennyson.

She picked up her spoon to take a sip of her soup and cover her social faux pas. "Yes?"

"I know it's too much to ask to pick up where we left off."

"Yes, it is." There was no need to let him think any differently. As awkward as it might be, it was best to speak honestly now.

He shifted, sweat trickling down his forehead. "I hoped we could at least try."

She licked her lips, trying to choose her words carefully and gracefully. "Jason, though I've forgiven you for what you did three years ago, that doesn't mean I'd ever want to be together again. You broke my trust. You abandoned me when I needed you most."

His cheeks reddened. "I was young and stupid."

She still wasn't convinced that he'd changed. "What are you doing with your life now, Jason?"

The red deepened. "I'm prepping to take over my father's company one day."

"Does that mean you're working?"

"No, not yet. But I'll have time for that later."

She leaned toward him, trying to get to the truth. "What are you doing here in Atlanta?"

He tugged at his collar. "You know I've always loved the Atlanta Hawks. They had a game."

"You didn't know I was going to be here?"

He shrugged and let out a forced chuckle. "Well, okay. Maybe I did know that."

She wondered exactly what his motivations were. Did he truly think the two of them could pick up where they left off? He couldn't be that naive. "Are you dating anyone?"

"No one serious."

In other words, he still didn't want to be tied down.

She'd had enough beating around the bush. There were questions she'd wanted to ask for the past three years—things she didn't want to talk about on camera. "Did you hear anything that night, Jason?"

Her question seemed to startle him. He looked dazed for a moment, and then squinted. "What?"

"That night, when I was abducted. You had no idea it had happened?"

"No, of course not. Why would you ask that?"

"Jasmine—what was her last name again?"

"Reynolds."

"That's right. Her room was right down the hall. I would think you'd have heard the commotion."

"Are you trying to say that I heard something and ignored it?" His jaw flexed, and anger lit his gaze. His food remained untouched.

"No, that's not what I'm trying to say. I'm trying to comprehend the events of that evening. There's always been something off about it."

"I already told you. I was with Jasmine. I regret it. I'm sorry." He took a long sip of his wine.

"You would have died if you'd been with me that night, you know."

His shoulders looked tighter than before. "I know. Believe me, I know."

The night flashed back to her. "It's just that, those men were pretty loud. You said you were shocked when you got back to the room and saw what had happened. How is that possible if you were right down the hall? The police were on the scene not long after."

His nostrils flared, and his hands clenched into fists. "Are you accusing me of something?"

She raised her hands, urging him to calm down. "I didn't say that. I'm just asking questions. Why are you getting defensive?"

"All of that stuff you said on camera wasn't true, was it? You didn't mean a word of it. It was just for show." His gaze trapped her, demanded answers, even accused.

Mallory sensed Tennyson bristle at the next table. She glanced over, and he looked ready to pounce if need be. Maybe it was only because she knew he was here and close that she'd had the strength to have this conversation.

"It wasn't for show, Jason. I've just had more time to process our conversation."

He locked his jaw and sneered. "I thought you were different."

"I am different." Why was this turning into her being the bad guy? Memories of their time together flashed back to her. He'd always been that way, hadn't he? She'd forgotten.

"I'm sorry I ever thought we could pick up where we left off."

"Me, too, because that was never going to happen." She kept her voice soft, but her words honest.

With heat simmering in his gaze, Jason tossed his napkin on the table and stormed off.

One thing remained certain in Mallory's mind: Jason knew more than he wanted to let on. As soon as she'd asked him about his whereabouts on the night she was abducted, he'd gotten defensive. He was hiding something.

She needed to figure out what.

CHAPTER 24

With Logan and Kori following behind, Tennyson drove Mallory to the TV station. He waited to see what Mallory had to say about her meeting with Jason.

He wanted to tell her about Narnie and about Walter Boyce, but he didn't want to fluster her before her TV interview. He would tell her as soon as they got back to the hotel tonight, though.

In the meantime, he'd e-mailed a private investigator friend of his to look into Logan's background. He still hadn't gotten a call back from Logan Hagen's reference with the Baltimore PD. The man's resume was impressive, his employer was well-known, and Logan seemed to be a stand-up guy. But again, Tennyson had to cover all his bases.

"Was I too hard on him?" Mallory finally said.

"On Jason? No. He needs some accountability." Someone like Jason had to hit rock bottom before he'd learn any lessons. Tennyson had seen his type before.

She raised her hands, palms up. "Is it just me, or does his story not add up? I mean, how did he not hear anything that night?"

"Those are good questions. Did he talk to the officials in charge of the investigation? They probably questioned him."

"I would imagine. Also, I'm not sure I buy the idea that Jason wanted to get back together or that he came all the way here for me."

Nor did Tennyson. He planned on keeping an open mind as to who was behind everything that was going on. He hadn't ruled out Jason, Grant, or even Ethan. Nor had he eliminated the possibly of Torres being alive, Sanchez being involved, or Inferno having its sights on Mallory.

"I'm probably reading too much into things," Mallory finally said. "My therapist says I have trust issues."

He remembered what Stone had said about women coming out of human trafficking never being the same. He didn't completely buy that. Sure, they might not be who they used to be. But they could still go on to live productive, happy lives.

"Everyone has trust issues in their own way," he told her.

"Even you?"

Claire flashed into his mind. Maybe one day he'd tell Mallory about Claire. He never really spoke about her or about what had happened with anyone. But there was a part of him that wanted Mallory to know.

"Yeah, even me," he said.

The words played on his lips.

Tell her.

Before he could open his mouth, Mallory gasped.

"What is it?"

She squeezed the skin between her eyes. "It's . . . it's nothing. Just my eyes playing tricks on me."

"Tell me what you saw."

"You'll think I'm crazy."

"It was Torres, wasn't it?"

She nodded. "In that car up there. The white sedan."

He gripped the wheel, remaining rational and in control.

"What are you doing? You've got to follow him," Mallory said.

"My job is to keep you safe."

"We can't let him get away. I have to know if that was really him. Please."

He kept the car at the same speed.

"Tennyson . . ."

He let out a breath and then accelerated. But traffic was heavy. He maneuvered around several cars, trying to get closer, but brake lights lit the street ahead.

"What if someone is dressed like Torres and trying to play with your head?" Tennyson asked. "What if this guy is the one who's behind the murders following you across the country? If he's the one who shot at me last night? Who left the perfume?"

She rubbed her temples. "This is a nightmare."

He wove into another lane, but traffic stopped. He couldn't get closer to the white sedan—not safely, at least.

"It's okay," Mallory said. "It was probably just my eyes playing tricks on me."

But was it? He didn't want to put Mallory in danger.

But neither of them could seem to get away from it.

• • •

Mallory finished the interview and let out a sigh of relief.

She'd been on tour for less than a week, but she already felt exhausted. She'd had no idea how draining it was to be on the road, to be in the public eye, and to always be "on." She still had nearly three months of this schedule. It would take her all the way into the summer. Hopefully then she could recuperate.

If she was still alive.

She shuddered at the possibility that she may not live through this.

The reporter, a perky woman named Alice, extended her hand. "Thanks so much, Mallory. You truly are an inspiration. I know our viewers will connect with your story."

"I appreciate you sharing it," Mallory said. "If I can help even one person . . ."

She stood and wiped her hands on her dress. Grant waited at the edge of the room, no doubt evaluating and critiquing every word she said. Certainly she'd hear later what she could have done better. His brain was always working like that.

Tennyson stood near one door, Logan stood at the other, and Kori remained near the stairway in the hallway. Three security guards.

The reality of the situation hit her again. How had she gotten to this place?

She envisioned what it would be like to be home. No, she didn't want to be at home. She'd never feel truly comfortable at her parents' old house. There were too many memories. But she imagined what it would be like to be at her own home. Maybe by the water. Somewhere quiet.

The image filled her with warmth.

That wasn't a reality right now. Right now, she had obligations to fulfill. Later, maybe she'd dream more about that little seaside hideaway. Maybe by the bay.

"You ready to head back?" Grant asked.

She nodded. "Yeah. Maybe we can grab some food to take up to the suite for dinner. I'd like to take it easy tonight."

Tomorrow they'd be traveling to Orlando.

Another thought remained at the back of her mind: Would there be another body here? She couldn't stomach the very idea of it—of people dying wherever she went. Yet she didn't know how to stop it, or what to do about it. Did she stop trying to advocate for these victims? That seemed like a shame within itself.

She needed to pray some more about it.

While Tennyson went to get the car, Mallory nodded toward the restroom in the hallway. "Let me make a quick stop, and I'll meet you out here."

Kori checked it out before she slipped inside, thankful for a moment alone to compose herself. She went to the sink and splashed some water in her face.

The reporter had asked her some hard-hitting questions. Had questioned her relationship with her parents. Her upbringing. Asked detailed questions about her time with Dante—questions that were supposed to be off-limits. She'd tried to gracefully skirt her way around the questions, fully aware the camera was recording her every move and every word.

She could already feel the scrutiny that came with vulnerability. She didn't like it. But if that was the worst thing she had to experience right now in her life, then she was doing well. When you'd lived a nightmare, you learned to take things in stride. Most of the time, at least.

Behind her, she heard a scuffle in one of the stalls and froze.

She slowly turned, holding her breath.

She saw no one.

Carefully, she peered under each of the stall doors, checking for feet.

No one else was in here.

She let out her breath. She must be hearing things.

She turned back toward the mirror, grabbed a paper towel, and wiped the water from her face. Would she ever be able to live in any state other than paranoia? She wasn't sure. She'd liked to think so. She had to believe it was a possibility.

"Everything okay in there?" Kori yelled from the hallway.

"Everything's fine," she called back. "I'll be out in one minute."

With one last glance toward the stalls, she started toward the door. She heard another scuffle.

She froze again. What was that? Was someone hiding in the stalls? She'd checked. She hadn't seen anyone.

One thing was for sure: she wasn't going to stick around long enough to find out.

•   •   •

Mallory waited with Grant, Logan, and Kori in the marble-lined lobby of the TV station for Tennyson to pull up with the car. Though the space was luxurious, it was also small. A fountain took up the center part of the room. There were two elevators on one side of it, and a reception desk against the back wall. Two security guards stood at the front, checking everyone with a metal detector as they came in.

Mallory scooted closer to the wall as a group of high schoolers came in. They were apparently going to film some kind of special for the station on the fifth floor.

She swallowed hard. The lobby felt crowded, and she was jostled back and forth.

"Tennyson should be here any minute," Kori said. "A group of a hundred high schoolers weren't on our security plan for today. A detail that somehow got left off the information the station sent us."

Mallory nodded, pressing herself closer to the wall and wishing she could get out of here. "I know. Thanks."

"Maybe we'd be better off waiting outside," Logan said.

"Tennyson told us to stay here," Kori reminded him.

"Maybe I should call him."

Logan seemed nice enough, Mallory supposed. But he wasn't Tennyson. The fact that she felt such an easy, quick bond with Tennyson frightened her. He hadn't let her into his head, even. Who knew what he was thinking? Besides, she had to stand on her own two feet, not with a man by her side. Not that any man would want to be by her side, not with a past like hers.

"Good job with the interview back there, by the way," Logan said.

She crept closer to the wall and finally felt its cool marble behind her. She breathed a little easier. "Thank you. It doesn't really get easier to talk about. Not yet, at least."

"It's a marvel that you're talking about it all. Most people want to bury those parts of their lives."

"I wish I could. But it never stays buried for long, does it?"

"Sure enough, a storm will come along and expose what the dirt once concealed. You're right."

She smiled, warming up to the man slightly. At least he understood her a little. That was important.

Just then, the metal detector at the front began wailing. Mallory swung her head toward the sound, just in time to see a man darting past the security guards. The guards near the door tackled the man. Shouts echoed in the room as a sense of danger filled the air. The crowd scattered around her, and mass chaos broke out.

Logan reached out his arm to shield her.

Mallory held her breath as she watched the security guards restrain the man who thrashed on the floor. Just as they pulled him to his feet, the man seemed to get a burst of energy. He jerked away from the guards' grasps and lunged toward the other side of the lobby.

"He's got a bomb!" one of the guards yelled.

Before Mallory could process what was happening, an explosion shook the room.

A hand reached around her bicep. She tried to remember her self-defense moves, but everything happened too quickly.

Before she could react, she was pulled into darkness.

CHAPTER 25

Just as Tennyson pulled the SUV up to the entrance, he heard a rumble. He saw smoke. Heard glass breaking.

Something was wrong.

He threw the SUV into park and darted inside, praying everyone was okay.

Praying Mallory was okay.

He stopped inside the doors, quickly observing the chaos around him. Smoke filled the air. Sections of the wall were missing. People cried.

Where was Mallory? He searched the clusters of people. Grant stood plastered against the wall, his expression frozen like a deer in the headlights. Logan, Kori, and Mallory were nowhere to be seen.

That was because they'd gotten her to safety . . . right?

Unease swarmed in his gut.

This wasn't a part of their plan. They should have gotten Mallory to safety. These high schoolers weren't supposed to be here. And something had caused a commotion in the center of the room.

Mallory . . . where was Mallory?

He rushed across the lobby toward Grant, adrenaline surging through him. "Where's Mallory?"

"She's right—" He started to point his thumb beside him but stopped. "She was right there, just a minute ago."

He glanced at the floor. Kori lay there, smut on her face from the explosion.

"Grant, call the police. Check on Kori. Where's Logan?"

"I . . . I don't know."

"When you find him, tell him what happened. I've got to find Mallory."

All his senses were on alert. He scanned the crowd one last time but didn't see Mallory anywhere. Where could she be?

The elevator doors were only a foot away from Grant. Had she slipped inside one of the cars? Had someone grabbed her and pulled her inside?

He looked up as the numbers lit, showing which floor the car was on. The light stopped on the seventh floor.

He bypassed the other elevator and took off toward the stairway, taking the stairs two at a time until he reached the seventh floor. He knew time was of the essence. If someone had taken Mallory, two minutes could mean the difference between life and death.

He stepped out of the stairwell just in time to see someone—possibly two someones—disappear around the corner.

He sprinted after them, hoping one was Mallory. Praying she was okay.

He rounded the corner. The person disappeared into a room. It was Mallory. One of them was Mallory. He couldn't miss that blonde hair.

"Stop!" he yelled.

He reached the room. His lungs strained for air. Sweat covered his skin.

He rushed inside, only to find darkness surrounding him. Where were they?

His nerves went on edge. Was this a trap?

He gripped his gun and remained close to the wall. They were in here. He could sense them.

He moved carefully around the room, listening for a sign of their location. As he skirted by something, he heard his sleeve tear. Felt his skin tear.

He'd cut himself on some kind of construction equipment, he supposed. But that was the least of his worries at the moment.

He had to find Mallory. With each second that ticked by, the odds and the risks became greater. That was unacceptable.

The fact that any of this had happened in the first place was unacceptable.

He continued to skirt around the room, giving his eyes times to adjust to the darkness. The whole floor appeared to be under construction, and dangerous equipment was everywhere.

At that moment, a gasp sounded on the other side of the space.

Mallory. That was Mallory. He felt certain of it.

He shifted his position, moving back toward the door. The last thing he needed was for her captor to make a run for it.

Suddenly, he heard a shout. In an instant, someone lunged toward him, landing in his arms.

Mallory. Mallory was in his arms. She wasn't even fighting it. Gratefully, he inhaled her strawberry scent. Felt her soft hair. Heard her low whimper.

The door opened, and the man ran out.

He started to go after him but held Mallory instead. "Are you hurt?"

She sniffled on his shoulder. "No, I'm fine. Go."

"I'm not leaving you."

"Then take me with you. We can't lose him, Tennyson. He has the answers we need."

Against his better instincts, he led Mallory down the hallway. The man was nowhere to be seen.

He couldn't have gotten far away. Tennyson listened for any whispered creaks or footfalls. He watched for any flickering shadows. Felt the air for any change in intensity.

His heart pounded in his ears. It was quiet. Too quiet. Was someone hiding, waiting to strike?

He took each step with caution and anticipation.

There was someone else on this floor. The question was where. Where were they?

He stayed closed to the wall, using all of his senses to alert him when necessary. His gun was raised, ready for action. But most of all, he had to keep Mallory safe.

The door at the end of the corridor flew open. Tennyson shoved Mallory behind him and raised his gun.

A figure stepped out. Tennyson couldn't see his features. But he saw the shadow of a gun.

"Tennyson?"

Tennyson lowered his weapon, his heart rate plunging.

Logan stepped into the light, his hands raised. "It's me."

Tennyson glanced around once more, not willing to let down his guard. "Did you see anyone run that way?"

Logan shook his head, beads of sweat glimmering in the dim glow of the exit sign above him. "No. Is Mallory okay?"

"I'm fine. But the guy got away. He could still be on this floor."

"Keep searching," Tennyson told him. "I need to get Mallory to safety."

As soon as they stepped into the stairwell, Tennyson absorbed Mallory's face in the dim glow of the light overhead.

"Are you okay?" he questioned.

She started to reach for him but paused, dropping her hand.

"I'm fine." A tear streamed down her cheek. She quickly wiped it away. "Or not."

Tennyson wanted more than anything to reach out to her. To do something to make her feel better. But pulling her into a hug would only upset her more. "I'm sorry, Mallory."

"No, I'm sorry." She let out a shaky laugh.

"Don't apologize."

She wiped under her eyes with the bottom of her finger. Mascara, heavy from her TV appearance, stained below her lids. "It took me back in time to the night those men grabbed me and killed my parents."

Tennyson couldn't imagine what she'd gone through mentally. He couldn't pretend to understand.

"I hadn't really thought about it in a long time. I mean, I hadn't *really* thought about it. I tried to forget about it, to be truthful." She paused. "I thought I was going to relive that year all over again, Tennyson, and that thought caused something to break inside me."

"I'm not going to let that happen. I'm not letting you out of my sight again." He shifted. "Did you get a good look at him, Mallory?"

"No, I didn't. He was behind me the whole time."

"Did you recognize his voice?"

"He didn't say anything."

Tennyson fought a sigh. He wasn't getting very far with this.

Mallory stepped back and took a deep breath, as if trying to pull herself together. "Maybe it is time for me to take a break. I don't want these guys to win, but wisdom tells me that stepping out of the limelight for a short time period would be good."

"I think you're right."

"I don't know where I'll go."

"I do," Tennyson said. "I know the perfect place."

Her gaze met his. "I'll have to trust you on that."

Something about her admission of trust caused heat to shoot through him. He liked the sound of that. But he didn't want to disappoint her.

Then her eyes zeroed in on his arm.

"You're hurt."

He looked down and saw he was bleeding. He hadn't even noticed it until now.

"I'll be fine."

"You should go to the hospital. You might even need stitches."

Something about her concern warmed him all the way to the bone.

Then he remembered Claire. He remembered Kori's warning about not getting too close. Claire might be alive if he'd kept his distance, if he'd been able to remain objective.

She was dead as a result. Tennyson couldn't let himself forget that.

Even if Mallory made it really easy to forget.

CHAPTER 26

The next morning, Mallory and Tennyson cruised down the highway toward Cape Thomas. Grant and Logan were driving a second vehicle following behind them. Kori led the way in a separate car at the front of the pack. Although she'd been knocked out at the TV station when the blast ripped through the lobby, she seemed to be doing okay now.

The convoy had stopped two hours ago, long enough to grab a quick bite to eat. Then they were on the road again.

No one had said much during the meal. In fact, everyone seemed pretty sober after everything that had happened. Mallory had been especially quiet, and she was grateful that Tennyson let her have space to collect her thoughts.

After the TV station debacle, she'd spent three hours being questioned by police, while paramedics had treated Tennyson's wound. Now the tour was over. Maybe it should have been over long ago. Maybe she'd been fooling herself into thinking she was doing the right thing.

Dante could be alive. Someone wanted her dead. And it was hard to talk about being a victor when someone was trying to victimize her.

Mallory felt Tennyson shift beside her. She sensed a new heaviness about him and braced herself for whatever he had to say.

"There's something I need to tell you, Mallory." His voice was quiet and still.

Her muscles tensed at the foreshadowing. "Okay . . ."

He pressed his lips together before drawing in a deep breath. "I'm sorry to put it this way, but there's no easy way to say this. Narnie is missing."

Mallory gasped, certain she hadn't heard him correctly. "What?"

"I'm sorry, Mallory. I know the two of you weren't close, but . . ."

Her head felt like it was swimming through muck. "What . . . ? How . . . ?"

"Her hotel room in Atlanta was ransacked. She hasn't been seen since then."

Mallory's chin dropped down toward her chest. Atlanta? She didn't know where this was going, but she didn't like it. "I can't believe it. Do you know anything else?"

"From what I heard, she was apparently threatening to go to the FBI with some information on Walter Boyce."

"Walter?" Every other sentence Tennyson spoke shocked her. She hadn't been expecting any of this. Wouldn't have been able to guess it even. She'd known Narnie was ruthless but . . . this?

"There's rumor that Walter was helping Torres transport his weapons overseas."

She let out a laugh at the absurdity of his statement. "Walter would never do that. He's a good man. One of my father's best friends."

"Even good men can be bought." He paused. "I'm sorry, Mallory."

His words echoed in her mind. She tried to settle down, to make sense of them. But, on the other hand, she didn't want them to. "I just can't believe this. Is there no end to what people will do to get more, to have more—money, power, success—whatever their poison is?"

"It's unsettling, I know."

She closed her eyes and pressed her head back into the seat. Walter. Could he have been in on this? And if he was, what did that mean about her father? Could Jason have been correct—did he have a backroom deal going with Dante?

She couldn't stomach that thought.

Not to mention Narnie . . . Though she had trouble feeling sorry for the woman, she didn't want her to suffer. Mallory had always hoped there was a chance for redemption. She still hoped there would be a chance for that.

Could things get any worse?

●　　●　　●

As they crossed the Chesapeake Bay Bridge Tunnel, Tennyson's phone rang. He grabbed it from the console and saw it was the detective in charge of the investigation in Atlanta.

He put the phone on speaker so Mallory could hear.

"I promised to give you an update," Detective Goodwin said. "First of all, you'll be happy to know that everyone in the building is okay. We have some injuries, but the bomb wasn't strong. It was more the kind meant to get attention than to injure."

"I'm glad everyone is okay," Mallory said. "Even the man with the bomb?"

"He suffered some burns, but he should recover. The only thing he's said is that he was paid to plant the bomb."

"What do you know about him?" Tennyson asked.

"His name is Marvin Harris. He has no known priors, but his neighbors said he's been acting suspiciously lately."

"Suspiciously how?" Tennyson asked.

"Keeping strange hours. Lots of late-night visitors."

What if Marvin had been a distraction? Tennyson wondered. Whoever the person was behind Mallory's almost-abduction had known Mallory would be in the lobby. He'd known that if everyone's attention was on someone else, that would give him the best opportunity to grab Mallory.

Tennyson's stomach clenched.

What would have happened if Tennyson hadn't come in when he did? Would the man have escaped out a side exit with Mallory? Off the roof? What had his plan been?

Tennyson wasn't sure. But he didn't like the thought of it.

"There was one other thing the neighbor said," Detective Goodwin continued. "Apparently, this guy Marvin has been a die-hard fan of Ms. Baldwin. There's evidence to indicate he's been following her. He even had some photos he took of her at various places."

Tennyson remembered the pictures he'd seen, the ones a stalker had taken and sent. "Yet he claims he was paid off?"

"That's correct."

"Did he say anything about sending messages to me?" Mallory asked.

Tennyson knew what she was thinking: Could this man be Nameless?

"What type of messages?"

"Mallory has been getting anonymous e-mails from someone," Tennyson explained.

"He wasn't sending them—not that we know of, but we'll look into it."

Were there two different things going on here? Did Mallory have a stalker and someone from Inferno who was following her? That's how it appeared. And it didn't make Tennyson feel better.

The web was getting more complicated by the moment, and more difficult to untangle.

Just as he hung up, Mallory's phone buzzed.

"I've got a text message."

"Who's it from?" Tennyson asked.

"Jason." She narrowed her eyes as she read the words there. Her lower lip dropped. "He's threatening to go public with the information about my dad meeting with Dante. Why would he do that? Nothing has even been confirmed."

His jaw flexed. "I have no idea. Maybe you should call Jason and see where his head is."

"What if he really has something?" she asked quietly. "I want to believe my father would never do anything to put the family in danger, but . . ."

"Then we'll handle it."

"I feel like I might break into a million pieces in the process," she whispered.

"Even if you do, I'll help put you back together," he said. He reached out his hand and offered it to her.

To her surprise, she accepted it. She wrapped her fingers around his and squeezed.

CHAPTER 27

As Mallory dialed Jason's number, her heart pounded fiercely in her chest.

Jason wanted to go to the media with information that was just conjecture.

He'd ruin her family's reputation. However, that wasn't even the most important thing to her. The truth was important, but this had "slimy" written all over it.

Why would Jason do this? It just didn't make sense.

She could hardly breathe as she finished dialing. Voice mail picked up. She'd bet anything Jason was simply avoiding talking to her.

"Jason, this is Mallory. Call me. Please." She hit "End" before looking back up at Tennyson. She squeezed the phone in her hands, trying to keep herself calm. Her white knuckles indicated she might break the phone if she didn't try harder. "I'll try him again later."

"You have no idea why he would pull a stunt like this?"

She shook her head, reflecting on her last two conversations with him. Sure, the last one had gone south. But this?

"I have no idea. It just doesn't even seem like Jason. He's the type who takes action, but only when things work in his favor. You know, when it helps him in some way."

"How could this help him?"

She tried to sift through her thoughts. "I'm not sure. I mean, he's poised to take over his father's company. With that would come more power and money. I suppose that could have something to do with it. Greed can lead to a multitude of sins."

"If he's really concerned, maybe he should go to the FBI. Not to the media."

"Exactly. It doesn't make sense." Justice was justice. If her father had done something wrong, she couldn't cover it up. But things needed to be done properly.

"Maybe he wants more attention for himself."

She remembered Jason's smug face. How he'd only ever looked out for himself. How he hadn't called her after her ordeal. She hadn't realized until recently the hard feelings she had because of that.

"This would be one way to get some attention." She bit down, trying to process her thoughts. "I knew when I saw him again that nothing had changed. He's still as self-centered as ever."

"This would be taking it to the extreme, don't you think?" Tennyson asked.

"That's what I don't understand."

"You rejected him. Maybe that cut deeper than you assumed it would. This would be attention plus some vengeance."

"If this is his way of getting even, maybe he's not right in the head." She crossed her arms and stared out the window for several minutes in silence.

Her thoughts shifted from Jason, to Dante, to her future. To her ability to truly love again, something she often questioned after her ordeal.

A question had been lingering in her mind for a while now. Maybe this was the time to ask it. She wasn't, however, sure how Tennyson would respond.

"Can I ask you a question?"

"Of course."

"What did Ethan mean by you wanted all kinds of women—single, taken, it didn't matter?"

Tennyson seemed to freeze. "You want to know the truth?"

Mallory nodded. Of course she did. "Yes, I do. The truth is all we've got sometimes."

His features seemed to age ten years before her eyes. What exactly was he about to tell her? She sensed it was deep and heavy and full of pain.

"Before I made SEAL Team Six, I was on a different SEAL team. We were training nationals in Iraq so they could defend themselves against the insurgents who were threatening to take control of the country."

Tension crawled up Mallory's spine. Whatever he was about to announce, it was big. She could feel it, could feel that whatever happened had profoundly affected Tennyson.

She waited for him to gather his thoughts. Resisted the urge to touch him, to comfort him. She wanted to hear what he had to say. She wanted to know him. To truly know him.

"An admiral contacted me. Said his daughter was in the area where I was training. She was working with the CIA, and he wanted me to keep an eye on her. I wasn't supposed to let her know that the conversation ever happened, of course. She would have been mortified."

This was the girl. The one whose photo Tennyson still carried with him.

His voice softened. "Claire. The woman I told you about before. She'd graduated from Harvard. Could have done anything she wanted with her life, but she decided to work for the government. She had a passion for justice—not unlike you."

Tennyson offered a quick, reassuring smile.

Mallory didn't know where the story was going, but she could sense it was nowhere good based on Tennyson's body language. She braced herself as he continued.

"I got to know her. She was fascinating. We were stationed in the country for four months. Claire and I knew we were in love a week after we met the first time. Our feelings were that intense. We saw each other whenever we could."

Something about his words caused pangs in Mallory's heart. Did he feel that way about her also? Was there even room in his heart to try to love someone like he'd loved Claire? That was a question and thought for pondering at another time.

"The rebel group who was trying to overthrow the government continued to attack US troops," Tennyson said. "Their weapons were high-grade, beyond what they would have gotten off the streets. It became obvious that someone was supplying them with the necessary gear to overthrow the government."

She knew where this was going, but she wasn't sure she wanted to hear the rest. However, she couldn't stop herself. She had to know. No matter how much it hurt or tore her up inside.

"Claire figured out that Dante Torres was the man behind it all. He was smuggling the weapons into the country somehow. She got a lead on a new shipment that was coming in, but she had to prove it was real." He dipped his head a moment—but only a moment—before focusing intensely on the road ahead of them. "I begged her not to go."

"And?" Mallory pressed her lips together, waiting to hear the rest.

"She told me she wouldn't. Not without backup. I mean, that was her job. It was what she was hired to do." He drew in a deep breath. "She told me to meet her one evening. Our relationship was all under wraps. She was undercover. I was a military man in a country where a lot of people hated Americans. It was no time for love. All of our meetings were in secret."

"What happened?" Mallory hardly wanted to ask the question.

"She asked me to meet her just to throw me off her trail." His voice cracked. "She never showed up. She never had any intentions of doing so. I'll never know her exact reasons, but I suspect she wanted to keep me out of danger."

"What was she doing in the meantime?"

"She went to gather intelligence about the arms deal. I figured out where she was going and rushed to help her. I was going to stay in the distance, make sure she didn't even know I was there. But make sure she was safe."

Her heart pounded in her ears as she waited for the conclusion of his story. She knew where this was going—she could feel it in her gut—but she wanted to hear it anyway.

"I arrived just in time to see Dante Torres pull his trigger. Claire had been made somehow. Torres wasn't about to let her escape knowing what she did."

Dante. He truly was an evil man. A man who'd deserved more justice than he'd gotten when he killed himself. She reached across the seat and rested her hand on his shoulder.

"I'm so sorry, Tennyson."

His jaw hardened. "I was going to shoot Torres right then and there. But everything went black."

"What happened?"

"Ethan Stone showed up."

"Ethan Ethan? The same Ethan who was in our hotel suite?"

He nodded. "He was working for the CIA. The two of us never liked each other. Probably because we were both in love with Claire. He knew if I pulled the trigger then, all their work would be destroyed. They needed to bring these guys down the legal way—not by route of a rogue Navy SEAL pulling the trigger."

"I never heard about any of this."

"CIA. There's no glory, per se. Claire became a nameless star on the memorial wall in Langley."

"Her father?"

"He's never forgiven me. I can't say I blame him."

She squeezed his shoulder, fighting the desire to pull him into her arms and tell him everything would be okay. They were in the car. She couldn't do that. But she longed to make things better. To comfort him. To help carry his burden, just like he'd helped to carry hers.

"It wasn't your fault. She did everything she could to keep the fact that she was going there from you."

He nodded slowly, his gaze still fixed on the road. "I know. But I beat myself up for years. All I could think about was getting vengeance—I called it justice back then—on Dante Torres."

"You have just as much reason to hate him as I do."

"But hate can consume you. It can make you a prisoner."

"Yes it can." She knew his words were true, but hearing them out loud only drove the point home.

She didn't want Dante or his men to have any more control of her life ever again. Ever.

• • •

Tennyson watched as the landscape changed from tree-dotted farmland to stretches of nothing but open sky on the horizon. They'd arrive at their destination soon.

Part of him wanted this trip to continue. Something seemed to have shifted between him and Mallory on the way here. Their conversation had bonded them.

He hadn't told that story about Claire to anyone since it happened. Wheaton knew parts of it. But sharing it with Mallory had felt right.

As had touching her. Holding hands. Feeling her hand on his shoulder.

They passed through gate and pulled up to Trident headquarters. She would be safe here. For a while, at least.

"So this is where I'll be spending a fair amount of time, huh?" Mallory leaned forward to get a better look at the building.

Trident's headquarters was located on twenty-five acres off the Chesapeake Bay. Part of the land had been used for farming up until Wheaton had purchased it. Right on the other side of the property was a separate parcel where the guys going through the program would live while they were in training.

It was an old hotel—only a decade old, actually. The building was surprisingly modern for the area: rectangular, industrial, artistic almost. The previous owner had tried to make a go of it as a hotel for several years, but had ultimately given up because there hadn't been enough business here.

Tennyson nodded and put the car in park. "I think you'll like it here. There's something about the water that can soothe the spirit. It's soothed mine, at least."

"This isn't far from Hope House, is it?"

"No, it's not. Right down the street." Tennyson turned toward her before she could join the others who were getting out of their cars. "Are you sure you're okay?"

She didn't answer right away, and he actually appreciated the forethought she was giving his question. He didn't want an easy answer such as an obligatory "fine." He wanted the truth.

"I don't know what I am right now, Tennyson. All I can think about is going back to the life I 'lived' in captivity for that year. It wasn't really living at all. I feel like I'm close—so close—to going back to that dark place. I can taste it. My body can sense it."

"I can only imagine what you're feeling."

The sun hit her face, giving her an almost angelic look that Tennyson drank in. She was so beautiful—inside and out. She didn't deserve any of the things that had been thrown at her.

"I've really tried to believe that everything that's happened has just been a terrible mistake or that the person behind these so-called threats was just socially awkward or cluelessly trying to play a prank. I don't know. It was probably naive of me. I've always had a tendency to want to stick my head in the sand rather than face reality."

His heart yearned to help her—to really help her. To sweep her away from all of this—forever. But he couldn't do that. His feelings for Mallory were growing, but he was hired help. Besides, he couldn't lose his focus on keeping her safe. "Is having your head in the sand your coping mechanism?"

She nodded. "Yeah, I guess you could say that. It's not a very good one. But I can't ignore everything that's happening. It would be foolish of me. This is more than a prank or someone taunting me. I realize that my life is on the line."

He remained quiet, listening.

"I guess I'm tired of living like the freedom I have could slip away at any minute. It's no way to live."

"Maybe we can help you get part of your life back here, Mallory. I'll support whatever choice you make, but I really feel like it would be best if you laid low for a while. At least until we figure out a few things."

"We have a lot to figure out." She reached for his hand and squeezed it. "Tennyson, if you hadn't come along yesterday . . ."

"Shh . . . don't think like that."

"I can't help but think like that. You've been a real lifesaver more than once."

"You're worth saving . . . however many times it takes."

Their gazes caught, and Tennyson felt his stomach squeeze with feelings he hadn't felt in a long time.

"Let's get you inside," Tennyson said, his voice hoarse and tight.

She nodded.

That's when he realized he was still grasping her hand. She hadn't pulled away or looked startled. Holding her hand had felt so natural that he'd hardly noticed.

Again, he reminded himself to keep himself in check.

How many times would he have to remind himself of that?

CHAPTER 28

"This is where you'll be staying." Tennyson opened the door to a small, dorm-like room. A little bed was tucked against the wall, as well as a dresser, small sofa, and desk.

None of this was ideal. She wanted to be on the road, not sequestered away. This was temporary, she reminded herself. A bump in the road.

"I'll be staying on the other side," Tennyson continued. "There's actually a bathroom connecting the two rooms, just in case you need anything. Logan and Kori are staying in the rooms across the hall, and Grant will be on the other side of you. He's downstairs talking to Wheaton right now, but he said he'd be up in a few."

As she looked at Tennyson, she remembered the moment they'd shared in the car and her cheeks warmed. It was so simple. Just holding hands. But to Mallory, it felt like moving a mountain—a huge leap of faith. Was there room in her life for a man? Did Tennyson even share her feelings?

Flutters rippled through her when she brought her eyes up to meet his. "Sounds good, Tennyson."

The smolder in his glance made her catch her breath. Did he even realize the effect he had on her when he looked like that? When his gaze was filled with so much care and concern?

He stepped back, almost as if he felt something too but didn't want to. "The premises are guarded. I'm sure you saw the fence as we passed. It's hard for anyone who hasn't been approved to get on campus."

"It sounds like quite the setup." The words sounded lame, not what she wanted to say. But it was all that would come out.

"It will be great once we open. They're still doing some construction on the other end of the building. But this hallway is secure."

Mallory walked across the room and shoved the curtain aside. Glimmering water stared back at her, as peaceful and serene as Mallory hoped her soul would be one day. "So nice to have a view of the bay."

Tennyson stood behind her, close enough that she could feel his body heat. Close enough that desire welled in her. That if she just turned around, they'd be face-to-face . . .

But Mallory didn't allow herself to do that. There were still professional boundaries in place. There were still doubts, uncertainties, and so many obstacles to overcome.

"It's beautiful, isn't it?" Tennyson murmured.

"It really is. I think I could stare at it all day." The endless expanse of horizon, the gentle ripples across the blue water, the blue sky that seemed to promise hope . . . maybe this was the place that would truly help heal her bruised and battered soul.

"I was hoping you might feel relaxed here," Tennyson said.

Mallory couldn't help but turn toward him. His gaze met hers, and something simmered between them. His pupils widened as his eyes moved to her lips. They'd done this dance. Two steps forward. Two steps back. Pulled together. Drawn apart. They'd be fools to think this would work between them, wouldn't they?

They were from different worlds. She was damaged, made whole again only through her faith. He was a man who could do no wrong.

Up on a pedestal? Absolutely. The worst place to be, in many ways. Because no one ever stayed up there for long.

Despite everything Mallory knew, they stepped closer to each other.

Did he want to kiss her? Because she wanted to kiss him.

At just that moment, someone burst into the room.

Mallory and Tennyson both jumped back from each other.

Grant.

"We got another e-mail from Nameless," he announced, oblivious to whatever had almost happened. "You'll want to see this."

.   .   .

Tennyson reread the words, his gut churning with each new phrase.

> YOU THINK YOU CAN HIDE, BUT YOU CAN'T.
> YOU THINK YOU CAN RUN, BUT YOU CAN'T.
> WHEREVER YOU GO, I'LL FIND YOU.
>
> YOU'RE MEANT FOR ME AND ONLY ME.
> DON'T EVER BELIEVE DIFFERENTLY. IT DOESN'T
> MATTER WHAT ANYONE ELSE SAYS. IT DOESN'T
> MATTER HOW YOU THINK OR FEEL. THE TRUTH
> IS THE TRUTH, AND I'M DETERMINED TO
> PROVE IT TO YOU.
>
> BE WAITING, MY DEAR. BE WATCHING, DOLL.
> NO ONE KNOWS THE DAY OR HOUR WE'LL BE
> REUNITED—NO ONE EXCEPT ME.

"He used 'doll,'" Tennyson said. A rock formed in his gut. Were the answers under their nose the whole time? Was Grant behind this?

He'd never respected the man, but he didn't think he'd sink this low either. Nor was he this stupid.

Grant raised his hands, his eyes wide and flabbergasted. "I get that it's weird, but it wasn't me. I can promise you that. Why would I show you this e-mail if I knew it would incriminate me? I'm smarter than that."

"Maybe this guy is someone who's closer than you think," Logan said. He and Kori had followed Grant into the room only seconds later. "He knows enough to know Grant calls Mallory doll."

"We should be able to narrow our list of suspects based on that information," Kori said.

"He's definitely taken the threat to the next level," Grant said. "I hope this little minifortress can offer us some peace, because this is getting downright creepy. I'm going to call Agent Turner and every detective we've talked to. I'm going to demand answers. Enough is enough."

Mallory sank into the desk chair, looking unusually pale. "Does that mean he knows where I am? He mentioned running and hiding."

"Not necessarily," Tennyson said, resisting the urge to comfort her. "We can stay here for a while and we should be okay. Plus, the location is secure. I checked, and no one followed us."

"This guy is a nut job!" Grant paced to the window, looking more stressed than Tennyson thought was possible.

None of this was helping to calm Mallory. The tension was getting to everyone, it appeared, and the room felt like a pressure cooker.

"Is Nameless connected to Sanchez and the incidents that have been taking place?" Mallory's wide eyes were desperate for answers as her shoulders slumped. "All along I suspected they could be connected, but I didn't want to believe it."

Tennyson wished he could give those answers to her.

"It's hard to say," Tennyson said. "Like Grant said, we need to contact law enforcement. Enough has happened that they need to move these incidents up higher on their priority lists. I hope this guy will mess up and someone will be able to track his IP address. No one is flawless when it comes to this stuff."

Mallory turned toward Grant. "Have you called all the places where we were supposed to stop on the tour? How are they handling the change of schedule?"

Grant turned from the window. "They're not happy of course. But they understand."

"What reason are you telling them?" Tennyson asked.

"I'm telling them that an unexpected emergency has come up. The publisher isn't happy—they were counting on this book for a boost in sales."

"There are more important things at stake here than book sales," Tennyson snapped.

"I didn't say otherwise." Grant glared at him. "But Mallory needs to know the stakes. This is her nonprofit. Her future."

"So, what's the plan? Just stay locked away here indefinitely?" Mallory asked. Her shoulders were a little straighter. She'd processed this new information and was now pushing forward.

It was just one more thing that Tennyson admired about her.

Keeping her tucked away here indefinitely was exactly what Tennyson would like to do. He wanted to hide her away, safe and secure, until all the threats against her had been removed. But he knew that wasn't realistic.

"I'd just suggest giving this a week," Tennyson said. "That will give the FBI a chance to do their job. Hopefully they'll get some leads. It will also give you a chance to get refreshed."

She blinked up at him, as if his words surprised her. "Refreshed?"

"There's been a lot going on. Maybe some downtime will be good for you. We don't want you to get overwhelmed. Wouldn't you agree, Grant?"

Grant stared at him a moment before nodding. "Of course. This past week has been stressful. Plus, you're set to speak before the congressional committee in eight days. Creating harsher laws for the people involved in human trafficking has always been one of your top priorities. You want to be at the top of your game for that. I know how important it is to you."

"You're right," Mallory said. "That meeting is very important. I guess . . . I guess I just don't want to sit around with nothing but time on my hands. When that happens . . . I start thinking too much. Remembering too much. It's better if I keep myself busy."

"We can work on some blog posts. Write some letters. Practice your speech. We could even do some live feeds. We'll keep you busy." Grant nodded, as if sure of his plan.

It wasn't a bad one. There were benefits to staying busy.

"We might even be able to go over to Hope House," Grant continued. "It's close enough and out of the way enough that we could make that work. I know how important your work is to you."

Her eyes lit up at that suggestion. "I like that idea. Working one-on-one with people has always been my preference anyway. It will help me feel like I'm not wasting my time."

"Then let's regroup again in the morning," Grant said. "Sound good?"

"Sounds like a plan," Mallory said.

• • •

That night, Mallory awoke with a start. Her eyes strained to come into focus.

Where was she? Not a hotel room.

That's when it hit her.

She was back in her bedroom at Dante's. Her eyes soaked in the lacy white canopy on the wooden four-poster bed. Everything was entirely too feminine and lacy around her—not her style at all. It was Alessandra's style.

Mallory's stomach roiled. How had she gotten back here? Was this just a bad dream?

She didn't know.

She threw her legs out of bed and walked to the bookshelf. There was the picture of her mom and dad that Dante had given her. In his own twisted way, he'd tried to be kind, even though he was really a monster.

Tears rushed to Mallory's eyes as she looked at the portrait. She missed her parents so much. And while she didn't miss who she'd been, she missed her old life. She missed having people to fall back on. Being without any worries. Thinking that bad things only happened to other people.

Now she was all too aware that bad things happened to everyone. For some, the bad things became living nightmares.

She glanced around her room again, hoping Gabriella would stop by today. The housekeeper was one of the only bright spots about being here. The woman listened. She really listened. She'd helped to wipe away Mallory's tears. She'd patted her back and offered motherly compassion.

That was, until she'd tried to help Mallory escape.

It had happened when Dante had begun trusting Mallory. He offered her more freedom, probably figuring she was too scared to run. Maybe assuming that, even if she did, they were on an island, and Mallory wouldn't be able to get far without the sea claiming her.

Then one day Gabriella had whispered, "There's a boat coming with supplies. You can hide in the cargo compartment and make it back to the States."

It had seemed too good to be true. But Mallory knew it was worth the risk. Otherwise, she just might grow old and die here . . . with Dante.

She nearly doubled over at the thought.

That day, while she was in the courtyard overlooking the blue waters of the Caribbean, Gabriella gave her a signal. Mallory knew that it was her chance. Now or never.

She moved swiftly down the seashell path toward the boat. Palm fronds brushed her skin. Mosquitoes hovered near her. All she could think about was the boat.

She looked left. Then right.

Her breaths were too shallow. Her motions too quick to be careful. No one else was around. Not at the moment.

As she reached the docks, she heard men talking and ducked behind the boathouse. Dante strolled past, speaking with a man she'd never seen before. Sanchez was also with them.

They were speaking Spanish . . . again. She desperately wanted to understand what they were saying, but she couldn't.

El envío está en camino.

Dante. Dante had said that.

Why couldn't she have paid more attention in Spanish class? *Envío* . . . what did that mean?

Maybe she could figure it out later. When she was safe.

They passed, and Mallory crept around the corner of the building, desperately hoping they hadn't seen her. Sweat dotted her skin, not only from the humidity. Fear caused the moisture to scatter across her forehead and hands.

As she took another step and peeked around the corner at the men, something snapped beneath her. A twig.

Sanchez paused. Looked behind him.

She drew back quickly, her heart pounding furiously. Had he seen her? Was her dress billowing out from around the building with the wind? Or what about her feet? Could they be seen from around the corner?

Each moment stretched on, feeling like an hour. Finally, Mallory heard the footsteps moving again. The conversation reengaged.

After they passed, Mallory knew this was her opportunity.

She darted toward the boat. Cleared the dock. Didn't hear a thing.

She stepped aboard, feeling freedom. Feeling hope.

But the emotion was short-lived.

Arms circled her from behind, jerking her back.

She turned.

It was Dante.

No se supone que estés aquí, Alessandra, he murmured.

He was taking her back to her prison. Just as freedom had been so close . . .

She'd rather die than live one more day with this man.

"Mallory . . . Mallory. Wake up. It's just a dream."

The voice jostled her, and then faded.

At once, Mallory was being rescued again. She'd huddled in the closet when she heard the men coming, praying she wouldn't be seen. Uncertain what was going on. Had one of Dante's enemies found them? Were they here for revenge? What would they do to her as a means of torturing Dante?

Bombs exploded. Gunfire pummeled the air.

She realized she was going to die. All she could do was pray.

Then she'd seen the light. A literal light.

Tennyson had appeared carrying a flashlight, shining it in her face. And he carried her to safety, away from the nightmare she'd been living, like a knight in shining armor.

"Mallory, it's going to be okay. I'm here."

That was what Tennyson had said to her. Surprisingly enough, she'd believed him.

"Mallory!"

Her eyes jerked open. She saw her room. Saw Tennyson.

Only this wasn't a dream.

She was in Cape Thomas. At the Trident headquarters. Tennyson was kneeling beside her bed, concern in his eyes.

"You were having a nightmare," he whispered. "I thought something was wrong."

Without thinking, she threw herself into his arms and buried her face in his chest. She relished the feeling of his strong arms around her. She thanked God for bringing him into her life. Then and now.

He kissed the top of her head. Rocked her back and forth. Wiped her tears with his fingers.

"Don't go. Please," she whispered.

"I won't."

And, eventually, she drifted to sleep. In his arms.

For the first time in three years, she felt truly safe.

CHAPTER 29

Mallory awoke with a start the next morning. Her nightmare—really more of a memory, a reliving of the past—rushed back to her. Every gory detail of it. She'd felt like she was there again. She'd even been able to smell the island compound's flowery scent.

But Tennyson had come to her rescue—both two years ago and last night.

She pushed herself up in bed, allowing the white sheets to fall to her waist. Sunlight hit her face, and silence stretched around her.

Tennyson . . . he was gone.

She cringed when she thought about how vulnerable she'd been . . . and how Tennyson had been a total gentleman.

Her cheeks warmed when she remembered his arms around her. She'd never once questioned his integrity, and that meant a lot. Especially considering everything she'd been through. Everything that had been taken from her.

She never thought she'd be able to trust again, but Tennyson had proven to her that she could.

She knew she was falling hard for him. Too hard. Too fast.

He was getting over her walls, bringing them down, despite her best efforts to stop it. Could she be stronger with a man by her side instead of weaker?

After she showered and dressed, someone knocked at her door. When she saw Tennyson standing there, the warmth on her cheeks went from uncomfortable to flaming. Especially when she soaked in his broad shoulders. His well-formed muscles. His firm abdomen. All hard to ignore in his formfitting T-shirt.

"Good morning." She pushed a wet strand of hair behind her ear, certain he could see her thoughts.

"Morning." His warm eyes made tingles dance up and down her spine before spinning in her stomach.

Get it together, Mallory. You're in danger, and what do you do? Contemplate whether or not you're falling in love.

His voice sounded low as he leaned toward her. "How are you this morning?"

Okay, other than the fact that I'd like to bury myself in your arms again. Drink in your woodsy scent. Be with you forever.

Her cheeks burned hotter. She cleared her throat, her embarrassment bringing her back down to reality. "Sorry about last night."

"Don't be sorry. I heard you yelling and thought something was wrong. That's when I realized you were having a night terror."

"I have them more than I'd like to admit, and they're really more like memories that I've tried to repress."

"It's the first time I've heard you."

"Well, that's something to be thankful for." She cleared her throat again, not meaning to go there. Instead, she glanced at the papers in his hand, desperate for a change of subject. "What's going on?"

Tennyson led her to the couch and waited until she was seated. Then he lowered himself beside her and showed her a photo. "Do you recognize this woman, Mallory?"

She licked her dry lips before picking up the picture. She could do this. She had to.

Mallory knew what was coming: another dead body.

She fully expected to see another blonde whom she didn't recognize. Instead, a brunette's lifeless, battered face was there.

She gasped and dropped the photo. Nausea rose in her so quickly that she grabbed the trash can beside her. But nothing happened. Not yet, at least.

"Mallory?"

She rubbed her eyes, trying to get the image out of her mind. Trying to pretend like none of this was happening.

She should look at the photo again, but she didn't want to. "That's . . . that's Gabriella, Dante's housekeeper. She was . . ." What was she? How could Mallory even describe their relationship? "She was my friend."

"When was the last time you saw her?"

"Two months before I was rescued. But I thought . . . I thought I'd gotten her killed. She tried to help me escape, but I was caught. I never saw her again after that. But she wasn't killed, was she? Not right away. Instead, it was much worse. She must have been sold into the sex industry."

Her hand flew over her mouth. Poor Gabriella . . . she'd only wanted to help Mallory. She didn't deserve this. How many people would be hurt because of Mallory?

"What happened?" she whispered.

"Her body was found in Atlanta last night. She'd been branded, just like the other girls. Strangled. Left near the hotel."

Mallory hung her head, her burdens feeling as heavy as the universe itself. What would it take to end this? To stop these senseless deaths? "This just gets worse and worse. I don't understand. I don't understand! Why is someone doing this?"

Tennyson pulled her into his embrace. She melted there, relishing the feel of his arms around her.

"We're trying to figure it out," Tennyson murmured. "Agent Turner is going to come here today, as well as Ethan Stone."

Her head jerked up. "Why Ethan?"

"The NSA is having him work with the FBI on this case. He knows about Inferno, just like I do. He's a good person to be working with, to have on your team. I wasn't on board with this at first, but now I think this will be a good idea."

"Whatever it takes to get to the bottom of this. I just want it to stop. I never anticipated any of this when I launched Verto. I only wanted to help . . ." Her voice cracked.

Tennyson's arms tightened around her. "I know."

"And I need to know if what Jason said was true or not."

"About your father knowing Torres?"

She nodded, her body suddenly achy with dread. She needed to face the truth, even if it turned her world upside down. "I'm going to call the CEO of my dad's company today and see if I can get any information out of him."

"Sounds like a good idea."

Mallory didn't know if it was a good idea or not. But she had to get some answers, even if the truth devastated her.

• • •

After Tennyson left to wait for Turner and Stone, Mallory called the CEO of Baldwin Appliances.

His name was Stanley Becker, and he'd always seemed like a nice enough man when she'd met him at family barbecues and company picnics. However, Mallory wasn't sure how this conversation would go.

Her throat felt dry and achy as she waited for him to answer. The questions she had could put the most easygoing person on edge. But they had to be asked.

Finally, a woman's voice came on the line. "Office of Stanley Becker. Vanessa speaking."

"Hi, Vanessa. I'm trying to reach Mr. Becker." Mallory pulled her legs under her on the couch, trying to relax. She failed.

"I'm sorry. He's not available. Can I take a message?"

"This is Mallory Baldwin."

Silence stretched for a moment. The woman obviously recognized her name. Mallory had almost grown up at the Baldwin Appliances headquarters, chasing balls down the hallways and building castles for her dolls out of old refrigerator boxes.

"Mallory Baldwin? Let me see if he has a moment. Hold, please."

Mallory's heart thumped in her chest as she waited. How would she even bring this subject up? She had no good ideas. Every possible conversation she imagined starting led to bad conclusions, but it was a risk she needed to take.

Stanley had been her father's right-hand man, and he was an obvious choice to take over the company after her father's murder. Mallory had remained hands-off after she was rescued, knowing that Stanley would do a better job than she ever could.

"Mallory." His warm voice came over the line. "I wasn't expecting to hear from you. You ready to come to work at your father's company?"

She frowned at the very idea. The four years she'd worked there had bored her to tears. Appliances were not her life's passion. "No, sir. I'm afraid not."

"That's right, you're doing that book tour. Maybe when it's over."

"No, I meant it when I signed over my rights. I have no interest in the appliance business. You're doing a great job."

"Well, there's always a place for you here. Never forget that."

Her heart slowed slightly at his warm tones. "Thank you. I'm actually calling about something else. It's a conversation I wish I could have in person, but that's not possible right now. I hope you understand that."

"How can I help you?" His voice immediately sounded crisper and more professional.

"Mr. Becker, when my family went on that trip to the Caribbean, I thought it was simply so we could all get away and reconnect after my granddad passed away. Do you know if my father had any business to attend to while he was there?"

"Business? At the resort?"

"Not necessarily at the resort. Just in the Caribbean."

"He never mentioned anything. Not that I can remember. Why do you ask?"

She licked her lips, trying to figure out the best way to word it. "I'm not really sure. Someone told me he saw my father meeting with a man on the night of the party, right before he died."

"Your parents' deaths were senseless and a real shame. But they weren't connected to the company."

She pressed her lips together, hearing the tension in his voice. "I didn't say they were. I just didn't want to leave any unanswered questions."

"I'm sorry that someone put those doubts in your mind. You don't need any additional stress right now. You just need to heal."

"I was mostly just curious. I feel like answers are important for closure." Which was why she had to stop sticking her head in the sand.

"Of course. If there's anything I can do, please let me know."

"There is one more thing. What do you know about Walter Boyce?"

Quiet filled the line. "Walter? He and his company have been allies of Baldwin Appliances for years. He and your father go way back, as I'm sure you know."

"Of course. Do you still work with him?"

"We do."

"What about Arthur Sigmund? Does he work for you?"

"Arthur Sigmund? The name doesn't sound familiar."

"He's married to my father's former stepdaughter."

"Oh." Realization rang through his voice. "That Arthur. Yes, I do believe he's still here."

"What does he do for you?"

"If I remember correctly, he works in distribution. Why?"

Distribution? Could he have found out something about Walter Boyce through his job at Baldwin? "I was just curious."

"Mallory . . ." Warning sounded in Stanley's voice.

"Yes?"

"I'm not sure what you're getting at, but be careful when drawing any conclusions."

Her spine stiffened. "What makes you think I'm drawing conclusions?"

"You're your father's child. Thorough. Tough. Always thinking. I have a feeling there's more to these questions than you're letting on."

She said nothing.

"Be careful what you go sticking your nose into," he finally said. "I'd be doing your father a disservice if I didn't tell you that."

"I will. Thank you." She hung up and leaned back on the couch for a moment, letting herself process the conversation.

There wasn't much to process. Stanley didn't think her father was conducting any business in the Caribbean. Mallory didn't know how to find out more information without also raising suspicions. The truth may have died with her dad and Dante.

Someone rapped at the door. Tennyson. "I just finished talking with Agent Turner."

Mallory held her breath. "And?"

"He said that, as far he knows, no one ever suspected that your father was involved with Dante Torres."

Her shoulders slumped with relief. "Good. But what about what Jason saw?"

"It could have been a mistake. This could be some kind of ploy on his end. Only Jason knows that."

She rose and walked toward the wall, leaning against it. "If Agent Turner is correct, then the truth is that my family just happened to be in the wrong place at the wrong time. Dante's men just wanted to rob us because we were wealthy Americans."

"Or you could have been the end goal," Tennyson said quietly.

She froze. "Me?"

He nodded. "That's right. He saw you in town and you reminded him of Alessandra, his wife that he missed very much. He saw the chance to regain something that he lost."

"Then my family died because of me?"

"That's not what I meant. None of this is your fault." His voice softened. "I shouldn't have brought it up."

"No, I'm glad you did. I don't want to run from the truth."

Something flickered in his gaze. "No matter how painful it might be?"

"No matter how painful. It's only after you face the truth that you can find healing."

Tennyson opened his mouth to say something. Mallory sensed it was big. Maybe a revelation about Alessandra? About what had led him to this point in his life?

Before he could say anything, there was another knock at the door. Grant stepped inside and began reviewing the revised schedule.

But Mallory couldn't help but wonder what Tennyson was about to say.

CHAPTER 30

Tennyson excused himself when his phone rang, and he saw it was Leigh Sullivan.

Maybe they'd finally learn the truth about Dante Torres.

"Leigh, thanks for calling. I'm hoping this means you have an update." He stepped into his room for privacy.

"I do, actually. Not only was reexamining the remains approved, but it was given top priority, thanks in part to Admiral Kline."

"Was it Torres?" Tennyson asked, getting right to the point.

"Of course, you realize how difficult it can be to identify someone when their body has been burned so severely."

"I do realize that. But I also know you're one of the best."

"Since you're not one prone to flattery, I'll take that as a compliment." She let out a sigh. "The dental records matched what we know about Dante."

"What about DNA?"

"It was very difficult to obtain Dante's DNA, but there were definite markers in place that matched. The man was the right size, the right weight, the right build, the right age. Plus, you saw his face before he lit that igniter."

Tennyson had seen his face. Even though it had been dark, the man had looked like Torres. Until Grant said he might still be alive, he hadn't thought anything about it. But now Tennyson was reexamining everything he thought he knew.

"Is there any chance it wasn't him?" Tennyson asked.

"Any chance? Of course there's a chance. There was one thing that bothered me, to be honest."

"What was that?"

"Dante supposedly broke his arm when he was a teenager. There was a regrowth mark where his bones grew back together."

"You didn't find that marker on this man?"

"Well, I did. It was even in the right location on his humerus. What was strange was that the break seemed to be more recent."

Tennyson's throat tightened. "Can you be sure the break wasn't older?"

"I have no way to verify it. The fire could have damaged the evidence, after all. But I'd guess the break happened when the man was an adult, not a child. There's one more thing I'd like to do. I want to send the bones for some specialized testing. It will tell us, based on mineral content, among other things, what area of the world this body lived in."

"You can do that?"

"We can. I'll let you know as soon as I hear something."

Even if Torres was alive, the question Tennyson struggled with the most was: Why would Torres come after Mallory now? Why not do it when she was isolated?

What if what Jason said was true? What if Mallory's father was somehow involved?

The questions only made the burden on his shoulders feel heavier.

All he could think was that this was going to get worse before it got better. Tennyson didn't want to believe it was true, but he couldn't shake the feeling.

• • •

Mallory and Tennyson met with Agent Turner and Ethan Stone after lunch. They went through all that had happened up until now and asked her questions about everything imaginable, then set up a workspace at Trident. Wheaton had joined them for part of the meeting, as had Grant, Logan, and Kori.

When the meeting ended, they headed to Hope House. Mallory needed to do something, or she'd go crazy. Tennyson had already talked to Savannah, who ran the shelter, who said it was okay.

Mallory would be meeting the various women there and speaking with them, hearing their stories, trying her best to minister to their broken hearts after they'd survived the unthinkable.

Excitement buzzed through her—more excitement than she'd felt in writing the book or making public appearances. This was what she really wanted to do. To connect. To make it personal. To help individuals instead of trying to reach the population at large.

"You ready for this?" Tennyson asked as he put the car into park.

He'd been mostly silent on the way here, and she appreciated the quiet time. Tennyson possessed a silent strength that she admired and found comfort in.

She nodded. "I am. Thanks for helping to arrange this."

"It was no problem."

Something about the way he said the words made her want to reach over and run her fingers across the smooth lines of his face.

But that would be inappropriate, she reminded herself. There were professional boundaries in place—among other issues. She shoved those thoughts aside. They'd already crossed boundaries they shouldn't. Mallory knew she should regret it, but she didn't.

Was she letting herself down by even being open to the possibility of loving again? Was she abandoning everything she'd vowed to accomplish? Or was there a possibility that two really were better than one—as long as the two were filled with mutual respect for each other?

Once at the shelter, Kori positioned herself outside one door, and Logan the other. Tennyson and Grant went inside with Mallory.

After talking with Savannah for a few minutes, Mallory met with various women, trying to speak hope and encouragement into their lives. One woman stood in the background the whole time, staring at Mallory with hollow eyes. Her arms remained folded across her chest, and she didn't offer as much as a smile.

"She just came in a couple of days ago," Savannah explained. "Women arrive here in all different states. Some are angry. Some are scared. Some are simply thankful. Trina hasn't opened up yet, so we're giving her space."

"You know anything about her?"

Savannah let out a soft sigh. "I know she was rescued just across the US border, in Texas. She was a runaway who grew up in Florida. From what I can gather, she had a hard home-life and decided to meet face-to-face with a man she'd met on the internet. You know the story. He seemed too good to be true. He basically groomed her, took away any self-reliance she had, and forced her into prostitution."

Mallory's gut churned with disgust. "How old is she?"

"Nineteen."

"Do you mind if I try to talk to her?"

"Feel free to try. Just don't be surprised if she won't open up."

Mallory nodded and made her way toward the woman. As she got closer, she noted the woman's blonde hair and blue eyes—not very different from her own. But this woman had dark circles under her eyes. Her frame was nearly skeletal. Her hair was limp.

"My name is Mallory."

The woman stared at her, eyes hollow and without the first sign of emotion.

"I understand you just got here a couple of days ago," Mallory continued.

Again, no response.

"I know the place you've been in," Mallory said. "I've been there. It's raw and gut-wrenching and a nightmare that most people can't even imagine. If they wanted to. And no one wants to. It's easier for them to block it out, isn't it? But I understand."

She'd hoped her words would reach the woman somehow. But there was still nothing.

"I don't know your story, but if you ever want to talk, I'm here to listen," Mallory said. "I believe restoration is more than possible. It can be a reality. Our past doesn't have to define us."

"Everyone, it's time for our group therapy session," Savannah announced. "If you'd all meet me in the study, we can start. Grab the folder with your name on it as you come in."

Mallory took a step back, disappointed that she hadn't reached Trina. She'd tried. That was all she could do. For now, at least. There was still the hope that she might connect with her later.

All the women in the room began filing toward the study in the distance. Mallory gave Trina one last look, waiting for her to say something.

Instead, the woman pushed herself from the wall, staring at Mallory with a hard gaze.

As she passed by Mallory, she leaned in close.

"He's still alive," she whispered.

Then she grabbed her folder and disappeared into the counseling session.

CHAPTER 31

Mallory stood at the edge of the room, her thoughts spinning.

He's still alive.

What was Trina talking about? Torres? Had she seen him? Did she know that for a fact?

"Trina . . . ," she called, her voice cracking with tension and emotion. She needed more information. Not knowing wasn't an option.

The woman kept walking toward the room where the therapy session was being held. She paused at the doorway long enough to shoot Mallory one last look before the door closed.

Mallory couldn't read the look. Was she apologetic? Gloating? Warning?

She couldn't tell.

Mallory's heart pounded in her ears, each beat deafening.

He's still alive.

Trina's haunting whisper dwelled in her mind. Mallory squeezed her eyes shut. Certainly she'd misunderstood. Certainly Trina was talking about someone else.

But as she'd told herself earlier, it was better to know the truth. Earlier, the possibility of Dante being alive was only a theory. But what if Trina had proof? What if she'd seen him with her own eyes?

"Mallory?"

She turned at the sound of Tennyson's voice. He'd been waiting for her against the wall but suddenly appeared beside her. His eyes wrinkled with concern as he observed her.

"Yes?" Her voice didn't sound right. It was too shaky, too thin.

"Are you okay?" He touched her elbow.

Just the feeling of his skin on hers started a new kind of adrenaline rush surging through her.

He's still alive.

She forced herself to focus. To steady her breathing. To come back down to reality. "I need to talk to her again."

Tennyson looked toward the door in the distance. "Who? The woman who just walked past and into the session?"

Mallory nodded.

She'd misunderstood. That was it. It had to be. Trina was talking about someone else.

"You may have to wait until her session is done." Tennyson narrowed his eyes. "Is there anything I need to know? You're not acting okay."

She glanced around, not wanting anyone else to hear what she had to say, then leaned closer. "Trina wouldn't speak to me the entire time I've been here—until just now. She walked past and whispered, 'He's still alive.'"

Tennyson's muscles went rigid. "Torres? Has she seen him?"

"That's what I want to ask her."

Tennyson glanced around the room, tension radiating from him, before he took her arm and led her outside. They didn't speak until they were near the water, at the place where the breeze off the bay would drown their words.

They stood face-to-face, probably too close. Her hair whipped into her eyes, and her heart pounded furiously against her chest.

"Mallory, I talked to my friend Leigh Sullivan today. She's been reexamining Torres's remains."

Her lungs froze. "And?"

"There are things that don't match, Mallory. She's sending the bones for more testing."

She ran a hand over her face, her stomach sinking with dread. "I've been in denial, Tennyson. I haven't wanted to believe it could be true, despite everything I've seen. Everything that's been going on. But what if it is? I'm never going to live without fear again."

He stepped closer and lowered his voice. "I'm not dropping this until we have answers, Mallory."

"Maybe Trina meant that Dante was still alive through his men." She nodded, her theory making more and more sense. "You know? They've taken up his mission, keeping his spirit active and his vision for the future solid."

Tennyson shifted. "What was that vision? Did he ever talk about it with you?"

The intensity of his questions made her feel off-kilter. "There was a lot of Spanish, so I couldn't understand most of what he said. However, there was one man he'd speak with . . . I believed he was an American who spoke broken Spanish."

"You never saw his face?"

She shook her head. "I could hear conversations through the vent. I'd try to make out what I could. I did hear them mention ROZ several times."

"The arms company?"

She nodded. "That's right. The FBI believes that Dante was working with them and purchasing weapons. The investigation has been ongoing. At least, that's what I understood. Once they got the information from me, they haven't exactly kept me in the loop."

"Let's get back to the house. I'm interested in hearing what else Trina has to say. Maybe there's a good explanation for this."

Tennyson took her arm, and they walked at a fast clip toward the house. As they neared the building, she spotted Logan and Kori standing there, guarding the perimeter, just as they'd been instructed.

Savannah met them at the back door. The lines on her forehead clearly showed something was wrong.

"Where's Trina?" She held the screen door open and ushered them inside.

Mallory blanched. "What do you mean? She's in the counseling session. I saw her go in before I stepped outside."

Savannah shook her head. "She left early. Said she had to speak with you, Mallory."

Dread pooled in Mallory's stomach. "I haven't seen Trina since I stepped outside. I just assumed she was still in session."

Savannah's eyes widened. "We need to look for her. Now."

CHAPTER 32

Tension formed between Tennyson's shoulders.

When he and Mallory had been at the shore, he'd been facing the house the whole time. He hadn't seen Trina leave. Part of the backyard area had been blocked by a few trees, so she could have gone in that direction.

Either way, unease sloshed inside him.

Something was wrong.

Tennyson snapped into guard mode. "Which way did she exit?"

Savannah nodded toward the front door. "She stepped out that way."

"How long ago?"

"Probably ten minutes."

Tennyson glanced at Logan and Kori. "Did you see her?"

Logan shook his head. "I was watching you two the whole time."

"Did you see anyone else come and go?"

"No."

"All the other women are still in session," Savannah added.

There was only one person missing.

"Where's Grant?" he asked.

"He stepped into my office to make a phone call," Savannah said.

"Before or after Trina stepped out?"

"A few minutes after."

"Stay here," he told Mallory. "Logan, Kori, stay with her. Don't let her out of your sight. And call the police."

Mallory remained quiet and stepped closer to the wall of the house.

Right now Tennyson needed to find Trina.

The woman who knew Dante was alive.

Where could Trina have gone?

On instinct, he followed the edge of the property out toward the street. A footprint in the dirt seemed to confirm his theory that Trina may have gone this way. He didn't know for sure that it was Trina's, but it very well could be.

The track led across the gravel road toward a field. He followed the trail, stopping at the road leading to Hope House.

Had Trina gone here? To this street?

He stepped into the center of the road and paused.

At the very end of the road, a car sped away.

The only place down here was Hope House.

Someone was leaving.

Most likely with Trina.

• • •

"What do you mean someone left with Trina?" Mallory kept her voice low so she wouldn't frighten any of the residents, even though her undertones clearly sounded panicked.

They stood in foyer, all in a tight circle: Mallory, Tennyson, Logan, Kori, and Savannah.

"The car had too much of a head start," Tennyson said. "There was no way for me to catch up. I couldn't even see the license plate."

Mallory rubbed her temples, determined to think this through. Her gaze met each person's in the circle.

"Who would have picked her up? Who knew she was here even?"

Certainly someone had an answer. Or did they? Who really knew Trina? The woman had seemed like a closed book.

Savannah shrugged, worry written in the fine lines that had appeared across her face. "No one. No one should have known. More than that, Trina didn't have anyone to pick her up. She was literally all alone in the world."

"Something must have happened." Tennyson stepped back from their huddle and glanced around. "Has anyone seen Grant yet? I thought he was making a phone call."

At that moment, Grant stepped out of Savannah's office. A wrinkle formed between his eyes as he stopped in the doorway and noticed everyone staring at him.

"What's going on?" He must have sensed their tension because the usual sparkle left his eyes.

Mallory stepped toward him, finding it suspicious that he'd missed all the commotion. "Where have you been?"

"I was calling Ashley and wanted some privacy. Savannah said I could use her office. Will someone please tell me what's going on?" He sounded more irritated than apologetic.

"One of the residents here is missing," Tennyson said.

"What do you mean missing?" Grant's eyes crinkled at the edges as if he were truly surprised.

"She's gone," Mallory said. "She went outside and disappeared."

"Maybe she left," Grant said. "We all know the women here have been through a lot. It's left many of them unstable, to say the least."

"That's not really a fair assessment." Anger rose in Mallory at the generalization. She thought Grant had understood the plight of these women more than the average person. Had she been wrong about him this whole time? Maybe Tennyson was right when he had an issue with him.

Grant raised a hand. "That's not how I meant it."

"We don't have time to argue about this now. We need to find Trina and figure out what happened." Tennyson turned to Savannah. "Was anything said in your session that could have triggered this?"

Savannah's eyes traveled to the left, to the right, and then back, before she finally shook her head. "No, I don't think so. We'd really only just begun when she slipped out."

"Where are the rest of the women now?" Grant said.

"They're still in the study," Savannah said.

"Is there a way we could question a few?" Tennyson asked.

"You tell me the questions, and I'll ask them," Savannah said. "They're still fragile."

"Of course," Tennyson said. "The only purpose in questioning them is to find Trina. That's it."

Logan lifted his chin. "What do you want me to do?"

"Call Agent Turner. Let him know what's going on."

He nodded and pulled out his phone as he stepped away.

"Kori, stay with Mallory," Tennyson continued.

Mallory shook her head. "I'm helping."

"I'm not sure that's a great idea."

She could handle this, and she wasn't going to let anyone tell her any different. "Of course it is. If something happened to upset her, I want to know what. It could have been me, for all I know. I could have upset her. I was the last person who spoke with her."

He stared at her a moment before nodding. "Okay then."

Savannah spent the next hour questioning the women, but no one had seen anything. All their stories matched: one minute, everyone was sitting in the session. The next minute, Trina excused herself and fled the building.

So how had the car known when to pull up? How had Trina known it was here or that it was time to leave?

The pieces weren't fitting together, Mallory realized. They were missing something . . .

Mallory stood in the middle of the study, where the women had been meeting when Trina ran out. Had something in here triggered the reaction? If so, what could it be? It was an old study, full of chairs . . . the same room Mallory had spoken in at the beginning of her tour.

She sensed someone behind her and turned. Tennyson. Her pulse skyrocketed before coming back down to a normal level. Why did it always do that when Tennyson was around?

She rubbed her throat, hoping Tennyson didn't see her affection for him in her gaze. "Anything?"

He joined her. "No, nothing. It's strange."

Mallory fought back a sigh. "I agree that it's strange. It would be one thing if Trina got up and walked away alone. But the fact that there was a car . . . that's what bothers me. It was like she planned it. Or someone planned it."

"I agree."

Mallory wandered down the row of seats and paused. Where had Trina been sitting?

She noticed a lone folder on one of the chairs. Each woman had entered the room with one of those folders. Could this one have been Trina's?

Her heart stammered as she opened it up. On top was a note that read:

*MEET ME OUTSIDE OR I'LL GUN DOWN EVERYONE
IN THE HOUSE.*

CHAPTER 33

Mallory sank into the seat, trying to process what she'd just read. "It's Nameless."

Tennyson sat down hard beside her, peering at the note in the folder. "Why would you say that?"

"It's written in all caps just like he sends my e-mails." A sick feeling gurgled in her stomach.

"That could be a coincidence."

A bigger question hammered at her thoughts. She turned toward Tennyson, not liking any of the conclusions she drew. "How did that note get there, Tennyson? Was Nameless in the house? How would he have gotten here?"

He frowned. "We need to talk to Savannah. Maybe she can help fill in some of the gaps."

At that moment, Savannah appeared at the door, and Tennyson waved her over.

"What's wrong? You found something, didn't you?" Savannah asked.

Tennyson showed her the note.

As she read the words, her face paled. "Where . . . ? How . . . ?"

"That's what I was hoping you could tell us," Tennyson said. "When were these folders put together?"

Savannah's face grew paler by the moment. "I put them together last night and laid them out on the table this morning."

"So someone put this note in here between last night and the meeting," Tennyson said.

"I suppose . . . but no one has come and gone. It's just been us. And who knew Trina was here? No one. It doesn't make sense." Savannah's hand went over her mouth.

"No one else has come and gone?" Tennyson clarified.

Savannah shook her head. "No one except you all."

Mallory didn't like the sound of that. But no one on her team would do this. Somehow, that note had gotten here another way. It didn't make sense.

"Do you have any type of video surveillance?" Tennyson continued.

Savannah's eyes lit up. "We do. Kade and Jack insisted that it was a good idea. As usual, they were right."

"Can I see it?"

"Of course. Follow me."

They all gathered around a computer in Savannah's office. Tennyson scrolled through the footage there. But everything from today was just static. It was gone. Erased.

"It's almost like someone used some kind of jammer." Tennyson leaned back in the chair, his face all tight lines. "All the video footage from last night and today has been erased."

"Do any of the women have access to this computer?" Mallory asked.

Savannah shook her head. "No, I keep this door locked at all times."

"I think we should check the browsing history. Just to be safe," Mallory said quietly.

"Of course."

As Tennyson pulled up the internet, Mallory took a deep breath. She could do this. She could find answers. She had to do something.

Because the conclusions she'd started to draw for herself were overwhelming, made her feel like she was drowning.

Tennyson hit the history drop-down list. Most of the websites that popped up seemed common: the bank, search engines, e-mail, a shopping site.

Had Trina sneaked in here and alerted someone to where she was staying? Why would she do that?

Mallory knew that some women came to depend on their pimps, began to feel like they were family. These women began to believe the lies that were fed to them day after day about how they couldn't survive without their pimps, without their captors.

Mallory knew better. But she also knew what it was like to be desperate. Changes were so hard to make. Sometimes it was easier to stay in a bad situation than it was to face the unknown.

There was nothing here, she realized. If Trina really had come in here and tried to make contact with someone, Mallory hadn't seen any evidence of it.

What was going on?

* * *

Despite everything that had happened, they'd had no choice but to head back to the Trident headquarters a couple of hours later. A visit that was supposed to bring peace to Mallory had only served to do the opposite.

Grant knocked on Tennyson's door and cracked it open after Tennyson hollered for him to come in.

"I've got to go run a quick errand," Grant said, sticking his head inside. "You'll keep an eye on Mallory?"

"Of course," Tennyson said.

Where could Grant be going at a time like this? Everyone was tightly wound. Mallory was worried out of her mind.

And he was doing errands?

All Grant's whispered phone conversations nagged at Tennyson. Plus, there was that cloak-and-dagger visit to the restaurant in Atlanta. Had Grant put that note in Trina's folder when they arrived?

Grant was hiding something. Tennyson couldn't deny it any longer.

As Grant disappeared, Tennyson stood and grabbed his car keys. If he was going to do this, he didn't have much time.

He motioned to Logan as he headed down the hallway.

"What's going on?" Logan's gaze flickered with curiosity.

"I need you to keep an eye on Mallory. I have to run somewhere."

His piercing eyes studied Tennyson as he said, "Of course."

Tennyson took another step away, knowing that time was of the essence right now. "Don't let her out of your sight."

Tennyson peered out one of the windows near the stairway in time to see Grant slip into his car. As soon as he took off down the road, Tennyson rushed outside to his own car. He got behind the wheel and followed Grant from a far distance.

He shadowed him onto the main highway, past the miles of crops and fields that had just been planted. Finally, Grant pulled off the road in the neighboring town of Cape Charles. He found a parking space along the quaint main street of the downtown area.

Tennyson slowed so he wouldn't be spotted.

He found a dark parking lot on the opposite side of the street and pulled into it. For now, he had an unobstructed view of Grant.

Grant stepped from his vehicle, looked around, and then hurried to the sidewalk.

He walked several feet before stopping near a man wearing an overcoat and sunglasses. The two leaned together and whispered.

What was this about? Was Grant selling information on Mallory? Giving away the secret of her location?

The man reached into his pocket and handed something to Grant.

Wasting no time, Tennyson climbed from his car and strode toward Grant's vehicle. He leaned against the driver's side door, waiting for

Grant to return. There was no way he was walking away from this without an explanation.

Grant started back down the sidewalk, his steps brisk.

Until he looked up and saw Tennyson standing there.

His eyes widened. He slowed before stopping in front of Tennyson.

Guilt stained his eyes. He knew he'd been caught.

"I can explain," Grant said, running a hand over his face.

"Then start talking."

CHAPTER 34

"It's not what it looks like." Grant raked a hand through his hair.

"All of your secret phone calls and excuses for doing errands that you're not really doing—it looks suspicious, especially in light of everything that's happened recently."

"I know. Believe me, I know." He let out a long sigh. "I've been trying to get my financial affairs in order."

Tennyson crossed his arms. "Why?"

He lowered his gaze. "My daughter . . . she's wonderful. A delightful child. So full of life and curiosity. But she has a rare genetic disorder. There's not even a name for it yet. I found a treatment, but insurance doesn't cover it because it's still considered experimental."

That wasn't what Tennyson had expected to hear. "I've always taken you as someone who's well paid. You certainly act like it."

"I am well paid. But my bills suck up all of my income. Bigger paychecks mean bigger houses and a better car. That equals less cash flow."

"Okay . . ." That made sense, he supposed, but it still didn't explain everything.

"So I've been trying to sell my stocks, and cash out some savings. I've even put my home on the market."

"How much is this treatment?"

Grant raised his eyebrows. "It's a lot. Two hundred thousand minimum. And that's only if nothing goes wrong."

"That's a lot of money. Why are you being so secretive about it?"

"I like to keep my personal life private. Mallory has enough on her mind as it is. She doesn't need to be bothered with this."

"People desperate for money can do desperate things."

Grant frowned. "I am doing desperate things—but they're desperate things that are within my means. If this doesn't work, a friend has offered to help us with fund-raising."

Tennyson stared him down another moment, trying to ascertain the truth in his words. Was he telling the truth? Or was he a great liar?

"Please, Tennyson. I know the two of us don't see eye to eye, but it's only because we're both trying to look out for Mallory's best interests."

He wasn't letting him off the hook that easily. "Who was that man you were just meeting?"

"He's interested in purchasing one of my cars. He e-mailed me about it this morning."

"You don't even have your car with you."

"He purchased it sight unseen." Grant stepped closer. "Tennyson, Ashley—my daughter—is everything to me. I need this job with Mallory—yes, that's true. But I also care about Mallory, and I care about the cause she's promoting."

Something about the look in Grant's eyes sold him on his story. Maybe he didn't always agree with the man or approve of his methods, but right now, he seemed sincere.

Tennyson nodded and stepped away from the car. "I'll keep this quiet. For now."

* * *

Mallory anxiously waited for Tennyson and Grant to return.

Where had they gone? Was something wrong?

She'd lit a few candles. It probably seemed strange, but she always carried a few with her in her suitcase. Her therapist said they would help her relax and unwind, offering a tangible visual to focus on. Right now, she was glad she'd listened to his advice, especially as she watched the lightning in the distance.

She tried to keep herself occupied. She read her Bible. She prayed for Trina. She tried to cast her cares on the Lord.

As she said amen, her phone rang.

It was Philip, Jason's best friend. She'd left a message for him an hour earlier.

"Hi, Philip. Thank you for calling me back."

"It's been a long time," he said. "To be honest, I really wasn't expecting to hear from you."

Philip sounded older now, and somehow wiser. Mallory had never particularly liked him. He'd mostly enjoyed getting drunk and finding his flavor-of-the-month to date and showcase. But if anyone knew Jason, it was Philip.

"I have a question for you," she started, rehashing the spiel she'd developed in her mind.

"Shoot."

"It's about Jason."

"You know the two of us don't talk anymore, right?"

"I wasn't aware of that."

"We haven't been friends for a couple of years now. Honestly, when you disappeared, it was a huge wake-up call. Not just for me, but for other people in our circle. We grew up after that, you know? I think we were all embarrassed, too. Didn't know what to say to you. So we didn't say anything. That's worse, isn't it?"

That was the least of her worries at the moment. "Don't worry about it, Philip. But you could do me a favor and answer a question for me. I can't go into details, but I'm trying to find out some information about Jasmine."

"Who's Jasmine?"

"Jasmine Reynolds, the girl that Jason was with on the night I was abducted."

Silence stretched. "That Jasmine."

Curiosity flickered inside her at his tone. "Why do you say it like that?"

"You want the truth?"

"Of course."

"With Jasmine, it wasn't what you think it was."

An ache darted through her heart. "What do you mean?"

"Jason paid to be with a girl that night. Maybe her name really was Jasmine. No one really knows."

CHAPTER 35

Mallory's mind reeled. Did she just hear Philip correctly? Jasmine wasn't simply a girl Jason had picked up that night? That was . . . reprehensible, to say the least.

"Are you sure, Philip?"

"I'm more than sure. Mallory, you know what kind of connections Jason has. His family owns a tech business. He used his resources—and the dark web—to help buy and sell women for the past four years. Maybe longer."

Nausea pooled in her gut. Would Jason really be that vile? She'd known he was unscrupulous, but . . . this?

Mallory felt like she would be sick. All the candles in the room didn't help her now.

She thanked Philip and hung up.

Her heart catapulted into her throat when she heard a knock at the door.

"Come in," she called, still gripping her phone.

Tennyson stepped inside, his eyes locking on her. "Hey."

She pushed her hair behind her ear, still processing the conversation she'd just had with Philip. "You're back. Everything okay?"

He closed the door and walked slowly toward her. "Yeah, it's fine. Do you have a minute?"

"Of course." She studied his somber expression and could only guess he had more bad news. It just kept rolling in, didn't it? "No hints as to what you were doing?"

He sat beside her and frowned. "Talk to Grant. He should be the one to tell you."

"Now I'm concerned. Is Grant involved with this?"

"No, it's not about all of this. Just talk to him."

She nodded slowly, fighting the urge to fidget. "Okay, I will."

Tennyson's hand went to her knee, causing warmth to explode in her. Such a simple act caused such a strong reaction in her.

"How are you holding up?" he asked. "There's been a lot to absorb lately."

"Here's a new one: Jason has apparently been buying and selling women on the dark web. He's a part of this whole mess. In fact, Jasmine wasn't even a one-night stand. Jason paid for her."

Tennyson closed his eyes, his features scrunching with restraint. "Oh, Mallory. I'm so sorry. A real man would never do that. You know that, right?"

She nodded, still feeling dumbstruck. "Yeah, I do. I just can't believe it."

"So Jasmine . . ."

"Probably wasn't her real name even. I'll never find her or be able to ask questions about what she saw that night."

"The FBI has a whole team on this now. With Leigh's unanswered questions about the body, they felt it warranted to look into things more."

"At least that's good news."

His gaze turned away from her and scanned the room. "Candles?"

"I thought it might storm." She suddenly realized how it might look and jumped to her feet. "You know what? I'll blow them out. I think the storm might miss us . . ."

Before she reached the last one, she felt Tennyson touching her arm.

"Mallory?"

"Yes?" She turned toward him.

Silence stretched between them as they stood in front of each other. He was close. Close enough that she could feel his body heat. Smell his cologne. Feel the energy crackle between them.

His fingers laced with hers, palm to palm.

Just then, the lights flickered and went out. Thunder rumbled. Darkness surrounded them, except for the glow of one lone candle.

"I guess you spoke too soon," Tennyson said. "The storm is overhead."

"I don't feel afraid with you, Tennyson," she whispered, her throat aching as the words emerged. It was the first time she'd voiced the thought aloud. That she'd dared to admit to Tennyson that he was different from every other guy she'd met.

His eyes widened, softened, warmed. "You don't?"

Her heart hit her rib cage so hard that Mallory was sure Tennyson could feel it. She'd been fighting these feelings for so long . . . and she was tired of it. Tennyson wasn't like every other guy. He wouldn't make her feel small so that he could feel more important.

"No, I don't. In fact, no one's ever made me feel so safe before."

"Good," he murmured.

He let go of one of her hands, and with his thumb, he brushed her cheek. She closed her eyes and leaned into his touch.

Her hand reached around his neck.

She expected to feel fear, stark and gripping. But she didn't.

She only felt desire and tenderness.

Tennyson tugged her closer before hesitating. "Are you sure?"

"Yes." She meant it.

He leaned closer until his lips brushed hers. Tingles exploded up and down her spine at his nearness. At his touch. At the realization that she could love again.

When she didn't pull back, Tennyson drew her closer. Their kiss deepened. He wrapped his arms around her waist, and her hands explored the ripple of his back. The lines of his neck. The firmness of his jaw. Breathless, they both stepped back. His hands cupped her face. Her hands fisted his shirt. All she felt was heartbeat. Desire. Swollen lips.

"I didn't know I could feel this happy," she whispered.

He shifted, like something was wrong.

"Tennyson?"

He squeezed the skin between his eyes and turned away.

"Tennyson?" she repeated, a hole gnawing at her gut, and all her warm feelings quickly cooling.

"Mallory, there's something I need to tell you."

She stepped back. "What's that?"

He took her hand and walked her over to the couch. "Let's sit down. Please."

They sat beside each other, knees touching, fingers interlaced. Lightning flashed and thunder continued to crash, echoing across the water in the distance.

Something wasn't right with Tennyson. He looked . . . nervous. And he never looked nervous.

"This isn't easy for me, Mallory." He rubbed his lips together, apology staining his eyes.

"What is it, Tennyson?" Part of her wanted to withdraw her hand, but she refused. She was willing to give love a chance. She never thought she'd be able to say that. That meant resisting her normal impulse to pull away when uncomfortable.

She didn't have to pull away, though. Tennyson released her hand and ran his fingers down his face. He closed his eyes, and Mallory could tell that whatever was on his mind was heavy and burdensome.

What could it be? Did he know something that she didn't?

"That night you were rescued from Dante?"

"The night you rescued me," she clarified.

He nodded stiffly. "We'd had our eye on his compound for a while. Stone was giving us intel from the inside."

"Okay . . ." Mallory had no idea where this was going.

"We knew about three months earlier that Torres had a woman in captivity."

The color left her face, but she said nothing. Only listened. Hoped the conclusions she was drawing were wrong.

"We didn't know the details," Tennyson continued. "We assumed maybe he had a concubine or a professional escort. We had to make a choice, though."

Her throat tightened. "What choice was that?"

"If we went in to rescue the woman, it might blow our chances of capturing Torres."

Her heart pounded in her ears. She didn't want to believe what she was hearing. This had to be a misunderstanding . . . right?

"All I could think about was Torres. Vengeance. Making him pay the price he deserved. I'd lived it for the year before that."

"So you chose to let me remain a human slave because I wasn't as important as your operation?" The words felt like acid as they left her lips.

"It wasn't like that, Mallory—"

"Then what was it like? I wasn't important because I was most likely just some girl that had been sold as a slave? My life wasn't important? Isn't every life important?"

"Every life is important, Mallory. We didn't know it was you."

"But what if it wasn't me? What if it was some poor girl form India who'd been sold into human trafficking by her family so they could put food on the table? Would she still be important?"

"Of course she would."

"I'm not sure I believe you." She crossed her arms. "I think I was wrong about you, Tennyson. I don't want to believe it. But . . . I just don't know."

He stood, somberness emanating from him. "Sometimes you make the best choice possible knowing what you know. It's all you can do. Sometimes it's the wrong call, and you have to live with those regrets for the rest of your life."

"Yeah, I guess you do." Mallory looked away.

"I hope you can forgive me."

"I'm not sure, Tennyson. I'm honestly not sure. I need you to leave now."

She felt him watching her. Finally, she heard his footsteps. The door opened and closed.

He was gone.

And so was any hope that Mallory would ever love again.

CHAPTER 36

Tennyson got back to his room and raked a hand through his hair. That had been a disaster.

One minute, he'd been swept up in the moment, relishing and enjoying his closeness to Mallory. That kiss . . . it was one he'd never forget. He never wanted to forget.

The next minute, reality had set in. He'd known he had to tell Mallory the truth. He should have done it sooner, but he just couldn't bring himself to utter the words. To bring his shame to light. To admit the wretched decision he'd made.

He slipped into the bathroom and splashed some cold water on his face.

He'd just ruined one of the best things to ever happen to him. Was it even possible to make this right?

Someone knocked at his door. His heart raced. Was it Mallory? Had she forgiven him?

He knew he was hoping for too much, yet adrenaline still surged through him.

He opened the door and saw Kori.

"Hey, I wanted to go over a few things with you." She stepped inside but paused when she saw the look on his face. "You look terrible."

"Thanks." He walked toward his couch.

"You want to talk?" She followed behind him.

"There's not much to talk about."

"This is about Mallory, isn't it?"

He didn't say anything, just sat down and stared into the distance. She gently lowered herself across from him. "Did you tell her?"

He nodded. Kori knew the truth. Her husband had been on Tennyson's SEAL team. He'd survived the battlefield, only to die of a heart attack a year ago.

"I take it she didn't receive the information well?"

"You could say that." Their conversation replayed in his mind.

"It's a lot to take in." She let out a long breath. "I have to say, though, that saving Mallory early would have sacrificed the safety of thousands, maybe even millions, for the well-being of one. She'll eventually see that."

"What if she doesn't?"

"If she doesn't, then she's not the one for you, is she? But she needs time. Everyone knows it was a hard call to make, Tennyson."

"Thanks for the talk, Kori."

"Anytime, Ten Man."

She stood.

"You wanted to tell me something?"

"I just wanted to talk about our plan of action. It can wait until tomorrow."

When she left, Tennyson knew he needed to distract himself with work. The only way to possibly make this right was to ensure that Torres never got his hands on Mallory again.

Tennyson grabbed his computer and got online. Jason's family owned a tech business, while Mallory's family had been in the appliance field. Was there any connection between the companies?

He pulled up the website for Jason's family's business. Tech could cover so many areas. After scrolling through the pages, he determined that the business was mostly involved with online support for companies.

Tennyson leaned back. Online support? Did Baldwin Appliances use them?

He did another quick search but came up with nothing. Maybe Mallory would know. There could be no connection there at all. But it was worth looking into.

At that moment, an e-mail pinged on his cell phone. He clicked on it, his apprehension growing with every second. Certainly he'd read that subject wrong.

He could only hope.

But when the e-mail came up, it proved he hadn't. The note was from a reporter, wanting a quote from him on Mallory. Did he believe her father had ties with Dante Torres?

Jason had gone to the press with that story after all. How could he?

Anger burned inside him. Was there anyone out there willing to do the right thing? It didn't seem like it.

Maybe Tennyson should lump himself in the same category.

CHAPTER 37

Mallory couldn't sleep. All she could think about was Tennyson's revelation.

How could he? She understood the struggle of choosing the greater good. But had he even looked for another alternative? Or had he dismissed her as unimportant, as just another one of Dante's girls?

Lord, please help me. I'm a mess. I'm broken. But I'm yours. Let me rest in that alone.

She turned over in bed and fluffed her pillow, trying to let sleep find her. But her mind was going in too many directions. It didn't help that the lightning outside acted as a strobe light, followed by angry rumbles of thunder.

She pressed her head into the pillow, trying to tune it all out. She'd already ruminated enough about her kiss with Tennyson. Instead, she turned her thoughts to everything that had happened. The sooner she wrapped up her current situation, the sooner she could get away from Tennyson.

What had happened to Trina? Was she okay right now?

And poor Gabriella. What had her final moments been like?

And what about Jason? She'd always known he was selfish, but she never thought he would take it so far as to threaten her. Was he just trying to extend his fifteen minutes of fame?

Finally, Mallory threw the sheets off and sat up in bed. Maybe a shower would make her feel better, cleaner. That had always worked in the past. The warm water could loosen her tight muscles and hopefully lull her to sleep.

She let the water flow over her and wash away her worries. In theory, at least.

In reality, her thoughts went back to Tennyson over and over again. She'd really thought there could be something between them—something beautiful.

Their kiss had taken her breath away. But it was more than the physical. They connected emotionally and spiritually, surpassing what she could have ever imagined in a relationship.

Yet she'd been so, so wrong about him.

Lord, please give me wisdom. Discernment. I feel like I'm drowning again. I don't know what to do, but I can't handle everything falling apart again. I need you.

As the water continued to pound her skin, the bathroom suddenly went dark.

Her heart stuttered in her chest.

What was going on?

She cut the water and grabbed a towel from the rack beside the shower stall. Quickly, she wrapped it around herself, listening for any hint of what was going on.

Silence answered back.

· · ·

Tennyson tried to sleep, but he couldn't. He had too much weighing on his mind. Too much that needed to be done. Too much that he hadn't figured out yet.

As he lay there in the silence, he heard the water come on in the adjoining bathroom.

Was Mallory taking a shower? At this hour?

He couldn't even let his thoughts go there.

Finally, he threw the covers off and stood. He paced over to the window, trying to get a glimpse of the storm. As he peered out, a movement caught his eye.

He squinted. Was someone outside? He stepped into the shadows and watched another moment.

Something moved again. Against the outside wall of the building. Close to the back exit.

Someone was definitely out there. Not only out there, but trying to get inside.

Tennyson grabbed his gun and stuffed it into his waistband. He knocked at Mallory's door, but there was no answer. Shower, he reminded himself, quickly trying to turn his thoughts from that picture.

Instead, he checked the door and made sure it was locked. It was. He'd make sure Kori kept an eye on the room while he checked things out. She was already on guard in the hallway.

"Someone's outside," he told her.

"Could it be one of the Trident guys?" Kori asked.

"It shouldn't be, but I need to double-check."

Tennyson quietly crept down the stairs, listening for a sign of anything suspicious. He drew his gun, watching for the unexpected.

Just as he cleared the landing, the soft lights illuminating the area blinked before going off.

Was that the storm? Or the intruder?

Tennyson didn't know, but he didn't like either option.

He remained close to the wall. Everything felt still around him. Too still. Too calm.

Was that a creak?

It almost sounded like it.

He took another step into the stairwell entry, hoping he'd see Wheaton or one of his men and realize this was nothing more than someone who'd locked themselves out.

He saw nothing.

Just then, the door flapped open. The wind from the storm had caught it.

As he looked down at the wooden floor, he spotted wet footprints leading inside.

Someone was here.

Tension mounted across his shoulders as he followed the footprints toward the other end of the building. He pushed past the construction plastic covering the doorway.

The sheets rustled behind him as another gust of wind swept inside.

A creak sounded. Behind him this time.

Just as he turned, something rammed into his head.

And everything went black.

• • •

Mallory quickly dried off with a fluffy white towel and pulled her pajamas on. She needed to get to the nightstand. She was sure she'd seen a flashlight there. Darkness caused panic to crash into her, caused worst-case scenarios to rush to the surface of her mind. Scenarios involving Dante finding her. Claiming her again.

Her limbs trembled uncontrollably at the thought.

It's just the storm. The electric lines out here are probably less secure. This is nothing.

She scrambled from the bathroom toward her bed. Her heart pounded in her ears as she reached her bedside table and opened the drawer. The flashlight . . . where was it?

Lightning brightened the room, causing another wave of panic in her.

There's nothing ominous about a thunderstorm.

Still, why hadn't Tennyson come over? Was he sleeping through this? Did he even know what was going on? Tennyson seemed like the type who always knew what was going on.

Something was wrong, she realized.

He should be here.

The power should be on.

She should be able to find the flashlight.

Her lungs tightened until she could hardly breathe. Slowly, she crept along the wall toward the door leading to the hallway. Would she be safer there? She didn't know. All she really wanted to do was curl up in bed and wait for the power to come back on.

Or run over to Tennyson's room. To feel his arms around her. To hear his words of comfort and reassurance.

He betrayed you, Mallory. Just like every other guy. Get that through your thick skull.

She was better off here. Alone. Depending on no one. Keeping her fear silent.

As she reached the door, she froze. Out there, she'd be exposed. In the open. She should just stay here, in the safety of her room.

If only she could see something. Anything! She gave up on the idea of going into the hallway. Instead, she darted back toward her bed and dove under the covers. She hated the fact that she felt like a little girl. But she did. She couldn't deny it.

Dear Lord, be with me now. Please.

Lightning flashed outside again. Electric purple light filled the room.

It illuminated the space just long enough for her to see. For the room to come into view.

When it did, she screamed.

She wasn't alone. Someone stood right by the closet.

CHAPTER 38

"Jason?" Her voice caught. "What are you doing here?" She jumped from the bed in alarm.

He stood only a few feet away, a gun in his hands. The weapon wasn't pointed at her. Not yet.

Another flash of lightning revealed a crazed look in his eyes.

But it was more than what she saw that frightened her. It was what she could feel in the air: desperation. It radiated from Jason with enough force it was nearly visible.

He stepped closer, his breathing shallow and his gaze twitchy. "Why couldn't you just do what I asked?"

"What do you mean?" She backed up, her mind racing. How was she going to get out of this situation alive?

"I don't want to do this." He swung his head back and forth, sweat glistening across his skin. Lightning—now coming at regular intervals—illuminated what the darkness concealed. Maybe Mallory didn't want to see. The truth was a scary beast at times.

"You don't want to do what?" Mallory struggled to understand, to figure out a way out of this situation. She scooted back until she hit the wall.

A dead end. Nowhere to go. Trapped.

Her fears began whispering in her ear.

No, all wasn't lost. Tennyson. He was always two steps ahead of everyone else. Unless . . . what if Jason had hurt him? That would explain why he hadn't come over yet.

Despite his revelation, the thought of him being injured—or worse—caused a small gasp to catch in her throat.

Jason wasn't in his right mind. Mallory was certain of it. And somehow, she knew that she only had herself to depend on right now.

"They're going to expose me, Mallory." Jason's voice cracked with uncertainty, each word sounding increasingly tense and unhinged.

"Who? Who's going to expose you?" Her mind rushed through the possibilities, stopping only at the media. The media could expose him. Ruin him. His family's reputation.

He chuckled a little too hard, a little too crazily. "Inferno, of course."

Her heart thudded in her ears. Her fingers clawed at the wall behind her. Sweat trickled down her forehead. "You're involved with Inferno?"

Thunder rumbled overhead, which made her muscles tense even more. The direness of the situation echoed in her mind. One squeeze of his finger and she'd be dead.

Jason shook his head, rubbed the skin between his eyes, chuckled again. All like a neurotic man might do. "Inferno? No, I'm not. I wasn't. I didn't want to be."

"What are you saying, Jason?" She glanced around, looking for anything she could defend herself with. All she saw was her alarm clock. Her suitcase. A journal.

She had nothing.

She felt powerless. And she hated feeling powerless. Absolutely hated it.

Never again, Mallory. Never again. Isn't that what you told yourself?

She tried to remember the defense moves Tennyson had taught her.

"I'm saying that sometimes things are out of my control." His words came out faster, harder. "This is one of those moments. I never wanted it to come to this. Can't you see that?"

She pushed herself back, farther into the wall. Wished she could disappear there. Wished she wasn't such a failure when it came to choosing men.

"You can change the course of your story, you know." Mallory's voice came out shaky. But her only choice right now was to try to convince him that this was a bad idea.

Jason stepped closer, raising the gun in his hands. "But I can't. They're going to ruin me."

"Hurting me will catch up with you eventually, Jason."

He stared at her a moment before shaking his head. "No, it won't. They'll think you couldn't handle the pressure. That you went off the grid. No one could blame you after everything you've been through. After what Dante did to you. It's chipped away at your personhood."

She refused to let his words get to her. "What is Inferno making you do?"

Keep him talking, Mallory. As long as he's talking, he's not hurting you.

"If I don't bring you with me, they're going to let the world know who I really am."

"Who are you?" She scooted down the wall, inching closer to the door, to escape.

"I'm a loser, Mallory. You don't know what I've done." He frowned. No, that wasn't a frown. It was a cry, followed by a low moan.

"Tell me, Jason. You'll feel better if you get it off your chest." Even though she already knew.

"That night you were abducted?" Sweat glistened on his upper lip.

"Yes?" Her lungs squeezed as she waited.

"I knew what happened. I knew who'd taken you."

Her throat burned as dark emotions clawed their way to the surface. "What do you mean?"

"I was with a girl I paid for. Not a girlfriend. Inferno knew this. They told me if I said anything, that they'd tell the world that I liked to buy my women."

Nausea roiled in her again, followed by the smack of betrayal. "So you stayed quiet? You traded my life for your reputation."

He nodded too quickly, too frantically. "It was complicated. Survival in its rawest form."

"You let me be kept as a slave for a year so you could take over your father's company?" Tears sprang to her eyes.

"I told you I was a bad person."

"I trusted you, Jason." Mallory pulled herself together. She had to convince him that he was above all this. She couldn't take him out herself, nor could she defend herself against his gun. She crept closer to the door.

"I'm not very trustworthy. You need to come with me, Mallory."

"You're going to have to take me dead. Because I'm never going back. Not willingly."

She continued to inch closer to the exit.

"I don't think you understand." His hand trembled, along with his voice. "You have to come back with me. They're going to kill me."

"No, you're going to have to kill me. It's not going to happen."

His free hand balled into a tight fist. "Why do you have to be so difficult, Mallory? You've always been so difficult. Nothing's ever easy with you."

"Yet you're the one holding the gun and making demands of me. Just shoot me, Jason. You're not going to take me alive."

"Maybe this will give you incentive: I've got Tennyson."

•   •   •

Tennyson pulled his eyes open. His head throbbed with such intensity that it took him a moment to remember what had happened.

Then it hit him. The storm. The electricity going out. The intruder.

He reached for his gun, but it was gone.

Whoever had knocked him out had also taken his weapon.

He hopped to his feet, a little too quickly. His head swam.

He didn't have time to worry about how he felt. He had to get to Mallory. Now.

Each step made his head pound harder. He pulled out his phone and called Logan. He didn't answer.

The lights were still out as he rushed up the stairs. Kori lay crumpled on the floor.

He put his fingers to her neck.

She was still alive. Her heart still beat strong. She'd be okay.

He paused by Mallory's door.

As he reached for the door handle, he heard voices inside. Two voices.

One was a male's. But it wasn't Logan's. If he had to guess, it was . . . Jason's.

His heart surged with concern. He crept into his room, grabbed his extra gun, and then slipped through the connecting door into the bathroom. This would be the best way to take Jason by surprise.

He hoped.

Tennyson could hear Jason talking as he crept from the bathroom into Mallory's room. Jason's back was toward him, and as long as Tennyson remained quiet, he should be able to make this work.

He remained in the shadows. His head pounded fiercely. Jason had knocked him out with something big and heavy. He probably had a concussion, but he'd think about that later.

At the moment, the only thing he could think about was Mallory. She'd meant it when she said she'd rather die than go back to being a slave. He'd heard the truth in her voice, and he didn't want her to do anything stupid as a result.

That meant he had to take down Jason.

He had to be careful. The gun was wobbly in Jason's hands. All he had to do was pull that trigger, and Mallory would go down. Tennyson couldn't let that happen.

· · ·

Jason's announcement made Mallory's blood freeze.

Tennyson. What had he done to him?

She spotted movement behind Jason.

Tennyson. Was that Tennyson? *He is alive.*

He shook his head, and Mallory looked away, not wanting to give away his presence.

He was planning his attack. But timing was everything. Mallory knew that.

"You're not a killer, Jason. I know you better than that."

"You don't know me." His voice cracked with every other word. "I don't want to hurt you, Mallory."

"Then don't."

Jason raised his gun. "I'm sorry."

Tennyson lunged from the darkness, tackling Jason. The two wrestled on the floor.

In the darkness, it was hard to see who was who. All Mallory could tell was that one man was on top of the other. Punches were being thrown. Grunts filled the air.

Lightning again lit the room, and Mallory spotted Tennyson. He'd pinned Jason to the floor. The gun had flown out of Jason's hand, but it was still within reach.

As she started to lunge for it, Jason got a second wind. He threw Tennyson off. Before Tennyson could right himself, Jason grabbed the gun.

He was going to shoot Tennyson.

Mallory couldn't let that happen.

Just as Jason raised the gun, she catapulted herself across the room. She threw herself over Tennyson.

"Mallory, no!" Tennyson shouted.

As she did, the weapon discharged. Acidic smoke filled the air.

Tennyson? Was Tennyson okay?

Before she had a chance to ask him, she felt something warm prick her arm.

She looked down.

Blood.

She'd been shot.

That was the last thing she remembered.

CHAPTER 39

When Mallory regained consciousness, she was surrounded by white. A hospital, she realized. She was in the hospital.

As the room came into focus, she spotted Grant. He hurried from his chair toward her.

At once, she remembered—not her rescue, not the events that had gotten her here—but she remembered her kiss with Tennyson. The sweetness of it. How her insides had swelled with joy and elation. How all her fears about intimacy had resolved for a moment.

Then she remembered his revelation. How her fears had come back with a vengeance. How her swelling heart had quickly deflated.

How was he doing? Was he okay?

"Tennyson . . ." Her voice sounded dry and raspy.

Grant leaned over her, taking her hand in his own. "He's okay. He wanted to be here, but he's wrapping up some loose ends about Jason."

She let out her breath. "Good. And Logan? Kori?"

"Logan's standing outside the door, keeping guard for us. Kori is taking second shift. Jason knocked her out, but she's okay."

The gunshot flashed back to her. Had Jason been killed? She couldn't recall what happened after she'd been shot. "So Jason is alive, as well?"

Grant nodded. "He's okay also. He's with the police right now."

Mallory tried to sit up. She expected pain, but there was surprisingly little. Still, everything felt thick and gel-like around her. "How long have I been here? Why . . . ?"

"You've been here about twenty-four hours. You're in Norfolk."

She glanced down, taking a self-inventory. There was a bandage on her arm. An IV in her wrist. Various monitors, one on her finger, another on her chest. Those things didn't explain how she'd lost a complete day.

"I don't understand," she said.

The lines on Grant's face deepened. "The doctor believes your mind shut down because of the trauma of the situation."

She swallowed hard, not liking how that sounded. So much for being strong. "I see. Then I'm okay otherwise?"

"The bullet grazed your arm. You just have a few stitches." Grant leaned closer, his gaze full of fatherly concern. "I'm sorry, Mallory. I know this is upsetting to you."

"That's an understatement. But thank you."

"I try to imagine what it would be like if it was my own daughter in this situation."

She blinked, uncertain if she'd heard him correctly. "Ashley?"

He nodded, an unreadable emotion lingering in his eyes.

"You love her, don't you?"

"Very much. Her mother and I got divorced when Ashley was only five months old."

"I'm sorry."

"Me, too. I discovered there wasn't room in my life to be both a family man and to dive into my career."

"You chose your career?"

He rubbed his chin. "Before I had the chance to make things right, it was too late. My wife left me. She moved Ashley to California and started a new life with a man who eventually became her new husband."

"I see."

288

"Anyway, the doctors knew when Ashley was born that something wasn't quite right. She has a disease that's so rare that there's not even a name for it, but it's affecting the way her bones grow. We found an experimental treatment that's not covered by insurance. I've been trying to get the money together so we can start it soon."

"You should have told me. I would have helped."

"I didn't want to distract you from the task at hand. You were already dealing with a lot. I'm very protective of Ashley and who knows about what she's going through. One of my biggest regrets is that her mother and I didn't stay together. Things would be easier if we had. Easier on Ashley. But we can't undo the past."

"No, we can't. I'm sorry, Grant," Mallory said again. She could only imagine how hard that would be.

"Me, too." He shifted beside her and let out a deep breath. "I'm not sure how this happened."

"How what happened?"

He rocked back, looking ten years older than he had just yesterday. "How this tour has turned into a monstrosity."

"Is that what you really think?"

"When we were just starting, we had purpose, excitement, and vision. Now all we seem to have is trouble."

She'd never heard Grant speak so candidly. He was always upbeat, almost to a fault—except when it came to Tennyson.

"We were fighting injustice in one way during the tour. Now we're fighting it another way." Mallory could only attribute the strength in her voice and the peace in her spirit to a higher power.

He studied her a moment before finally saying, "What's going on between you and Tennyson?"

She drew in a quick breath, not expecting the conversation to go there. "What?"

"You can't hide it, Mallory. I can read it in your eyes. You like him."

"Just like I can read that you don't like him."

He let out a chuckle. "Don't turn this around on me. This was about you."

She sank her teeth into her bottom lip as she remembered her kiss with Tennyson—and the unpleasant aftermath that followed. "Our relationship is strictly professional."

"For now."

"For always," she corrected. "There are some obstacles that can never be overcome."

Even if she cared for Tennyson, every time she looked at him, she'd remember his decision to delay her rescue. She'd never get past that.

"One day you'll date again," Grant said.

His fatherly tone caused a wave of grief to wash over her. "I don't know about that, Grant. God got the oyster and the pearl mixed up when he created me."

"What do you mean?"

"Sometimes I feel like I'm a pearl on the outside when people talk about how strong and brave I am. But what they don't see on the inside is the oyster that's still there. The rough edges. The ugliness. The scars that will never go away."

Compassion warmed his eyes. "I've seen people overcome great tragedies in their lives, Mallory. That's only true if you make it true. I don't think there's any ugliness inside you."

"Dante stripped away my dignity." Her throat tightened at the words. She hadn't believed them in a long time.

"Not all of it. I'm not a Christian, but I've heard you talk about it enough. I know your identity comes from Christ. That's something that can't be taken away."

His words brought surprising comfort. "Thank you, Grant. I can tell you're a good father. And if you need money for your daughter's treatment, let me know. Please."

"Thank you. I will." He patted her knee.

Just then, a shadow appeared in the doorway. Tennyson.

Despite her desperate fight to stay in control, her heart raced.

"I'll let you two talk." Grant clamped down on Tennyson's arm as he went past. "Take care of her."

Tennyson nodded, the action tight, as he approached Mallory's bed. As he stood over her, he actually seemed to have concern in his eyes. In a hazy whirlwind, memories of what had happened with Jason filled her thoughts. Grant had filled in some of the details, but not all of them.

"So Jason was behind all of this from the start, huh? The notes? The murders? Everything?" Talking about Jason was safer than talking about her heart.

Tennyson stood stiffly beside her bed, his eyes telling one story and his body language another. His gaze showed his inner turmoil, his regret, his guilt. Physically, he almost seemed to be bracing himself.

"We don't know the extent of Jason's involvement yet. He claims that someone blackmailed him to do everything—to threaten you. To abduct Trina. To go up to your room."

"He abducted Trina?"

Tennyson nodded. "He told the FBI where he was keeping her. They sent a team out there and found her. She's doing okay."

"Thank goodness. Did you talk to Jason?"

Tennyson pressed his lips together. "I did."

"And?"

"Maybe you should rest up a little more before I dive into those details."

"I want to know."

He assessed her with his gaze and finally nodded. He pulled a chair up and sat at her bedside. She carefully pushed herself up, mindful of her hospital gown. Tension stretched in her gut as she anticipated what he had to say.

CHAPTER 40

"Like I said, Jason claims he was being blackmailed. Someone has been holding this over his head for a long time and was able to pull a lot of strings as a result. The police and FBI are still investigating the extent of his involvement in the crimes committed in relation to you. Hopefully they'll have some answers soon."

"I realize I still need a security team since we don't know who was behind the blackmailing," Mallory said. "We'll continue as we have been."

"Okay." Tennyson pressed his lips together like he wanted to say more, but didn't.

Tennyson's phone rang. Mallory listened closely, trying to determine what was making Tennyson tense even more. Finally, he hung up and turned to her.

"Who was that?"

"Agent Turner."

"Did he say if my father was mixed up in Inferno somehow? Along with Walter?"

Tennyson shook his head. "They don't think so. That was just a ploy to throw you off the trail of what was really going on. Everything the FBI has looked at indicates your dad—and Walter—were clear."

"That's good to know."

"That's right." Tennyson shifted. "Agent Turner did say that they believe someone working for Dawson Electronics may have been behind the blackmailing of Jason."

She froze. "Dawson Electronics? What sense does that make?"

"They're the biggest competitor to Jason's father's company. Someone on staff discovered Jason's philandering ways and began blackmailing him in an attempt to take the company—and the competition—down."

"They went as far as to murder?" Mallory asked.

"We're not sure."

Mallory shook her head. "Besides, why would they involve me in that? That's what doesn't make sense. It would make sense for them to simply go public with the information."

"Ultimately, it was a way to make more of a spectacle of Jason. Not only is he guilty of being highly unethical, but he is also guilty of taunting you. It makes him look crazy. And his excuses—true or not—only make him sound crazier."

"I guess so."

"The authorities are working on this now," Tennyson said. "What Jason did was wrong. And involving you was heartless. But maybe we can finally put this behind us."

She nodded, even though she felt a moment of grief. When all of this was over, would Tennyson return to his regular life? Wasn't that what she wanted?

Her head said yes, but her heart said otherwise. She was determined not to let her heart win.

"One other thing," Tennyson said.

"What's that?"

"Jason said he'll only talk further to me down at the FBI office. Kori is resting up so she can take the next shift, but Logan is at the door. Will you be okay?"

She nodded again. "Always."

CHAPTER 41

Mallory stared at the window of her hospital room and let the tears roll down her face. She hated—*hated*—feeling so alone.

But she'd told herself from the start that being by herself was the way to go. Why had she dared to think differently? It always ended in heartache.

As someone knocked at her door, she quickly wiped away the tears and sat up straighter.

"Come in," she called.

Ethan Stone stepped inside her hospital room, a bouquet of flowers in his hands.

"Hey there." He handed her the flowers. "I just wanted to bring you a little something."

"Thank you." She eyed him curiously. "If you don't mind me asking, what are you doing here?"

"I'm just checking on you. Is that okay?"

"Of course."

He stared at her a minute. "Tennyson's gone?"

"I'm surprised you didn't pass him on your way in."

He sighed, pulled up a chair, and straddled it. "Can I tell you something?"

"Do I have a choice?" She kept the words light.

"I know what happened between you. I know everything that went into the raid that night and how hard that must be on you."

She bit down. "Tennyson knew I was there and didn't rescue me. That's hard to get over. He could have at least told me earlier."

"It's not something that comes up casually in conversation. 'Hey, I could have saved you earlier, but I didn't. I just thought you should know.'"

"There are ways."

"You have to understand the scope of the mission. I know the phrase is overused, but we had to think about the greater good. It's hard to sacrifice one life—anyone's life." He softened his voice. "But Torres was in the middle of a dangerous arms deal that would have put millions at risk. It's a hard call, but it had to be made. With time, you'll understand, and I hope you'll give him another chance."

"I might be able to see his viewpoint, but I'm not sure I can get over it."

Ethan leaned closer. "Mallory, I haven't seen Tennyson look at anyone like he looks at you since . . . since Claire." His voice sounded surprisingly serious.

Her breath caught at his unexpected words. "Really?"

He nodded, almost sadly. "He really did care about her. And I can see that he really cares about you, too. That's not easy for me to say."

She stared at him, trying to find the right words. "You loved Claire also."

His neck looked tight. "I did. But she chose him. I can't blame her. I'm a little rough around the edges at times."

"Yes, you are."

He flinched dramatically. "Ouch. At least you're honest."

"Honesty is important." She let her words ring out.

His smile slipped. "Think about giving him another chance."

"I need some time." She stared at Ethan. "What are you doing now that this is over?"

He shrugged. "I'll be around for a while. There are still some threads that need to be tied up."

"Did you really think Dante was alive?"

"It was a possibility. It was hard to identify his remains, even for the most seasoned forensic anthropologist. You knew Torres just as well as anyone. You know he was brilliant and sneaky. He had to be in order to do what he did."

Her stomach clenched again. She didn't want to face the truth. Not that truth.

But right now she had no choice.

• • •

Tennyson stared at Jason as he sat across the table from him at the FBI office. "Why did you want to see me?"

"I'm in too deep, man."

"And you wanted to tell me that, why?" Tension grew between his shoulders. Something about this conversation wasn't right.

"I've been blackmailed."

"I know."

"I want to save face . . . but I can't. There's more to my story."

"Tell me what it is, Jason."

He dragged his gaze up to meet Tennyson's. "Inferno hates you."

"I've gathered that. But I thought this wasn't about Inferno."

"I lied. It is."

Anger rushed through his veins. "So you're saying Inferno was a part of this?"

He nodded.

Tennyson glanced at the two-way glass, knowing Agent Turner was there and listening to all this. "Why did you have to tell me in person, Jason?"

"You need to watch out for Mallory."

"I've been trying to do that, but it seems like this is coming from you a little too late, all things considered."

He raked a hand through his hair. "I know. It was complicated."

"When you involve yourself with Inferno, it gets complicated fast." He leaned toward him. "Did you ever see Torres?"

He shook his head. "No, not face-to-face."

"What's that mean?"

"I mean, he was referred to, but I never saw him with my own eyes."

"So you don't know if he's alive?"

"I can't confirm it."

"Why does he want Mallory?"

"People didn't like Mallory. Torres jeopardized missions so he could see Mallory and spend time with her. It was sick. And it caused resentment. Torres would want her alive. All of his men would want her dead. They're not done yet."

CHAPTER 42

Logan stepped into Mallory's hospital room and smiled. "I just thought I'd check on you. How you doing?"

"I'm hanging in. Ready to leave this place."

"Soon, I'm sure."

He set a glass of water next to her on the bedside table. "The doctor said you need to drink plenty of fluids."

She nodded. She'd heard the doctor say those very words, along with a list of other things, before he'd left.

Her arm ached as she reached toward the table to grab the drink. Her wound was minor, but it still left her feeling sore. The pain medication she was taking didn't help.

"Can I get you anything else?" Logan asked.

"I think I'm okay," she told him. "Thank you."

She stared at the glass. She had to get over some of her bouts of paranoia. It was time for her to move on, to act like the grown woman she was.

She took a sip and let the cool liquid refresh her.

"I heard Jason was arrested," Logan said, sitting down beside her.

"Thankfully." She took another sip of her water.

"At least he won't be able to do more damage."

Her head began to swim. Was it the pain medication kicking in? She'd always been sensitive to medications.

Maybe she just needed to lie down.

"Are you okay?" Logan peered at her, lines of worry wrinkling his forehead.

She nodded, even though she felt anything but okay. "Maybe everything's catching up with me."

"Maybe you should just rest."

"I probably should." She lay back in the hospital bed as her limbs began feeling like Jell-O.

That's when it hit her. This water had a strange metallic aftertaste. A taste she'd experienced before . . . when Dante had drugged her.

She dropped the glass. It shattered on the floor. Water sloshed everywhere.

Her gaze met Logan's as facts collided in her mind. "You drugged me."

Before her eyes, he transformed from the quiet guard Mallory had known into someone sinister.

Her breath caught as the implications of the moment washed over her.

"Logan . . ."

He grinned maliciously, all signs of his laid-back personality gone. "Sorry, love. You and I are going to take a trip down memory lane, though."

She tried to stand up, to escape. But before she could, the world around her spun.

Then blackness descended.

．　．　．

Tennyson stood after questioning Jason and stepped into the hallway. He saw that he'd missed a call from Leigh.

He glanced at his text messages and saw that she'd sent one saying: Check your e-mail. He pulled his e-mail up on the screen and braced himself for what he might read.

It was about the bones that had been tested.

He scanned the words there.

Though Dante had grown up in Mexico, the mineral samples from the bones determined that this person had grown up in South America.

South America.

His heart pounded in his ears.

That body wasn't Torres. This confirmed it.

That meant that Torres was still out there and most likely trying to get what he'd lost: Mallory.

Tennyson had to get back to the hospital.

He tried calling Logan. The man didn't answer. That was strange. Why wouldn't he answer his phone?

Unless something was wrong.

His adrenaline spiked.

At that moment, Tennyson's phone rang. Logan. Was it Logan?

He didn't recognize the number, but he answered anyway. It was Brian Mills, one of the men he'd called when checking Logan's references. He was about a week too late in returning the call.

"Walker speaking."

"I understand you were looking into Logan Hagen."

"That's right," Tennyson said.

"I was on vacation and just returned back to the office. I called as soon as I got your message. There's something you need to know."

"What's that?"

"Logan Hagen died two years ago in the line of duty. I don't know who you're talking to, but it's not the man who once worked for me."

Tennyson's heart sank and facts began to click together in his mind. One thing was certain: Mallory was in trouble. Big trouble.

· · ·

He reached the hospital and threw his car in park. Wasting no time, he rushed into the building. His adrenaline surged along with his heart rate as he ran up the stairs to the third floor.

He reached Mallory's room. An empty chair sat out front. A chair Logan was supposed to be sitting on.

The door to the room was wide open.

Tennyson cautiously stepped inside.

But it was too late. Mallory was gone.

CHAPTER 43

When Mallory opened her eyes, darkness swallowed her. Complete and utter darkness that swirled like an abyss around her. Taunting despair. Hopelessness. Stark fear that invaded her soul so deeply that her muscles, her limbs, trembled uncontrollably.

She pushed herself up. Her arm ached in protest. Her head swam. But she had to push past that.

She reached forward and felt nothing but air.

She listened but heard nothing but silence.

Use your senses, Mallory. You can figure this out. Stay logical.

She closed her eyes, trying not to let the fact that she could tell no difference between when her eyes were open or shut increase her panic.

She drew in a deep breath. The place smelled stuffy, hot and dusty. No real clues in that.

Metallic undertones of the drug she'd been given still lingered in her mouth.

Beneath her, she felt something rough. Wood, she realized with a small yelp as a splinter dug into her finger.

Despair tried to clutch her, but she pushed it away.

No, there had to be something here. She wasn't suspended in space. She just had to reach a little farther. Think a little harder.

She crawled, until finally her hands hit something cold. Something metallic.

A container, she realized. The blood drained from her face.

But where? What was beyond these walls?

Where had Logan taken her?

As if to answer her question, a loud creak cut through the air. Mallory jerked her head toward the sound. It was close. Incredibly close.

Acid spun in her stomach as she waited, anticipated what would happen next.

A sliver of light appeared.

A door was opening, she realized. Bright light flooded inside, blinding her.

Until a shadow covered it.

"Hello, my Alessandra."

She knew that voice. Knew the name it belonged to.

Dante Torres.

The acid churned even harder, burning her stomach, climbing up her throat.

She wanted to scramble backward, to get far away from him. But she didn't allow herself the opportunity.

She wasn't who she used to be.

She could face her fears.

"I thought you were dead," she said, still unable to see clearly as her eyes adjusted to the light. She protectively put her hand over her chest.

What was she wearing? An outfit that Dante liked. A lacy, beige sheath. Her hair had been fixed. She probably even had makeup on.

He chuckled and stepped closer. "I thought you knew me better than that."

"You used a body double?"

"Yes, my Alessandra. That's what I did. Clever, yes?" He stopped in front of her and reached down, cupping her face with his hand.

She jerked away from him as bile continued to rise. "Why do you have me now?"

"Because we're meant to be together." He was close enough now that she could clearly see his face. Smell his repulsive breath. Feel the burn of his fingers on her skin.

"Why now? It's been two years."

"I had to lie low. Have some work done. But now I'm back, and I'm ready to finish what I started."

"Which is?" *Keep him talking, Mallory. Keep him talking.*

He chuckled again, something akin to warmth in his eyes. "So inquisitive and feisty. I can see you've changed some since we were together last."

"You kept me drugged. You can hardly know who I really was."

"My Alessandra. I envisioned our reunion would be different than this."

"My name is Mallory." She shouldn't have said it. Shouldn't have potentially provoked him. Bitterness rose up in her. But along with the bitterness came her fighting instincts.

Victor, not victim.

"What are you going to do with me?" Her throat burned as she said the words.

"You're going to live with me. Soon, I'll be one of the richest men alive. Together, we can have whatever we want."

"Except freedom. You'll be one of the most wanted men alive."

Maybe she could find a weapon. But there was nothing.

"Don't you worry about that. I'll handle that side of things." He smiled down on her.

She licked her lips, fighting sickness. "What's going to make you so rich?"

"That's not for you to know. I'll find you nicer accommodations. Soon. Until then, sit tight."

At the thought of being stuck in here again, panic set in. Darkness. She didn't want to face the darkness again. It was like being buried alive.

"No—wait! Please. Not in here. Don't leave me in here."

"Don't worry, my love. I'll be back. This is just temporary. Soon you'll be all mine again." He brushed his hand across her cheek.

"Please. I can't stay here." The thought of it made her want to crawl out of her skin.

He stood, his gaze still fixated on her. "We're leaving tonight, and I'll take you somewhere no one will ever find us."

• • •

Where would Logan have taken her? The possibilities seemed endless, but Tennyson had to narrow them down. And he needed help. Wheaton—his first choice—was on the Eastern Shore. That left him with Ethan Stone.

He called his friend, found out his location, and picked him up five minutes later.

"Just stop for a minute," Stone told him in the parking lot of the hotel where he was staying. "Driving around won't bring us any closer to finding Mallory. Let's talk this through."

Flexing his jaw, Tennyson put the car in park. His friend was right, but he hated to sit by idly while Mallory could be getting farther way. "Okay."

"Torres used Logan to take Mallory," Stone said. "But where? Where would he take her?"

"That's the question I've been asking."

"He'll want to get her out of the country," Stone said.

"I agree. But how is he going to do that? I already called Agent Turner. The FBI is keeping an eye on all of the airports and ports."

Stone rubbed his neck. "But what about the small airports? There's more than one way to get her out of the country."

"There's an APB out across all the agencies. I doubt he'll slip past there. Too many people are looking for him—even at the small locations," Tennyson said. "Torres will need to sneak her out."

"So let's think like a terrorist. How's he going to do that?" Stone said.

Tennyson closed his eyes. "He's got a plan. There's no doubt about that. He's using some kind of company as a front."

"Dawson Electronics? Isn't that who they're saying was blackmailing Jason?"

Tennyson nodded. "According to Agent Turner, none of that is panning out. I think that was a cover."

"How about Jason's company?"

"It's clear also, best I can tell." Tennyson turned his thoughts over until a realization hit him. "Jason had his own company within his father's company. It was on his card that he gave to Mallory."

"What's the name?"

He pinched the skin between his eyes, trying to remember the name. "Rocket Tech! That's it."

Stone pulled out his laptop and began typing. "Rocket Tech has a warehouse in Norfolk."

Tennyson's thoughts surged. "That's it. What if they were working with Jason the whole time? What if he's been using his business as a front for their operations?"

"It's our best lead yet," Stone said.

Tennyson started the engine. "Let's go."

CHAPTER 44

The door opened again. Mallory didn't know how much time had passed. It felt like hours, but it could have only been minutes. In the darkness, everything blurred together. It felt muted yet electrified.

She fully expected to see Dante. She was prepared this time. She'd managed to work a piece of wood off the floor. The scrap was sharp enough to act as a knife.

Maybe she could throw Dante off balance for long enough to escape. She had no idea what was beyond the walls. But anything was better than being trapped in here and eventually returning to the life she'd been rescued from. Anything.

She stood at full height, ready to fight. Even with her raw fingers, achy arm, and wobbly legs.

But it wasn't Dante standing there.

It was Sanchez.

She lowered her hand in surprise. What . . . ?

He didn't seem anxious. No, each of his motions seemed to be taken with a nuclear-aftermath-like calmness. He was so calm that Mallory's own apprehension surged. Dante had plans that included keeping her alive. Sanchez did not.

"I tried to warn you."

She blanched, uncertain if she'd heard him correctly. "What do you mean?"

"I left you a note, telling you Dante was still alive. I told you to hide."

"You left that? Why?"

"Dante . . . he's reckless. He hasn't been right in the head for years now."

Her mind raced, desperate to draw the right conclusions. "You're trying to stab him in the back?"

Sanchez stepped closer, his hands tucked casually into the pockets of his slacks. Mallory stepped back, unsure what his intentions were. She was both frightened and fascinated by how easygoing he seemed. "You don't understand, do you?"

"Understand what?" She gripped the piece of wood behind her back, wondering when she could use it. Her heart pounded in her ears.

"My sister Alessandra . . ."

"Dante loved her." Her stomach turned at the thought.

"She was just like you," he said softly.

Mallory's heart stuttered. "What?"

A shadow formed over his eyes. "She didn't willingly come into a relationship with Dante. She was forced. Like you."

Mallory's gut twisted at the news. That couldn't be right. Alessandra was Dante's love. His wife.

But all along she'd actually been . . . his slave?

Bile rose in her throat. "I . . . I didn't know. I thought . . ."

He nodded. "I sold her out to be a part of his team. I've never forgiven myself. I won't make that mistake again. I tried to let you get away that day, Mallory. On the island? I knew you were hiding behind the boathouse."

Memories of that day flooded her mind. "I thought you might have heard me."

His gaze remained stoic. "I did. Unfortunately, Dante did also. He caught you."

Mallory took a step back, wanting to trust Sanchez, but unsure if she should. "Did you kill those women?"

"Dante had his men do it. He tried to replace you. It didn't work, and he wanted to send a message."

"How was Jason involved?"

"We needed to use his business as a cover to ship out our weapons, so we blackmailed him. He would lose everything. End up in jail. His family would be ruined."

It was a powerful motivation, especially for someone like Jason, who prided himself on image.

"He really did send those messages?"

She stared at the opening. Could she run?

Sanchez nodded. "Dante wrote them. Jason sent them."

Her heart thudded in her ears. "The perfume? Did Dante do that himself?"

"He did."

"Who tried to break into the hotel room that night? Jason?"

"He did under our directive."

"You're trying to help me?" Was she understanding him correctly? Nothing made sense.

He offered a quick nod of affirmation. "Yes, and you're wasting time asking these meaningless questions. You have less than five minutes to run. Go straight until you reach a block of blue containers. Then go left. Run as fast as you can."

She froze, Sanchez's words nearly not registering. Was this real? Was this her chance to get out?

"Why are you standing there?"

She flinched, coming out of shock. Then she took a step forward, her legs wobbly, her feet bare.

But before she reached the door, a gunshot exploded through the air.

Mallory screamed as Sanchez dropped to the floor.

CHAPTER 45

Mallory retreated from the pool of blood surrounding Sanchez's head. His lifeless figure appeared to stare at Mallory, even though he was dead. The blood running through her veins seemed to freeze at the thought.

Dante stepped inside.

"You killed him," Mallory whispered. She started to squeeze the makeshift dagger in her hands. It was gone. She must have dropped it when she heard the gunfire.

"He betrayed me." Dante scowled and lowered his gun. "He couldn't be trusted."

She backed up, until the frigid metal of the container hit her hands. "I don't understand what's going on here. Were you stalking me?"

His eyes warmed with misplaced affection. "My Alessandra, I would not stalk. I kept an eye on you." She wanted to keep him talking. To find out answers. To delay whatever the inevitable was.

She pressed herself farther into the chilly wall behind her, wishing she could disappear there. "What are you planning, Dante? What's going on?"

"Weapons are on the way to Berna. The rebels will use them and overthrow the government."

"Why would you do that?"

He tilted his head. "I thought you knew me well enough to know that."

"For the money?"

Satisfaction ignited in his gaze. "And the power. Of course."

"Why are the stakes so much higher now?" Where was that piece of wood? If Mallory looked for it, Dante would notice.

"Once the rebels overthrow the government, they'll have access to the country's nuclear weapons. Of course."

Her heart pounded in her ears. "What? They don't have nukes in Berna."

"You don't think their government would announce it to the world, do you?" He chuckled. "A government's power can be determined by what they do in secret."

"But with nukes . . ." Her mind drifted with the possibilities. None of them were good. In fact, they were devastating.

Tennyson's choice flashed back to her, as well as the grave consequences.

"With you by my side, I'll be invincible again. I'll be calling the shots. You understand that, my love?" He stepped closer and reached for her.

She scooted back, on the verge of being violently ill. "Why do I need to be by your side? You don't need me."

"But I do. We were meant to be together. Can't you see that, Alessandra?" He shifted and touched her face again. "I'm nothing without you. You complete me."

Her stomach twisted and bile rose in her. She tried to jerk away from his touch, but she had nowhere to go.

"We'll never be apart again," he announced, trailing a finger through her hair. "Never. Now I've got to finish my preparations. We leave tonight."

•   •   •

Tennyson, Stone, and Wheaton showed up at the warehouse just as darkness was beginning to fall. Tennyson had called Wheaton, and he'd agreed to meet them. They parked in the woods and made their way on foot toward the fence around the property.

This could be nothing.

But Tennyson prayed that he'd be able to find some answers. To find Mallory.

Lord, help me.

If she wasn't here, he didn't have any other options. Their time was running out. That was a possibility he didn't want to face.

Usually at this time of night, everything would be quiet in a location like this. But Tennyson clearly saw movement near some of the shipping containers in the distance. He grabbed his binoculars for a better look.

"You've got to be kidding me . . . ," he muttered.

"What do you see?" Stone crouched beside him.

He handed him the binoculars. "They're preparing to move out."

Stone squinted into the eyepiece before shaking his head. "That's what it looks like."

"Do you think they have Mallory in one of those containers?" Tennyson's muscles tensed with every word.

"It's a good guess."

Anger climbed up his spine. "We've got to get her."

Stone's hand gripped his shoulder, pushing him back down. "We can't do anything rash. Let's watch for a few more minutes and develop a plan of action."

"He's right." Wheaton pulled out his phone. "I'm going to call Agent Turner and let them know what we've discovered."

Tennyson didn't argue. He needed his friends to keep him level-headed. Rash decisions could lead to destruction, and he couldn't afford that. Not when Mallory's life was on the line. He'd let her down once. Never again.

"They're on their way, but they're still at least thirty minutes out," Wheaton said, sliding the phone back into his pocket.

"We don't have that much time." Tennyson's muscles stretched taut. He wouldn't let Mallory slip away. He wouldn't do it.

Just then, a gunshot sliced through the silence.

His blood froze.

Tennyson stood, ready to pounce when he thought about who might be at the opposite end of that gun. Stone jerked him back down again. "Torres won't kill Mallory."

Tennyson wished he felt that confident. "How do you know that?"

"You know that, too. Think it through. Torres wants her alive. He could have killed her already otherwise."

Tennyson took some deep breaths and tried to rein in his emotions.

He took the binoculars from Stone and glanced in the direction of the gunshot. A moment later, someone stepped from one of the containers.

Tennyson's breath caught.

Dante Torres.

It was him. Tennyson had no doubt.

He was alive and up to no good.

The man's plan had worked, and he'd successfully faked his death for the past two years.

No longer.

Torres yelled something in Spanish to the men in the distance.

Una hora y nos vamos. One hour and we're gone.

One hour? They might have enough time to wait for the FBI.

But Tennyson could bear to risk it. "I'm going to get her," he said.

They huddled and developed a plan of action. It was risky. But if Mallory disappeared from this warehouse, Tennyson knew he'd never see her again. He couldn't let that happen.

One by one, they climbed the fence and landed on the other side. A guard patrolled the perimeter, but they knew they had approximately three minutes to get over the fence and to disappear from sight before he returned to this area.

Once over, they split up. Tennyson headed toward the container. He remained in the shadows, listening for any signs that someone had spotted him. So far, it was quiet, except by the dock area. There, a group of men talked beside a barge. Their voices carried on the air of the otherwise still night.

Dante had disappeared inside the warehouse itself, but it was only a matter of time before he came back out.

Tennyson peered around the corner of the container. A man stood guard there. Of course.

He glanced across the property. Stone nodded at him before making a soft whistling sound.

The guard turned toward the noise. As he did, Tennyson lunged forward and brought the butt of his gun down on his head. The man sank to the ground. Tennyson grabbed his weapon and tucked it into his waistband. Then he tugged at the door.

To his surprise, it opened. He held his breath, a moment of fear washing over him. He didn't want to think about worst-case scenarios. But the image of finding Mallory dead pummeled him.

He shined his light on the floor. Blood. His heart leapt into throat. No . . .

He had to confirm it. He stepped inside. As he did, he sensed movement beside him. He barely had time to register the dead body of a man.

Sanchez. Was that Sanchez?

He jerked his head to the left. Facts clicked in place one by one. Arms raised above someone's head. Clutching a makeshift weapon. Ready to plunge it into him.

He caught the arms before the sharp edge could prick his skin.

"Tennyson?" a soft voice said.

"Mallory?"

In the next instant, she flew into his arms.

"You're okay," she cried. "You're okay."

She was alive. And safe.

Thank You, Jesus.

He wanted to relish the feel of her in his arms, but he'd have time for that later. "We've got to get you out of here."

She pulled away and nodded, but her limbs were still shaky. "Let's go."

Just as they stepped outside, Tennyson heard a gun cock.

He looked up.

Dante Torres stood there.

His gaze shot to the left. Stone had his arms in the air. This wasn't good. Not the outcome Tennyson had anticipated.

CHAPTER 46

"Alessandra . . . my love," Dante muttered, a smirk on his face.

Mallory held her breath. Dante would shoot Tennyson without a second thought. She knew it.

She couldn't let that happen. Not because of her.

Too many people had already died because of her.

"Don't hurt him." Her voice was a trembling mess as she clung to Tennyson's arm. "Please, Dante."

"You like this man, do you?" Dante stepped closer, observing Tennyson with a calculated gaze.

"He's a good man. He's kept me safe while we've been apart." Her words caused bile to rise in her throat.

"Mallory, don't do this," Tennyson said. "Please."

"Maybe he likes you too much?" Dante continued inching closer, still calculating, formulating, planning.

"No, he just wants to protect me. You owe him a debt of gratitude." Mallory didn't want to go with Dante. Her entire body rebelled against it. But she wouldn't let Tennyson die to ensure that.

No, she loved Tennyson. She knew she did.

She glanced around. Four men surrounded them, weapons aimed on Tennyson. Stone stood in the distance, his hands in the air. Was it just the two of them? Or had they brought backup? Was this a no-win situation?

Dear Lord, please give me Your wisdom now. I don't know how we're going to get out of this.

"You're telling me I should thank this man?" Dante said. "The man who tried to kill me."

"Dante, he's been kind to me." She softened her voice. "Please. I haven't asked much of you. But let him go."

"Mallory—I know what you're doing. Don't." Tennyson edged closer to her. His voice sounded hoarse and tight and pleading.

His words clutched her heart, but it didn't matter. No more bloodshed on her account. If she had to die to save others, so be it.

Her goal had been to bring healing and restoration to women. She'd done the opposite. Women had suffered and died because of her.

Dante reached his hand toward her. "Okay then, my love. Come with me. We'll leave this behind."

Mallory stared at his outstretched arm. Her chest squeezed with the reality of the situation. As soon as she went with him, that would be it. Her life would be with Dante . . . as a slave. Locked away. Absent of freedom or choice.

No part of her wanted to return to that life.

But she had no choice.

"You're not going to hurt them?" she said. "You promise?"

"Don't do it, Mallory!" Ethan yelled.

She swallowed so hard that it hurt. Her heart pounded fiercely in her ears. Her eyes darted from person to person.

"Tell your friend to put his gun down," Dante said. "I won't hurt him."

"Tennyson . . ." she started, realizing she still gripped his arm.

At that moment, the man holding Ethan rammed something into his head, and he sank to the ground.

Mallory gasped.

"He was a mole, my Alessandra," Dante said. "He must pay."

"No one else needs to get hurt." Her voice cracked. The situation was spiraling out of control. Her mind raced to keep up.

"People get hurt every day," Tennyson reminded her, his voice controlled but tense. "You think you can stop all of that?"

"I want to stop what I can." She licked her lips. She knew she couldn't change Dante's mind. But if she could save Tennyson . . .

"You're so sweet, my love," Dante murmured. "You make me a better person."

Her stomach roiled at the look in his eyes. He believed his words. "Let him go, and I'll come with you."

Tennyson bristled under her hand. "I'm not leaving you, Mallory," Tennyson said through gritted teeth. "Get that thought through your head."

"I can't let you die, Tennyson."

"No one's dying here today. Not you. Not me. Not Stone even."

She wished she felt as confident.

All the weapons remained trained on Tennyson. Except for Tennyson's. If he took a shot, five other guys would be waiting to take him down.

Just then, gunfire rang out from above the container. Tennyson pushed her to the ground and followed suit.

Mallory squeezed her eyes shut and prayed. Because she had no idea what else to do.

• • •

Tennyson knew exactly what was happening. Wheaton had climbed to the top of one of the containers and was picking Dante's men off one by one. He watched them fall to the ground.

Without missing a beat, Tennyson popped to his feet. He raised his gun, fired at Torres's hand, and the man's gun flew to the ground.

Torres moaned and grabbed his injured wrist.

The other members of Inferno were down. Wheaton stood guard.

Now it was between Tennyson and Torres.

Tennyson thought he'd ended this two years ago, but Torres had the upper hand then.

Not this time.

This time, Tennyson was in control. He gripped his gun and stared at the terrorist leader, a man who didn't look nearly as imposing now that he'd been cornered.

But Tennyson wasn't finished with him yet.

He raised his gun to Torres's chest. This was the moment he'd dreamed about for years. Since Claire. He finally had the chance to kill the man who'd made him lose everything.

Except, despite the hurt and the pain, not all was lost.

God had brought him a new hope and purpose. Even though he'd always mourn Claire, healing was possible. Not all was ruined, nor would Claire want him to live like it was.

He'd even found a new love—if Mallory would ever forgive him.

No, Torres deserves to die. Especially after what he did to Mallory.

"He's of more help to the authorities if he's alive, Tennyson." Mallory rolled over, her eyes wide and blood trickling down her forehead. "Imagine the information he can give them."

"You really want to keep this guy alive?"

"No, but I don't want you to have to live with his death," she said quietly.

Her words caused his heart to pound wildly in his chest.

Live with his death. Tennyson had thought it would bring him satisfaction . . . but would it? He shook his head, trying to clear his thoughts.

Lord, what should I do?

Mallory was right. Tennyson couldn't shoot Torres. Vengeance would only satisfy him for a moment. Justice would be handing Torres over to authorities.

"I'll make sure the government has something much worse in store for you than being shot by me," Tennyson said, releasing his breath.

His choice had been made, and he knew it was the right one.

"Put your weapons down! FBI!" Agents surrounded them.

Tennyson lowered his gun as an agent grabbed Torres. His body seemed to deflate as the adrenaline wore off. Mallory stood, and her arms caught him. Or he caught her. He wasn't sure which one. They buried themselves in each other.

"You came for me," she whispered, her breath tickling his ear.

"I told you I always would."

Her embrace tightened. "Do me a favor? Never let me go."

Warmth spread through him. "My pleasure."

EPILOGUE

"This is your place?" Mallory crossed her arms over her chest and stared out over the bay as the sun set. Unlike that first night in Cape Thomas, at the beginning of her tour, now she felt no fear. No storms raged in the distance; clear skies and calm water stretched before her instead.

From behind, Tennyson slipped his arms around her. Their cheeks touched, and Mallory relished the soft scrape of his stubble. "This is it. For now. It's not quite the mansion you grew up in."

"I don't need a mansion."

"What do you need?"

Mallory uncrossed her arms and turned until they were face-to-face. She looped her arms around Tennyson's neck. His warm eyes made her heart flutter out of control. The past few days had only solidified her feelings for this man. She wanted to stare at this face, to drink it in, for the rest of her life.

"I just need you," she murmured.

His gaze went to her lips, and he tenderly stroked her cheek with his thumb. "I love you, Mallory."

"I love you too, Tennyson."

His lips covered hers, and her entire body both relaxed and exploded with delight. The depth of connection she felt with Tennyson exceeded what she could have ever imagined or hoped for. She somehow knew deep down inside that total healing was possible—through God and with Tennyson by her side.

Like water, love had the power to sustain life or to devastate it. Love would sustain her now.

She rested there in his embrace, relishing how safe she felt. Never wanting to let him go. Ever.

The past few days had been a whirlwind. She'd been debriefed over and over again. Dante was being held by the government, and he'd be going away for a long time.

With Dante behind bars and Sanchez dead, Inferno's proverbial head of the snake had been severed. Authorities hoped that meant the organization had disbanded. Using the information that Jason had told them, they planned to intercept the newest shipment of arms before it got to the insurgents in the Middle East.

Narnie had also turned up, and she was okay. She'd been planning, with the help of her husband, Arthur, to send a ransom note to try to milk money out of Mallory. Her love of money had led to some very poor choices—choices that she could end up doing jail time for. Maybe she'd finally learn her lesson.

Tennyson took a step back, but the look in his eyes was enough to take her breath away. She'd never had a man look at her like that before. His eyes were so full of love and affection . . . She'd be a fool to ever let him go.

"I know you never planned on this, but your book is now a best-seller," Tennyson told her.

"It's not exactly the way I wanted that to happen. But all of this has increased the awareness of human trafficking. That's the good news."

"You sure you're okay with this change of plans for your tour?"

She nodded. "I don't need any more drama. I'll continue doing interviews to promote Verto, but the public appearances just need to be put on the back burner for now."

"Is Grant still coming by later?"

"Yes, he is. As much as I don't agree with all of his choices, I do think that, in his mind, he was looking out for me. I'm not ready to turn my back on him. I'm certainly glad that people didn't turn their backs on me."

Tennyson's eyes glowed with warmth and affection as he stared at her. "I'm sorry."

She put her finger over his lips. "No more sorrys. Life is full of decisions."

Their lips met again, and Mallory knew that the words she'd written in her blog this morning were true.

I'm not who I used to be. I'll never be that person again. Instead, I'm stronger. I'm a fighter. I'm more determined than ever to be an agent of change in this world.

I have the power to do this.

And so do you.

It's your choice. Today and every day. Through the grace of God, I'm a victor not a victim.

ABOUT THE AUTHOR

Photo © 2011 Julie Scott

USA Today calls Christy Barritt's writing "scary, funny, passionate, and quirky." Her mystery and romantic suspense novels have sold more than a million copies, won the Daphne du Maurier Award for Excellence in Mystery/Suspense, and were twice nominated for the Romantic Times Reviewers' Choice Award. She has had more than fifty books published.

Christy has been writing for as long as she can remember and worked for ten years as a newspaper reporter. Her husband is a children's pastor, and together they have two sons. Christy splits her time between the Virginia suburbs and Hatteras Island, North Carolina.